ChangelingPress.com

Intergalactic Brides Vol. 1

Jessica Coulter Smith

Intergalactic Brides Vol. 1
Jessica Coulter Smith

All rights reserved.
Copyright ©2018 Jessica Coulter Smith

ISBN: 9781980283140

Publisher:
Changeling Press LLC
315 N. Centre St.
Martinsburg, WV 25404
ChangelingPress.com

Printed in the U.S.A.

Editor: Crystal Esau
Cover Artist: Karen Fox

The individual stories in this anthology have been previously released in E-Book format.

No part of this publication may be reproduced or shared by any electronic or mechanical means, including but not limited to reprinting, photocopying, or digital reproduction, without prior written permission from Changeling Press LLC.

This book contains sexually explicit scenes and adult language which some may find offensive and which is not appropriate for a young audience. Changeling Press books are for sale to adults, only, as defined by the laws of the country in which you made your purchase.

Table of Contents

Brielle and the Alien Geek 4
- Chapter One 5
- Chapter Two 17
- Chapter Three 29
- Chapter Four 40
- Chapter Five 50
- Chapter Six 59
- Chapter Seven 76
- Chapter Eight 85
- Chapter Nine 93
- Chapter Ten 100

Victoria and the Alien Doctor 115
- Chapter One 116
- Chapter Two 123
- Chapter Three 135
- Chapter Four 150
- Chapter Five 160
- Chapter Six 170
- Chapter Seven 179
- Chapter Eight 188
- Chapter Nine 196
- Chapter Ten 207

Avelyn and the Alien Daddy 214
- Chapter One 215
- Chapter Two 225
- Chapter Three 235
- Chapter Four 251
- Chapter Five 260
- Chapter Six 275
- Chapter Seven 296
- Chapter Eight 305

Jessica Coulter Smith 316
Changeling Press E-Books 317

Brielle and the Alien Geek
Jessica Coulter Smith

Brielle has waited faithfully for her fiancé to return from Terran Prime, only to discover she's been engaged to a lying, cheating bastard, who tosses her out on her rear the moment he's back on Earth. Not one to go down without a fight, Brielle will do anything to ensure her survival -- even sign up for a bride exchange on another world.

Syl has lived his life in his lab, always preoccupied with his experiments. But the moment he sees Brielle, he realizes that perhaps his life has been missing something after all. Wanting and having are two different things. What would an exotic-looking female like Brielle want with an alien geek like him?

Chapter One

The coffee scorched her throat as she gulped the hot brew. Her hand clutched the cup tightly as she watched the men and women exit the space shuttle. She rubbed the back of her neck and then clutched her purse strap as she waited. It had been nearly a year since she'd seen her fiancé, and over six months since she'd had contact with him. As a medical doctor, he'd volunteered to travel to the space station on Terran to serve on their medical staff for one year. Why he was coming home two months early, she didn't know, but she wouldn't question it. She'd been lonely without Aaron by her side.

A familiar head of sandy hair appeared. She bit her lip, adjusted her clothes and then blew out a breath as she watched him, her heart thrumming against her breast. As he drew nearer, she saw there was a woman clutching his arm. A tall, busty blonde who was grinning from ear to ear. Had they met on the shuttle? Her brow furrowed as her heart slowed its pace. She frowned and looked around, but there was no one else waiting in this section except her.

Aaron looked up and spotted her. The smile on his face froze for a moment, and she thought she saw a hint of panic in his eyes. He came closer, stopping a few feet away, the blonde still clutching his arm. Brielle looked at the blonde, then her fiancé, wondering who the woman was.

Aaron cleared his throat. "Brie. Good to see you again."

"We agreed I would meet your shuttle when you returned. I was a little surprised when I received the call from the station that you were coming home sooner than expected."

"I didn't think you'd be here." He rubbed the back of his neck and shifted from foot to foot. "This is rather awkward."

"Why is it awkward? I know we haven't seen each other in nearly a year, but--"

"It isn't that," he interrupted. "Brielle, this is Melissa."

Brielle mustered a smile for the blonde. "How do you do? Did the two of you meet on the shuttle?"

"Um, no." Aaron fidgeted. "I've been seeing Melissa for the last four months. Brielle, I don't know how to say this, so I'm just going to spit it out. Melissa and I are engaged."

Brie's gaze bounced from her fiancé to the blonde and back again. "I don't understand. You're engaged to me. We've been engaged nearly two years."

"I didn't plan for this to happen; it just did. I met Melissa during a routine exam and things just clicked between us. Hurting you is the last thing I'd ever want to do, but I can't deny what my heart wants. And it wants Melissa. I tried to contact you, to let you know, but communications have been down since February."

"We live together!"

He fidgeted again. "About that... I need you to move out. Melissa's lease is up on her place next week and she needs a place to stay. Since we're getting married, it only makes sense for her to move in with me. It was my place first, after all. Until you have your things packed, I'll stay at her place."

Brie clenched her hands at her sides, her nails biting into her palms. Heat worked its way up her body and she felt color bloom in her cheeks. She bared her teeth at her now ex-fiancé, and before she thought better of it, took a swing at the puppy-dog expression staring at her. Her fist connected with his left eye, the edge of his cheekbone bruising her knuckles.

"Ow! Ow! Ow!" Brielle shook her hand, but felt deep satisfaction at the color now budding around the bastard's eye.

Two security guards hurried her way, their hands on their weapons, as if they were going to draw on her at any moment. It figured. She was the one getting her heart ripped out, but they would surely take Aaron's side. Assholes always stuck together.

"Is there a problem?" the first security guard asked.

"This crazy bitch just hit me." Aaron gave her a furious one-eyed glare. "I want her arrested."

Brie folded her arms over her chest. "If I'm in jail, I can't pack my things. If I can't pack my things, you can't move your slut into the apartment."

"There's such a thing as Goodwill."

She gasped. "You wouldn't dare donate my belongings!"

"Arrest her!" Aaron demanded. "I want the bitch locked up."

The second security guard pulled out a set of cuffs and Brie turned her glare his way. "Of course you're going to take his side! Never mind that he's been engaged to me while shacking up with this bimbo for the past four months! Men! You're all alike."

"Not all of us," a deep voice rumbled behind her.

Brie spun to face the interloper, a sharp retort on her tongue. As her gaze fastened on the light lilac skin stretched across a broad chest, the words died on her lips. She looked up, captured by dark purple eyes. She'd of course heard of Terrans before, but she'd never actually met one. They tended to shy away from cameras so this was her first chance to see one.

Terran. Odd, when you thought about the meaning of the name. She was pretty sure it meant *Earth*. She supposed something had just gotten lost in translation. It wasn't like the Terrans spoke English as their native language, or wrote with the alphabet she'd grown up with. She'd have to ask about it another time, when her ex-fiancé wasn't being a belligerent asshole.

Like that was ever going to happen.

"Captain, this doesn't concern you," one of the security guards said. "The woman is human and so is the man she attacked. Your laws don't apply here."

"From what I heard, the man deserved what he got. If he were still on Terran, his punishment would be far worse. We value women on my world. To throw one away is a severe crime."

She heard Aaron gulp behind her. "But we aren't on Terran," Aaron said. "We're back on Earth, so the rules of your planet don't apply."

"That isn't technically true," the Terran said, pointing to a sign over their heads. "You haven't crossed the threshold yet. When you broke up with your fiancée, you were very much still under Terran rule."

Brie didn't know why the alien was helping her, but if he wanted to punish Aaron, she wasn't going to argue with him. Hell, she'd applaud his efforts and help him snap the cuffs into place. Arrogant bastard deserved whatever hand fate was about to deal him. She turned to face Aaron, wanting to see the fear in his eyes.

Her ex-fiancé was pale, deathly pale. The spineless coward's lips trembled when faced with the massive alien at her back. She felt the captain's heat envelop her as he leaned forward, his lips brushing her ear.

"What do you think his punishment should be? Locked in the dungeons for the next ten years? Forced to work the mining camps?"

"Is there a punishment where his balls are removed?" she asked, staring Aaron down. He reached for his crotch, and if possible, he paled even further. The man was shaking and she loved every minute of it.

The alien brandished a blade, the silver edge gleaming in the sunlight. "He hasn't broken a law that would yield that punishment, but I will be happy to take on the task. Any man who cheats on his woman shouldn't be able to procreate."

The guards began to swear. "Captain, you don't want to do this. Even your people would frown on such drastic measures. Incarcerate him if you must, but leave him intact."

He lowered the weapon. "Unfortunately, they're right. As much as I would love to do this for you, it's against our laws."

"Just let the spineless wimp go." She turned to face the alien once more, looking up to meet his amethyst gaze. "He obviously never loved me, and honestly, I'm not as hurt as I should be. It's painful to know he's chosen someone else over me, and my pride has suffered, but my heart isn't breaking like it should. What does that say about me?"

The alien smiled at her, a dimple flashing in his left cheek. "It means your heart was not engaged because he wasn't your... what's that Earth term? Soul mate?"

When she thought of Aaron's thin frame and pasty skin, compared to the hunky alien in front of her, she couldn't remember what she ever saw in the guy.

Sure, Aaron was usually soft-spoken and cultured, but he was a sissy. Brielle was tired of sissies. She wanted a real man, a man who could make her feel cared for and safe. She wanted strong arms to wrap around her at night, not spindly arms that couldn't lift a window without assistance.

"No," she agreed. "We weren't soul mates."

"On my planet, you would be a prize for any warrior. Why have you not taken part in the bride exchange? Your family would be paid handsomely if you should decide to take part. I can promise that you would have your choice of warriors."

"Terran warriors," she clarified.

He nodded. "And if you're into sharing, there are those on my planet who would be happy to oblige you, as long as you were accepting two or more males into your bed."

Brielle's breath caught in her throat. She could barely imagine holding on to one of these large males, much less two. She'd heard they were rather well-endowed and worried they would split her in two. She opened her mouth to respond, but snapped it shut. A bride exchange? As of this moment, she had no home. Her family wasn't about to take her in; they lived in a small cabin in the Kentucky hollows. Growing up, she'd shared a room with her three sisters, two of whom were still living at home.

The alien's smile broadened. "You're thinking about it, aren't you?"

"It seems I'm being evicted from my home," she said. "And I hadn't had a chance to tell Aaron yet, but I lost my job last week. So with no money to speak of, there's absolutely no possibility of me landing on my feet right now."

"There's an application you need to complete. It's rather lengthy, but we don't care about your finances. On Terran, women are precious, whether they are wealthy or poor." His hand lifted and he stroked her hair. "Your hair is like the sunset. I can promise that you would have your choice of warriors."

She glanced over her shoulder at Aaron, who was watching the exchange with an open mouth. She wasn't sure if she should be offended that he thought her of such little worth that no one would want her, or if she should smile and rub it in his face that she was going to be with someone far superior to him. She'd take a Terran warrior over a human doctor any day.

Brielle looked back up at the captain. "Where do I sign?"

His smile broadened even further, showing even white teeth. "Excellent. Please allow me to escort you to the processing station. The application is computerized and they will be able to answer any of your questions."

The alien placed a hand at her lower back and began guiding her through the building and toward processing. She could feel Aaron's eyes boring into her back, but she refused to look his way again. She was finished with him. It might be completely insane to agree to be an alien's wife, especially since she'd never put any thought into the matter, but desperate times called for desperate measures.

"Whitney," the alien called to the human woman behind the desk. "I have another candidate for you."

Brielle looked up at him in surprise. "Do you just wander the station looking for women to bring down here?"

He chuckled. "No. But you are not the first candidate I've brought to processing during my travels to Earth. Sometimes the women boarding the ships to Terran decide they want to participate. Others never want to step foot on my planet again."

"Why would they not want to return? You do have indoor plumbing, don't you?"

"Yes." He smiled. "There's indoor plumbing. Electricity too."

"Now if you could just find a way for me to email my sisters…"

He shook his head. "No written transmissions. We do, however, have Vid-Comms set up in all of the suites and homes on Terran. They were working again as of last night. As long as your family has access to one, you'll be able to speak to them."

Brielle shook her head. "They can't afford something like that. And the nearest Terran station is a few hundred miles away."

"If you're accepted into the program and select a Terran mate, I assure you that he will do everything in his power to make sure you can contact your family. He would never separate you from your kin. Families are important to Terrans." He smiled and stroked her arm. "Even soft pink ones."

"Just tell me what to do to get the ball rolling."

He motioned to Whitney. "She's going to walk you through the process."

"And will I see you again?"

"Possibly, but I will not be among the unmated males seeking a female. My mate would not approve."

Figures the sexy captain would already be taken. It seemed her luck hadn't entirely improved. But if the other Terrans were half as handsome as him, she would be thankful. It would definitely be an improvement over Aaron. Just thinking about the weasel made her lips curl in disgust.

"I hope that look isn't for me?" the captain asked with some humor.

"Sorry. I was thinking about my ex."

"Put him firmly in your past. Your future is on Terran. I have no doubt that you will be accepted into the program. And maybe your family could use the money gifted to them to set up a Vid-Comm in their home."

More than likely the money would go toward the mortgage, which always seemed to be behind, and in keeping the utilities turned on. Her family was so poor they were lucky to have that indoor plumbing she'd joked about a moment ago. Toast for breakfast, PB&J for lunch, and whatever Papa could catch for dinner. That had been her life growing up.

"Thank you," she told the captain as he turned to leave. "I wouldn't have thought to do this if you hadn't suggested it."

"You're most welcome. I hope things work out for you."

She nodded and turned back toward Whitney, who was watching them with a bored look on her face.

"Are you ready?" Whitney asked. "The application takes about an hour to complete."

"After I'm finished, how long before I'll know if I've been approved? I'm sort of on a deadline to exit my current home."

"I can put a rush on it and you'll have your answer in a day or two. Normally, it takes a week because they perform a background check to make sure you aren't a criminal trying to escape prosecution. That sort of thing. But with a rush order, they'll start proceedings right away. It will still be a thorough check, though."

Brielle nodded. "I'm not hiding anything. Just an empty bank account and an eviction from my ex, who wasn't my ex until he returned from Terran with some bimbo on his arm."

Whitney's eyes widened. "Um, let's get you started."

Brielle followed her over to one of the computers lining the wall. She sat in the swivel chair and watched as Whitney pulled up the application. The woman explained how the program worked, then left her to fill in the blanks on the screen. She was right in estimating it would take an hour to finish and included answering questions about her health, her family, and why she wanted to join the program. Brielle was tired when she clicked submit.

Now to sit back and wait. She hoped she would hear something in the morning, but she wouldn't hold her breath. She thanked Whitney on her way out. When she reached the parking lot, she cursed under her breath. Brielle had driven Aaron's car, thinking they would go home together, and the asshole had taken it and left her to fend for herself.

Trudging back the way she'd come, she checked her purse to see if she had enough cash for a taxi. As she stepped up on the curb outside the Terran transport station, she saw the captain again, standing next to an open limo door. He saw her and motioned her over.

"I heard you finished your application," he said.

"Yes. Whitney said she would put a rush on it for me."

He looked around. "Did you not drive here?"

"I did. The asshole took the car and left me here. I thought I'd try to catch a cab, but I don't have enough funds to cover the ride. I'll just catch the bus and walk the last few blocks to the apartment."

The captain looked up at the setting sun. "It will be dark before you get home. That isn't safe."

She shrugged. "I do what I must. It won't be the first time I've walked home in the dark, and if I'm not accepted into the program, I'll also be living in the dark since I won't be able to pay utilities."

He motioned toward the waiting limo. "Get in. I'll take you where you need to go. It's the least I can do since I detained you and made you lose your ride home."

"Are you sure it isn't an imposition?" she asked.
"Not at all."

Brielle slid into the limo and scooted to the middle to give the alien room. He ducked into the car and took the opposite seat from her, smiling. Once the door was shut, the car lurched forward.

"I need an address to give the driver," the captain said.

She rattled off Aaron's address and settled in for the ride, answering the captain's questions. He was very curious for someone not seeking a mate, but it made the time pass quickly and soon the car was pulling to a stop in front of her apartment. Brielle smiled at the captain and thanked him one last time before exiting the car and walking up the stairs to the apartment.

As she opened the door, the limo pulled away. She raised her hand to wave one last time and then stepped inside the darkened apartment. Brielle flicked on a lamp and set her purse and keys down. Toeing off her shoes, she made her way to the bedroom. There were still boxes in the storage room off the balcony and she would use those to start her packing. Whether she was accepted into the program or not, she had to be out of the apartment within a week or Aaron would no doubt come and toss her out.

The big alien had come along at just the right time, as far as Brielle was concerned. He'd extended her a lifeline and she was going to grab hold with both hands. It was a pity he wasn't available, but she was certain there was a decent, sexy alien out there just for her. She knew the males outnumbered the females on Terran. It was because of that difference that the bride exchange had been set up. In exchange for a woman offering herself as a Terran bride, her family would be compensated handsomely. If she was alone in the world, she could do what she wanted with the money. Donate it or keep it.

"Just think," Brielle told herself. "This isn't only a win for you, but for your parents too. They could use a little boost right now."

She pulled the boxes out of the storage room and dragged them to the bedroom, where she started filling them with her knickknacks. Next, she'd go through her clothes and decide what she was going to keep and what she would donate. It was going to be a long-ass night.

Chapter Two

Brielle clutched the letter in her hand as she approached the Terran transport station. Her bag was being delivered to the shuttle and the rest of her belongings would be placed in storage until she decided what she wanted to do with them. Until she had a mate and a home of her own, she wouldn't be permitted to take more than one suitcase with her.

The acceptance had arrived that morning, and they'd given her exactly three hours to pack and get to the transport station. If she missed this shuttle, there wouldn't be another one for four more days. It took a day, using hyper drive, to arrive on Terran, and a day for the shuttle to return home. As long as there was space for more humans on the planet, the shuttle would continue to make trips. But once the lodgings were at capacity, there would be no more trips until someone returned home.

The woman at the gate held out her hand. "Ticket?"

Brielle held up her letter. "I didn't receive a ticket, but this letter was delivered a few hours ago."

The woman scanned the letter and handed it back to her. "The front row is reserved for brides. Pick any seat."

Brielle thanked her and continued down the carpeted path to the shuttle steps. Once on board, she took a seat by the window. It would suck if she had to go pee and had to climb over people, but she wanted the view since it was her first time going up in space. And possibly her last, if she was able to find a Terran mate. She crossed her fingers and said a quick prayer that everything would work out.

She looked around as passengers claimed their seats and was surprised that no one else sat in the front row. When the stairs were pulled away and the shuttle door was closed, her heart began to race. Was she crazy to do this? To give up everything she knew to go live on another world with men she'd never met? Brielle had been independent her entire life, and she wasn't sure she'd be able to give up control to someone now.

What if they were controlling? What if she had to ask permission before doing anything? What if they were ugly? What if they smelled? The Terran captain had smelled nice, but what if the others weren't as hygienic?

With a sigh, she placed her hand against the cool glass and watched the scenery pass as they taxied down the runway. When the shuttle lifted into the air, her stomach did a flip. The ground rapidly disappeared as they climbed past the clouds and hurtled toward the atmosphere. Brie closed her eyes and when she opened them again, everything seemed so very far away.

"Please remain in your seats," the captain said over the loud speaker. "We will be breaking through the atmosphere shortly and it may be a bit bumpy. If you feel sick to your stomach, there are bags in the compartments above your seats."

Brie tightened her seatbelt and peered out the window. As the shuttle rocketed into space, she tried to keep her ears equalized, but she felt pressure building in them. She'd researched Meniere's disease the night before and knew that it was unlikely the flight would affect her. She opened and closed her mouth a few times and finally popped her ears, relieving the pressure.

The shuttle began to shake violently, but eventually evened back out. Brie looked through her window and saw the planet becoming smaller and smaller. She was now surrounded by vast space. Having broken her watch the other day, she had no idea how long she'd been on board, but it didn't feel like it had been all that long, and at the same time, it felt like forever.

She heard the sounds of people vomiting and cringed, scooting closer to the window. She'd read that people with Meniere's disease could feel nauseated during flights, but thankfully, that hadn't happened to her. She'd been smart and taken some Antivert that morning, before heading to the transport station. Meniere's disease tended to leave her dizzy and sometimes she felt pressure build in her ear. It only affected her right ear. During the worst episodes, she'd lost hearing in that ear for a short time.

"Welcome to space," the captain said over the speaker. "The easy part is over. I know time feels a little different out here, but we left Earth less than five minutes ago. We'll arrive on Terran in approximately eight hours at the continued speed of four thousand miles per hour. Terran is approximately ten billion miles from Earth."

There were murmurs in the cabin of the shuttle.

"I would imagine you've done the math and wondered how we can make it in eight hours," the captain said. "We'll fold space in approximately one hour. It can have an unsettling effect on humans, so the shuttle's cabin is stocked with special masks that will put you to sleep until we reach the Terran atmosphere. Reach above you and click the button on the hatch to your right. A mask will fall down. I want you to fit it over your face and breathe deeply. When you wake, we'll almost be to your new home world."

Brie reached up and pressed the button. A clear mask fell down. She fitted the strap behind her head with the mask covering her nose and mouth. As instructed, she took long, deep breaths. There was a tang to the air and she felt her body beginning to numb. Within moments, her eyes were sliding shut.

***

Brielle felt someone tugging the mask from her face and she swam back to consciousness. The sexy captain from the other day was smiling down at her. Brie pushed herself up in her seat and looked around. Everyone else had already disembarked.

"I was worried about you," the captain said. "Everyone else left about a half hour ago, but when we did a head count, you were missing."

She tugged her right ear. "I wonder if my condition had anything to do with it."

He frowned. "What condition? Are you ill?"

"Meniere's disease. It causes vertigo, pressure in my right ear, and sometimes deafness. I've had it for a few years now."

"I would take you straight to the med bay, but your mate may prefer to handle it. I wouldn't want to overstep."

"It's okay." Brie smiled. "I'm used to it. It can cause problems, but it's nothing I can't handle."

The captain nodded and held out his hand. "Come. Let's get you settled."

Brie slid her hand into his and slowly rose to her feet. The captain escorted her down the steps and into the station. There were groups of Terran males near the entrance.

"Are they here for me?" she asked.

"They are most curious about the bride coming to Terran. So yes, they are here for you. Some are not available and merely wished to see you. Others are hoping to claim you for a bride." He looked down at her. "Do they scare you? I can ask them to move."

"No, it's fine. I know they won't hurt me."

He smiled.

"Where am I to stay tonight? Did my bag make it off the shuttle?"

"Your things have been taken to one of the... I believe you call them studios. We keep a half dozen for brides to use when they first land on Terran. You won't be rushed to select a mate, but the sooner the better. I'm afraid they may pester you until you make a decision."

"Are women really so few on your planet?"

The captain nodded. "There is only one Terran female for every fifty Terran males. The youngest fully Terran female is in her thirties. We don't know why females are no longer born here -- full Terran females -- but our scientists have been working on it. However, there doesn't seem to be an issue with half-Terran half-human females being born. The doctor at this station has already delivered three in the past year."

"That's incredible."

The captain ushered her out of the transport station and into the sun. She looked up. Suns. She'd read there were three suns on Terran, and four moons, but seeing it was another matter. They were beautiful. She'd read that Terran never truly had a winter, with temperatures never dropping below seventy degrees. Being on Terran was going to be like visiting a tropical paradise. Well, without the water. Terran didn't have oceans, just lakes. Lots of lakes.

They came to a stop in front of a fifteen-story high building and the captain waved his wrist over an electronic pad by the door. There was a click and the door sprang open. He pulled it open further and motioned for her to go in ahead of him. The door shut behind them and he guided her toward the bank of elevators.

"Your studio is on the thirteenth floor. I've heard that can be an unlucky number for humans, but on Terran it's very lucky."

"What's on the fourteenth and fifteenth floors?" she asked.

"You would call them penthouses. There are two on the fourteenth floor and the fifteenth floor belongs to an inventor. He uses half the space as his laboratory and the rest as his home."

"Is he Terran?"

"Yes. There are a few Terrans who have chosen to live here, but most of the building's inhabitants are human. I think our council feels better having a few Terrans in the building, in case something goes wrong."

They entered the elevator and she turned to face him. "Am I the only bride right now?"

"Yes. The last bride we brought to Terran selected her mate three weeks ago. Another pilot will take the shuttle back to Earth. When a new batch of brides has been selected, they will be brought to Terran and will reside in the studios on the same hall as yours." He smiled. "Although I hope you will have chosen a mate by then. It could be weeks, maybe months. Because of your situation, we rushed things a bit. There is normally a one-week lag between application and acceptance, and then the bride is given several weeks to say good-bye to her family and choose what she will bring with her."

"I don't mind that I was rushed. This was an answer to a prayer." And she had been praying hard while she waited to hear from the Terran embassy.

The elevator came to stop and the captain led the way to her quarters. He passed his wrist over another electronic pad and the apartment door opened. When Brie stepped inside, she saw her suitcase waiting on the bed. There was a small couch, a Vid-Comm, a small bed, and a miniature kitchen with a table and two chairs. The furniture was nice, even if the space was tiny compared to the apartment she'd shared with Aaron.

"Will this do?" the captain asked.

"Yes, thank you." She motioned to the door. "How do I go about opening the doors around here? I don't have an implant in my wrist."

"Someone will arrive shortly to take you to medical where you will go through minor surgery to have an implant placed in your wrist."

Brie rubbed at her wrist. "Will it hurt?"

"No. The doctor will use a laser to open the skin and another to close it. Other than a faint line, you won't be able to tell you had the operation. The pink line will fade over the next few weeks, but the implant will give you access to your quarters and any public building on Terran."

"What about food and any other essentials I need?"

"It is recommended that you spend your meal times with the single males seeking a mate. If there are any other items you desire, the credits will be deducted from your mate once you select one. Shop owners will keep a tally of your charges until that time."

She nibbled at her lower lip. "I'll try not to buy too much. I'd hate to run up a tab my mate wouldn't be able to pay. That's not a good way to start a relationship."

The captain smiled. "You have a level head on your shoulders, but then I realized that when you punched your ex-fiancé. Considering his comments to you, I'm sorry I didn't let you hit him again. He certainly deserved it."

"I doubt that's going to endear me to anyone."

"You'd be surprised." His smile widened. "We love fierce women, and you, Brielle, are a fierce woman."

"You know my name, but I don't know yours. Hardly seems fair. Unless everyone just calls you Captain?"

"My name is Reyvor."

"Reever?"

"R-E-Y-V-O-R. But yes, that's how it's pronounced."

She held out her hand. "It's nice to meet you, Reyvor. Thank you for coming to my rescue the other day and again today."

Reyvor grasped her hand and shook it gently. "You're most welcome, Brielle. Come. Why wait? We'll get your implant surgery out of the way. Would you like to meet some males this evening or take a day to settle in?"

"I suppose the sooner I meet them the better. I came here to mate with one of your males. Only seems fair that I hold up my end of the bargain by starting right away. Delaying a day won't change anything, except make for a lonely meal tonight."

Reyvor escorted her through the city streets and into the doctor's office. It wasn't quite what she'd expected. It had stark white walls, like several clinics she'd been to, but one wall was entirely made of glass with a Vid-Comm taking up the majority of it. A movie from Earth was playing and caught Brie's attention.

"Wait here," Reyvor said. "I'll let the doctor know you're ready for your surgery."

"Stop."

He turned to face her.

"Why is it I can understand you? I just figured the Terran station had some sort of translator in the building, but I've been able to understand you since then too."

"I speak all of your Earth languages." He tipped his head to the side. "I see where this is going. Would you like to be implanted with a neural translator as well? The doctor could easily perform both operations at the same time."

"Yes, please. I'd like to understand everyone around me. I know not everyone here from Earth is from America, and I certainly don't know how to speak Terran."

He smiled. "We get a few other alien races here too, so don't be surprised if you see them wandering around. The most fearsome are the Bentares. Their skin is black as obsidian with white markings and stark white hair. Their eyes are light silver and rather unsettling to humans, or so I've been told. There has actually been some discussion of opening the bride program to other races, as Terrans are not the only ones lacking in fertile females."

"But I'm here to mate with a Terran, correct?"

He nodded. "In some cases, our Terran males have forged tight bonds with other alien races, and in those cases, they may wish to share a mate. If you prefer one male, you simply need to ask up front if they plan to share you with anyone."

"I've heard about brothers sharing on my planet, but I've never been part of a relationship that included more than one man. I don't know that I would be opposed to it, but it does make me a little nervous. It's unfamiliar."

"You don't have to do anything you don't want to, Brielle. Remember that. You're in control of your destiny here. Once you have a mate, they will watch over you, but Terrans are not like your Earth males. We would never think to order a female around. It goes against everything we believe in."

"Something tells me, when danger lurks, you're pretty good at ordering women around."

He nodded. "If it means guaranteeing their safety, then yes, but not on an everyday basis. Now, wait here and I'll return with the doctor."

She watched him disappear behind the glass. He walked through another door and disappeared from sight. Brielle looked around and settled on a chair across from the Vid-Comm playing the movie. It was one of her favorites from the eighties. She watched for about twenty minutes before Reyvor returned with another Terran in tow. The doctor, she assumed.

"Brielle," Reyvor said. "This is Xonos, the local doctor."

"Local? How many cities are there on Terran?"

"Three, but this is the main station. If humans wish to visit the other cities, they may, but they do not have as many shops as Terran Prime."

She nodded.

"Reyvor tells me that he explained the surgery to you?" Xonos asked. "Do you have any questions for me?"

"No." She rubbed her hands up and down her denim-clad legs. "I just want to get it over with. Should I be worried about waking up? Whatever gas was used on the shuttle knocked me out far longer than anyone else."

Xonos frowned. "You didn't mention that, Reyvor. I should run some tests before I give her anything. I'd hate to cause her damage."

Brielle stood. "I'm ready whenever you are, Xonos."

Xonos motioned for her to follow him. They went behind the glass wall and stopped at one of the hospital beds. He asked her to lie down and turn her arm over. He took several vials of blood and then walked over to a lab area, where he added different solutions to all but one. The last one he studied under a microscope.

"It's your DNA," Xonos explained. "The sleep agent we use is harmless, but it seems to bond to your molecules and make you sleep longer than the average human. It's most unique. I've never run across another sample like this one."

"What does that mean, as far as the surgery goes?"

"We'll still do both surgeries, but I won't give you gas. Instead, I'll give you an injection to make you sleep. You won't wake for at least an hour, but it's the only way to guarantee how long you'll be out."

She nodded. "Then let's do it."

Xonos smiled at her and held up a syringe. "This might pinch a little. The needle is a bit bigger than the others because the solution is rather thick."

Brielle braced herself and winced when the needle slid into her skin. The solution felt cool as it entered her bloodstream and after a few minutes she began to drift. Everything blurred at first and then the doctor's voice sounded like it was coming from underwater, and a moment later, Brielle was completely out.

When she woke an hour later, she was the proud owner of two implants, one identifying who she was and what she was allowed to access, and another that would allow her to communicate with anyone she came into contact with.

Chapter Three

Syl was more than a little aware of the woman who had moved in downstairs. He'd watched from his wall of windows as she entered the building, a trail of Terrans following in her wake, all anxious to get a look at their potential mate. If he hadn't been so busy, he might have joined their ranks. It wasn't that there weren't females on Terran; there just weren't any *available* females on Terran. Big difference.

He looked around his pristine lab and wondered when his work had become his life. For two years now, they had accepted mates from other worlds, predominantly Earth, but not once had he ever contemplated claiming a mate for himself. His work kept him busy and had, up to this point, kept him happy. But now he wondered if maybe there was something missing in his life.

It wasn't uncommon for him to take a trip off world every six months to visit the floating brothel nearby. He knew the women were clean, had insisted on them being tested regularly the first time he'd visited, threatened to bring it before the intergalactic council as a health hazard, but there was something lacking from the encounters. Yes, he was able to relieve some stress, but it was so... clinical. There was no passion involved; the women merely did their jobs, jobs they hadn't asked for to begin with. His conscience always pricked, knowing he was sleeping with a woman who had been forced into that lifestyle.

What would it be like to sleep with a woman because she wanted him? What would it be like to be wanted? No one wanted him, never had. Even his own mother hadn't known what to do with him when he was a child, always more interested in what went on in the labs than in the training fields. He came from a long line of proud warriors, and while Syl knew how to use a sword and various other weapons, it wasn't the life choice for him. He preferred beakers of solutions, test tubes filled with green goo, or assisting the weapons designer with new projects. He worked on everything from inoculations to laser weapons. There was never a dull moment.

And yet it wasn't fulfilling enough. Not anymore. He wanted something else in life, something he'd never thought to dream of before. Syl wanted a family, a mate to call his own and children who would either take after their beautiful mother or their brilliant father. He'd watched from his windows as families had gone on outings to the local park areas or the swimming pool, watched his friends pair off one at a time. When would it be his turn?

The new Earth woman was beautiful, from what he remembered. There had been a brief video that had played for all of Terran, a shot of her punching her ex-fiancé after she had discovered he'd cheated on her. In Syl's opinion, she should have done much worse to the male. He obviously hadn't been worthy of her, and to his way of thinking, she was much better off without him. He didn't understand what had prompted her to become a bride and move to Terran, and he wouldn't question her if they met face-to-face. If she wanted to share the story, she would in her own good time, he was certain.

"What do I know of females?" he muttered as he mixed two solutions. "My own mother didn't want me. Why would a mate?"

It wasn't that he was feeling sorry for himself, not exactly; he was just trying to be logical about the matter. Syl had always been a loner, except for his mentor, who was no longer allowed in a lab -- not after that small explosion a few years ago. It wasn't that he wasn't just as sharp mentally today as he'd been in his prime, but... well, he did tend to get easily distracted. He was also painfully alone, having never chosen a mate because he'd been consumed with his work, a fate that Syl was starting to think he would face as well, unless he made a change now, before it was too late.

He glanced outside at the waning suns. By now, the building's new occupant would have settled into her room and would be preparing for dinner. Had someone already asked her to join them? He was certain she would have had offers between disembarking the shuttle and arriving at the building. Terrans were direct if nothing else. Well, most were.

Determined to take the first step in changing his life, he set his instruments down, ditched his lab coat, and went to freshen up a little. When his hair was neatly combed with a fresh braid that trailed over his shoulder, he decided he was as ready as he'd ever be. The worst that would happen was that she'd already have plans. Either way, he could introduce himself and welcome her to the building.

When Syl reached her floor, he stepped out of the lift and approached her door. Everyone in the building knew which suite she was occupying as an announcement had been made prior to her arrival. He knocked and waited, hoping she was still inside and hadn't left for the evening already.

The door slid open and she stood before him, uncertain, her fingers fiddling with the hem of her tunic-style shirt and her teeth nibbling on her lower lip. Her fiery red hair cascaded down her back and across one shoulder, hanging nearly to her waist. Syl couldn't remember the last time he'd seen something quite so beautiful.

He cleared his throat, realizing that he was just standing there, staring at her.

"I thought I'd welcome you to the building," he said and then held out his hand, remembering that people on Earth shook hands when they met someone. "I'm Syl. I live upstairs."

She slid her hand into his, her fingers curling around his as the heat of her palm sparked against his flesh. He felt the hair on his nape stand up and an immediate reaction in his pants, something he hoped she didn't notice. Her gaze held him spellbound, the green depths sultry, promising many nights of passion to the male lucky enough to claim her.

"I'm Brielle," she said. "It's nice to meet you."

He cleared his throat again. "Do you already have plans for the evening? I was about to step out for a meal and thought I'd see if you wanted to join me."

You sound like you don't have a brain in your head. He could have kicked himself right now, knowing he was blowing his chance with her. Who wanted a male who couldn't carry on a decent conversation? Truth was he'd never had a chance to really interact with females before, except for those he was related to.

Her teeth bit into her lip again, her hand still securely in his. "Are you sure it won't be an imposition?" she asked.

Relief flooded him. "I'm positive. I would love the company."

"Just let me put on some shoes."

He glanced down and wished he hadn't. Syl couldn't remember a time he'd thought someone's feet were beautiful, but hers were. Long, thin and pale with pink polish on her toes. Her feet were delicate, much like her, despite the video of her punching someone. Syl didn't think she looked like a woman who went around striking males on a whim.

She slipped on some white canvas flats and stepped out into the hall, her door sliding shut behind her. Hesitantly, she reached out and placed her hand on his arm, allowing him to lead her through the building and out into what was turning into a beautiful night.

It was her first night on Terran, and while he could take her to the café that served Earth food, he thought she might prefer something with more of a local flare. He took her to his uncle's restaurant, which served popular Terran dishes. When they stepped through the door, his aunt hurried over with a big smile on her face.

"Syl! You've brought a guest with you this evening," his aunt said. "Come. You'll have the best seat available."

Which meant she wasn't going to make him sit by the kitchens like she normally did, and for that, he was grateful. He wanted to make an impression on Brielle, a favorable one so that she might agree to see him again. Now, if he could only think of something witty to say.

The tables were equipped with scanners that also displayed the items available to purchase. He explained the different meals to her; they made their selection and then he swiped his wrist across the scanner to pay for their food. He'd read somewhere, that on Earth, people paid after the meal, which he found confusing. Shouldn't you pay before they went to the trouble to make it? What if you changed your mind?

"What do you think of Terran so far?" he asked while they waited for their meals.

"It's really pretty, and a bit different from what I expected. I knew I was coming to a city, but this place could easily be on Earth. We have tall buildings, like the one we live in, and while your homes look different from ours, your community seems to be set up similar to ones I've seen on Earth."

"Is that a good thing?"

She smiled. "Yes, it's nice seeing familiar things."

"I told myself I wouldn't ask, and if you don't want to tell me that's fine, but you're a rather beautiful woman and I have a hard time seeing you as someone who would need to sign up for the bride program just to find a mate."

She grimaced. "I was engaged on Earth, but it didn't end so well. He came here to work in one of your medical facilities, and while he was here, he fell in love with someone else. He tossed me out of our apartment and I had nowhere else to go."

"What about your family?" His brow furrowed and his lips thinned, irritation flashing through him at the thought of her being left alone in her time of need. "Would they not take you in?"

"Oh, I'm sure they would have, but they live in a really small house and two of my sisters were already living at home. There really wasn't space for me, but if I'd asked they wouldn't have turned me away. I just didn't want to burden them. When Captain Reyvor realized my situation, he suggested I sign up for the bride program. It seemed like the perfect solution."

"Do you expect to find love on Terran?" He'd read enough about humans to know that was something most Earth women sought. There were even books written about males and females falling in love.

He'd read one of them once -- for scientific purposes, of course.

"I'm not sure that I believe in love anymore." Her lips twisted. "Maybe love is an illusion. What I do know is that love isn't required to build a lasting relationship with someone. There are common interests, a sense of humor and knowing that I can depend on him. My parents were married when they were young, because my dad got my mom pregnant, and they've been honest with us that love grew over time. It might not be that all-consuming love you read about, but I think the love they share is better than the kind that can flare hot, then burn out."

Sense of humor? Well, that left Syl out. It wasn't that he didn't find things funny; he just didn't know how to be funny. While other children had gone off to laugh and play games, he'd sequestered himself in laboratories and tried to puzzle out the next medical miracle. He was grateful their food arrived and hoped she'd change the topic. The last thing he wanted was another reminder of how lacking he was.

"I've said too much," she said, when he didn't comment.

"No. Just processing. So you would settle for a loveless mating in the hopes that love would grow over time?"

"Yes. Definitely. But... there has to be a spark there."

"A spark?"

"You know..." She waved her hand around. "Sexual chemistry. If I don't desire him and he doesn't desire me, then what's the point?"

Syl felt his cheeks warm, having never discussed sex with a female before. "I imagine any male who meets you will feel that spark. I saw the crowd gathered around the building, waiting for you to show up. Most of them were unmated males wanting a look at the potential bride."

"I've heard some warriors on Terran share a mate."

"Yes. But not all. I think the warriors form a bond when they're in battle that carries over into the rest of their lives. Many share the same home even if they aren't mated yet."

"You mean they…" Her cheeks flushed. "Are you saying they're gay?"

Syl frowned. "I don't understand that term. Are you asking if they're happy?"

"No." Her cheeks turned an even brighter shade of pink. "I mean, do they sleep together. Do they have a sexual relationship?"

"Oh. Oh! No. Nothing like that. I know some humans prefer same-sex couplings, but Terrans are different."

"Enough about me," she said. "What is it you do? Are you a warrior? Or are you the scientist I was told lived in the building?"

"I guess you could call me a scientist. I dabble in a little bit of everything, but yes, it's all science related. Right now, I'm working on a cure for one of your human illnesses. One of the mates, one of the first women to take part in the program, has recently been diagnosed with schizophrenia. I know on Earth, you have pills that can help control the illness, but I wish to eradicate it completely."

Her eyebrows rose. "You can do that?"

"We've already cured several of the illnesses you have on Earth. It's just a matter of finding the right combination."

"You must be pretty smart."

"I was told what I lacked in muscle I made up for in brain matter."

She eyed his arms and chest. "You lack muscle? You could probably snap me in half without even trying."

He felt oddly pleased with her observation. No one had considered him strong before, and he liked the fact that she did. Maybe taking a mate wouldn't be so hard, if all the women thought the way Brielle did. Maybe he didn't have to be a strong warrior to make a female feel safe and cared for. It was something he'd worried about.

They finished their meal and he was sad that their time was at an end. He wasn't sure he was the right male for her, but he'd enjoyed their time together. It just proved that he really did need someone in his life, someone to pull him away from his work, someone to laugh with. As he watched Brielle, longing hit him right in the chest. No, what he wanted was someone to love. If Brielle was correct, and love could grow over time, then maybe there was hope for him.

"I'll walk you back to your room," he said, rising from the table, wanting to prolong their time together.

Brielle stood and looped her arm through his. Syl led her through the restaurant and out into the moonlight. In the distance, the nearby planet of Thrax could be seen clearly, a red and purple orb in the night sky. He pointed it out to her.

"Once, people lived on that planet. It's said that the ground shook and opened in areas, releasing the gases you see surrounding the planet now, giving it those vibrant colors. Many of the people escaped and moved to other worlds, but a lot of them perished. No one goes there now."

"That's so sad. Did any of the people come here?"

"A few. Their males are orange with black-and-white stripes on their skin, similar to one of the animals on your planet."

She smiled. "A tiger."

He nodded. "You may see them as you explore more of Terran, but only one or two live in Terran Prime. The others reside in the outlying cities."

When they arrived at Brielle's door, Syl didn't want to let her go, and he wondered if she would ever consider dining with him again. As much as he'd love to lay claim to her, he knew it was only fair to allow her to explore other options, possibly finding a male better suited to her. There would be other brides, but he doubted any would sparkle like she did.

"I had a nice time tonight," Brielle said, a smile curving her lips.

"I did as well."

She looked at him expectantly for a moment and then unlocked her door. "I guess I'll see you around the building, since we're practically neighbors."

"I don't venture out of my lab very often, but I hope to see you again."

Was that disappointment in her eyes? Disappointment over seeing him again, or because he hadn't asked her to join him for another meal or outing? Females were rather confusing to Syl and he wasn't sure what he was supposed to say or do. He watched as she slipped inside her quarters and the door slid shut. It felt so final, watching the portal close.

Unsure what his next move should be, or when, he headed back to his floor and his waiting lab. Maybe working on his current task would clear his mind and make him see things in a different light. Or maybe it would give him the coward's way out of approaching Brielle again, on the off chance she turned him down. Syl was tired of being rejected, first by his family and later by his peers.

Chapter Four

It had been three days since her date with Syl, and she'd seen several males since then. But for some reason, the shy, quiet scientist haunted her at night. He'd made an impression on her and she hoped she would see him again. Brielle wasn't sure what the rules were on Terran as far as women approaching men. Would it be all right for her to seek him out?

She was sunning herself by the pool, contemplating that very issue, when something large passed overhead and Brie shielded her gaze, trying to get a better look. It was a ship of some sort, much larger than a shuttle. The black metal gleamed in the sunshine. Her brow furrowed as she realized they were too far from the transport station to attempt a landing, and yet they were getting closer. The air stirred as it neared the planet.

A feeling of unease came over Brie. Something wasn't right. There was no reason for the ship to be hovering like that, not unless they wanted something, or were searching for something. Or someone. She didn't know enough about the aliens in the area to know what kind of ship it was, but she knew trouble when she saw it.

A beam of light blasted from the ship and when it cleared, three aliens were racing toward her. They didn't look familiar to her, their skin an icy blue, their eyes black as midnight. Fear wasn't something she was accustomed to, but she felt it now. Scrambling off the lounger, she braced herself.

They stopped in front of her and the closest one reached for her. Brie smacked his hand away and took a step back. They followed her retreat.

"What do you want?" she demanded, trying to hide the quiver in her voice.

"Come with us," the tallest one said. "We won't harm you."

"If you try to remove me from this planet, I'm going to harm *you*. Go away!" She took another step back.

When they reached for her a second time, she punched the closest one, her fist connecting with his jaw. Pain radiated through her wrist and up into her arm, but she didn't back down. More hands reached for her and she lashed out, hitting and kicking, biting the hand that came near her face.

"We're going to have to sedate her," the tall one said.

"Like hell you will!" Brie bared her teeth at them. "No one is sedating me."

The third alien looked around. "We've drawn the attention of two warriors. They're rushing this way. Grab her and let's go."

As the aliens reached for her again, she fought like a wildcat. No way was she going down without a fight. If they wanted her, they'd have to drag her away kicking and screaming. She had no idea who they were or what they wanted from her, although she had her suspicions.

"Brielle!" She heard a Terran's voice, the deep husky tone telling her a warrior was on his way to aid her, but didn't dare look his way. She kept her gaze fastened on the aliens in front of her.

From the corner of her eye, she saw a glint. Something silver was coming toward her. She glanced the Terran's way and realized he'd tossed her a blade as he'd neared the group of aliens. She snatched it out of the air and brandished it with the awareness of someone who had been in more than one fight in her life. The next time a grabby alien reached for her, she lashed out at him, slicing his arm. Black blood oozed from the wound and he hissed in surprise.

Another alien made a grab for her and she lashed out at him too, slicing across his fingers. He jerked his hand away and she took a step back. The Terran launched himself through the air, landing in a crouch in front of her, and she saw a Bentares warrior a few yards away.

The Terran rose to his impressive height, blocking the blue aliens from her view. When the Bentares joined him, she found herself staring at a rather yummy wall of muscled males. She supposed there were worse ways to spend her time. Now that the two warriors were here, she knew the aliens wouldn't get away with kidnapping her. She knew they would keep her safe, even if she had been doing okay on her own. Eventually, the blue bastards would have won and she would have been on that spaceship before she could call out for help.

"The woman is ours," the Terran said.

Theirs? Not likely. She snorted.

"She's unmarked," one of the blue aliens said. She wasn't sure which one it was. "It means anyone can mate with her."

"How did you know she was here?" the Bentares asked.

"A mated friend of ours was visiting when she arrived. He got word to us that there was an available female on Terran. We would be very good to her," the blue alien insisted.

"You're not taking her," the Terran growled.

"A mate isn't worth this much trouble," one of them muttered. "Let's go, brothers. There are other females on other worlds."

Brie peered around the Bentares warrior and watched the blue aliens return to their ship. That was it? It was over that quickly? She'd been fighting for her life and all it took was two warriors to place themselves between the aliens and her and then the little blue creeps decided to take off?

"I think I'm insulted," she said.

The Bentares male turned toward her. "That they didn't fight harder to keep you?"

"No. I'm mad that no matter how hard I fought, they were determined to take me. But the minute you two show up, they suddenly throw their hands in the air and surrender. I cut two of them. Doesn't that count for something?"

The Bentares warrior smiled. "You were fierce, but the cuts you gave them were minor. It was like being scratched by one of your Earth kittens."

She folded her arms over her chest and harrumphed.

"Are you injured?" the Terran asked.

"No. I'm fine." She unfolded her arms. "I should thank the two of you for showing up when you did. If you'd been a few minutes later, I probably would have been on their ship and no one would have known what happened to me."

The Terran looked decidedly uncomfortable. "That isn't entirely true."

"Which part?" Her brow furrowed.

"We would have known where you were, once someone realized you were missing. All we'd have to do is activate the tracker in your chip and someone would have come to rescue you."

"Tracker?" She felt steam building inside. "You microchipped me like a puppy?"

"It's part of the chip that the doctor put in your wrist. It's only meant to keep you safe. No one would activate it unless you were missing," the Bentares assured her.

She knew that should make her feel better, but it didn't. Brie felt violated, but she'd agreed to have the operation. She just hadn't understood exactly what was being done to her. It wasn't like she could undo it; she needed that chip to get around Terran. What was done was done. Time to move past it.

"You seem to know who I am," she said. "But I have no idea who the two of you are. I haven't seen you before."

The Terran smiled. "I'm Kelvyk, but my friends call me Kel. The Bentares here is my brother-in-arms, Ryoku. We were on our way to the training grounds when we heard you fighting the Tourmalanes. They're not usually dangerous, but the women on their world are dying out. They're just as desperate for brides as we are."

"So why don't you work together?"

The warriors shared a look.

"What? I know the Terrans set up the bride exchange with Earth first, but what if you opened it up to more alien races? There are plenty of women on Earth who would want to be brides. You could open up agencies on other planets that have women who would be willing. Why not expand on what you already have so you can include more people and put an end to the abductions? Wouldn't it make more sense to work together than to fight each other?"

"She has a point," Ryoku said. "There are some races out there who only wish to enslave women, but those looking for mates could be allies with us. If we fought fewer battles over the women we bring here, we could focus on other matters."

"In other words, you want me to speak to my uncle," Kel said, a wry smile on his lips.

Ryoku shrugged. "If you mention it to him, he might actually consider it. But if I bring it up, he's likely to scoff and tell me the idea is ridiculous."

"Being the man's only living male relative is a bit taxing," Kel muttered.

"I don't understand," Brie said. "Who's your uncle?"

"Chief Councillor Borgoz. He runs things around here, for the most part. There's an entire council that puts the laws into place, but my uncle is head of the council." Kel gave her a lopsided smile. "He considers me his heir so he tends to listen to my suggestions, but he's never cared for Ryoku. He's incensed that I didn't choose a Terran warrior mate."

"Wow." She raised her eyebrows. "So you're like Terran royalty?"

"We don't have a royal house on Terran, but Kel is the closest thing we have to a prince around here."

"I feel like I should curtsey," Brie muttered.

Kel and Ryoku merely laughed.

"You should let us take you out for dinner tonight." Ryoku glanced at the setting suns. "It will be mealtime shortly."

Brie nibbled on her lower lip. It was the least she could do after they'd saved her, but there was something about this dynamic duo that had her on edge. They were different from the other males she'd met. They didn't have that desperate feel to them. Neither had come running when she'd begun meeting the single males, and she doubted either would be the type to fall at her feet, something one Terran had done just the other day.

The smile fell from Ryoku's face. "I understand if you'd prefer to just eat with Kel. I've heard Earth women tend to be frightened of Bentares warriors."

"I'm not scared of you."

"Then you'll have dinner with us?" he asked, his white eyebrows rising.

"Yes," she said, coming to a decision. "I'll have dinner with you, but I need to shower and change first. Can't go out like this," she said, motioning to her bathing suit.

"We'll meet you outside of your building in an hour. Will that give you enough time to get ready?" Kel asked.

"An hour would be perfect."

"Please allow us to escort you back to your building." Ryoku held out his hand. "We won't allow any harm to befall you."

She glanced over her shoulder. "The building is what? Twenty yards away? I think I can make it without incident. But thank you for the offer. I'll see you outside the main lobby in an hour."

Without giving them a chance to say anything further, she turned and began the short walk back to her building. It wasn't until she was safely locked behind her suite door that she breathed a sigh of relief. The two warriors were intense and put off strong vibes. Being in their presence was hell on her body. They would be hell on any woman, but lucky her, she was the only available woman on the planet. For now. Still, despite the physical attraction, she didn't feel they would be ideal mates for her.

She'd heard from Reyvor that another shipment of brides was arriving in another day or two. When the council had seen how bombarded Brielle was, they had worked quickly to bring more potential mates to Terran. Something Brielle was grateful for. The pressure to pick a mate, when so many were searching for a woman to complete their families, had sent the men to her in droves. She hated the disappointed looks when she didn't choose someone, or when she had to tell them there just wasn't a spark there and she wouldn't be seeing them again. It was like kicking a puppy.

Aware of her time limit, she quickly stripped out of her bathing suit and climbed into the shower, letting the hot water wash the protective oils down the drain. Her skin was so fair that Xonos has come up with a special oil for her to wear, kind of like sunscreen that would protect her from the suns.

As her hands brushed across her breasts, her nipples puckered. It had been so long since she'd had sex she wasn't sure she'd remembered how. She knew enough about Terrans to know a sexual encounter did not mean she would be mated to that warrior, but there just hadn't been enough of a spark between any of the men she'd dated since coming to Terran and her. Except for Syl.

Finished with her shower, she shut off the water and went to her meager belongings to find just the right outfit for her dinner with the two mouthwatering males. She had to admit they were both very good-looking, enough that she'd felt a spark of desire, just not as much as the spark she'd felt with Syl. She shook her head. Obviously, he wasn't interested since he hadn't returned to her door. *Unless he's gotten lost in an experiment and has forgotten the world exists.* It was something to ponder.

She settled on a strapless floral-print dress that complemented her fair skin and red hair. Selecting one of the strappy pairs of shoes she'd brought with her, she slipped them on and fastened the buckles.

It had taken her a day or two to figure out the Terran version of a hair dryer, but she'd mastered it now and dried her long locks. She almost needed an hour just for her hair, but she rushed through it, leaving it partially damp. It would end up with a bit of wave to it, but they didn't have flatirons on Terran. Maybe she should bring it up to one of the inventors she'd met.

Brie put on a clear deodorant and spritzed on her favorite perfume -- not enough that it would be overpowering, but enough to lure an unsuspecting male, assuming she ran into Syl in the building.

The two warriors had already seen her without makeup so she didn't see the point in putting on more than a sheer lip-gloss. Her cheeks were naturally rosy after all her time in the sun the past few days.

With a sigh, she realized she was as ready as she'd ever be, and a quick glance at the time told her she was already a few minutes late. Knowing the warriors, they had not only been on time but had perhaps even shown up a little early, meaning she'd kept them waiting.

Exiting the building, she watched as two figures stepped out of the shadows. Both men were dressed in leather vests and leather pants with calf-high boots. Neither had on a shirt, showing their bodies to advantage. She wondered if they even owned shirts. Brie had noticed most Terrans only wore leather pants and boots.

"You look beautiful," Kel said, taking her hand and looping it through his arm.

Ryoku took her other hand and placed it in the crook of his arm, placing his hand over hers. "Kel is right. You are even more tempting than when you were wearing so little."

Brie felt a blush rising to her cheeks and thanked them. Flanked by her escorts for the evening, they made their way down the walkways and travelled a few blocks from her building.

She smiled up at Ryoku. "You look rather serious, Ryoku. Is everything all right?"

"Everything is fine, Brielle. I'm just making sure we arrive at our destination safely."

"Surely you don't think there will be another attempt today." She looked around, the hairs on her nape standing at attention. "I haven't had problems for days. It had to be an isolated incident, right?"

"We don't want to take any chances with your safety," Ryoku told her. "You're very important to us."

"But you don't know me."

His gaze bore into hers. "I know everything I need to know."

She wasn't sure what to say that and faced forward again. They stopped outside of the human-owned café, something that was relatively new to Terran. She'd heard about it from one of the warriors she'd dined with, but no one had brought her here yet. She was looking forward to the experience. From what she'd heard, the woman who ran it was mated to a Terran warrior and had asked to open the café as a way to occupy her time. Truthfully, Brielle was surprised the woman's mate had allowed it.

As they slid into a booth near the window, she found Ryoku watching her, his gaze intent.

Chapter Five

After they had placed their orders, Ryoku studied Brielle. The sun glinted off her copper hair. He'd love nothing more than to reach out and stroke it. It looked so soft. He'd never been with a woman before, not a breathing one at any rate. He'd used the sex bots at the floating brothel nearby, as had Kel. They'd even shared one on several occasions, but neither had been with a flesh-and-blood female before. Would they be able to please her?

She chatted easily with them, proving that she would fit nicely into their lives. There were no awkward silences, no hesitance in her touch as she brushed his hand with her fingers. Despite the fact most women shied away from Bentares warriors, Brielle seemed to embrace being with both Kel and him. It gave him hope that maybe things would work between them. He'd heard she'd been out with several males since arriving, but there was no mention of her favoring anyone.

"When you're mated, will you feel the need to work, like the owner of this café does? Or will you be content to stay home and be a mate and mother?" Ryoku asked.

"I'm not sure. I know children take up a lot of time, but between now and the time those children arrive, I think I would be bored sitting at home while my mate went off and did whatever warriors do day after day. And during times he had to be away to fight, a job might keep the loneliness at bay and keep me from worrying about him so much."

Ryoku smiled. "You would worry about us?"

"I'd like to think I'd worry about my mate, or mates, if they went off to war. I'd even worry about you when you left to go train. Accidents happen, right?"

Kel took her hand and kissed it. "We've never had anyone worry about us before. Neither of us have parents who are living. My uncle would probably worry to some extent, but it's rare for a Terran male to worry about anything other than his mate and children."

"You don't even worry when you go to into battle?" she asked, her head tilted to one side and her brow furrowed.

"During a fight, you're too busy focusing on the men around you -- those fighting at your back, and those trying to take your head off. There isn't time to worry." Ryoku watched the emotions rolling across her face. "Remember when the Tourmalanes tried to abduct you today? How you fought back without thinking about anything but escape? It's not different when you're waging war, or defending your people."

"I guess I never thought about it." She pursed her lips. "Your job is really dangerous, isn't it? I mean, the two of you could easily be called off to fight and your mate would never see you again, right?"

"It's a possibility," Ryoku conceded, earning himself a harsh look from Kel. "But we've been fighting since we were sub-adults, barely eighteen. We met during a small skirmish on a planet not far from Terran and became brothers."

"Brotherhood forged in battle?" she asked.

Ryoku smiled. "Makes the bond stronger than that of blood. I would do anything for Kel."

"And I'd do anything for Ryoku," Kel said.

She narrowed her eyes. "Are you sure you two aren't..." She waved her hand. "You know."

Ryoku's brows slanted down. "Aren't what?"

"Gay," she said with a huff.

Ryoku had no clue what she was talking about, but looked to Kel for assistance. His brother-in-arms had his mouth hanging open and his eyes were wide, telling Ryoku that whatever their future mate had said, it had been shocking.

"What's 'gay' mean?" Ryoku asked.

"She wants to know if we sleep together. Intimately," Kel said.

Ryoku choked on the water he'd just swallowed. "What?"

"No," Kel told her. "We aren't gay. I think of Ryoku as a brother and nothing more."

"But you've shared women before, right? I mean, you wouldn't attempt to mate me together if you hadn't been in an intimate situation together before, right?" She glanced between the two.

Ryoku was glad his skin prevented her from seeing the blush he felt in his cheeks. "We've shared sex bots before, but never a living woman. The first time was by accident, but it made us realize we would enjoy pleasuring a woman together."

"Sex bots?"

"The floating brothels have them. It never felt right using a female who was either forced into that life, or one who had fallen so low she had no other options," Kel said. "We've actually never been with a living woman, not even separately. Does that make you wish for different mates?"

"Actually, it's rather sweet." She smiled. "But if neither of you have ever pleasured a woman, how do you know you can?"

She looked at them expectantly.

"We've watched videos from your Earth."

She snorted. "Porn? You're going to base your first time with a real woman off porn?"

Ryoku sat a little straighter. "You're going to mate with us?"

"Just because we sleep together doesn't mean we have to have an official mating." Although the look in her eyes said she wasn't sure she wanted to be intimate with them at all, despite the words that had fallen from her lips.

Ryoku shared a look with Kel and shook his head. Kel nodded his agreement.

"It's a mating or nothing," Kel said. "We want you, Brielle, don't mistake that, but we want you permanently. One night won't suffice."

"You've spent maybe a half hour with me, not including the fight today. I think it's a little premature to say you want me as your mate. You don't expect me to believe you fell in love with me at first sight, do you?"

"But it isn't the first time we've seen you. Captain Reyvor broadcasted a video of you punching your ex-fiancé across the Vid-Comms on Terran before you arrived. He commented that you were fierce, but he thought you would be loyal. Then when we saw you in action today, we knew we had to have you," Ryoku said.

"Let me get this straight." She took a sip of water. "You want me because I attacked my ex when he cheated on me, and because I fought against the Tourmalanes today when they tried to abduct me?"

"You're also beautiful and quite tempting," Kel said.

"Got it. Fierce and beautiful. So any woman who stood up for herself would be an acceptable mate to the two of you." She rose from her seat. "Since I'm just convenient and really any woman will do, I think I'll let the two of you enjoy dinner without me."

Ryoku's eyes widened as he watched her walk out of the café, just as their food arrived.

"I can have her meal sent to her quarters," the waitress offered. "And really, the two of you had it coming, her walking out like that... I'd have done the same thing."

"What did we do?" Ryoku asked.

"You made her feel common and like she was more of a convenience than someone you had to have. In her mind, you'd accept any woman who stood up for herself, which is most of us, so if you want her and only her, then you have your work cut out for you."

Kel punched him in the shoulder. "Way to screw everything up."

"What? How was I to know she wouldn't take it as a compliment?"

The waitress set their plates down and hurried back to the kitchen with Brielle's plate still clutched in her hand.

"Wait!" Kel called out. "We'll take it to her."

The waitress just shook her head, but boxed up the food and took it back to their table. "Don't say I didn't warn you. It wouldn't surprise me if the two of you ended up wearing this meal."

Ryoku glanced at Kel. "Think she'd throw it at us?"

"I think she's more likely to punch us." Kel's lips twisted. "Or draw one of our weapons and geld us."

"I wouldn't want to take a chance and hurt her." Ryoku frowned. "If she's tries to harm us, we'll just have to make sure she doesn't hurt herself and take our punishment like the warriors we are."

Kel nodded. "Probably a good idea. Let's eat quickly and take her meal to her. We can't let her starve just because you opened your mouth and stupidity came out."

Ryoku scowled at him.

"What?" Kel shrugged. "It's true."

With one last fierce glare at his brother, he turned to his food and ate quickly.

***

Brielle fumed the entire way back to her building, the scowl on her face sending most of the warriors in her path scurrying in the other direction. And she'd thought Kel and Ryoku were different! They were just like every other man out there, wanting to take the easy way. She'd be willing to bet that the moment more potential brides stepped foot on the planet they would turn their attention elsewhere.

"Everything all right?"

Brie looked up, her scowl turning to a smile when she saw Reyvor. "I'm just a little pissed at two of your warriors, but otherwise I'm fine."

"And what did they do to earn your ire?"

"They were typical men."

He laughed.

"What are you doing out and about without your mate? Don't tell me she's making you fend for yourself tonight."

Reyvor shook his head, but sadness entered his eyes.

"What's wrong?" Brielle asked, placing her hand on his arm.

"Anna is sick," Reyvor said, a sigh slipping between his lips. "Xonos has done everything in his power to cure her, but apparently there are some illnesses on Earth even we can't combat."

"Is it serious? Will she get well?"

She watched as he blinked moisture from his eyes. "Xonos said she may have a few weeks left. It's cancer and he said it's incurable. I knew she hadn't been feeling well, but she always brushed me off when I urged her to seek medical attention, and now the cancer has spread to the point Xonos can't help her."

"Oh, Reyvor." She wrapped her arms around him in a brief hug, wanting to give comfort, but not wanting to make the situation more awkward. "Is there anything I can do?"

He shook his head. "I appreciate the offer, though. Did you ever go back to Xonos to have your ears checked? Maybe he can cure your sickness."

"My dizzy spells haven't been so bad since moving here. I'll wait and discuss it with my mate, if I ever find one." Her lips twisted in a grimace. "I could have had one a hundred times over, but I think they're all of the opinion that any woman will do."

"And you want to be special."

"It's what every woman wants. Maybe I'll hold out until the other brides arrive. It will thin out the males and show me who is truly interested in me and not just desperate to have a female in his life."

"Sounds like a smart decision." He gestured toward her building. "May I walk you to the door?"

"I'd like that. I don't think I'm ready for any more males tonight. I've had my fill." She smiled. "Except for you."

Reyvor smiled and held out his arm. She placed her hand on top of his forearm and allowed him to escort her the rest of the way to her building. When they reached the front doors, she kissed his cheek.

"Thank you for everything you've done for me. If there's anything I can do for your mate and you please don't hesitate to ask."

He nodded, gave her a small smile, then turned and headed back the other direction.

Brielle scanned her wrist, opened the door to the building and hurried inside, making sure the outer door shut behind her. When she was back in her suite, her stomach rumbled, reminding her she'd missed dinner. No way in hell was she venturing back out tonight and braving even more males. She'd just have to go hungry for the night. Wasn't the first time in her life she'd gone to bed without supper, and if she didn't find a mate and uphold her end of the contract, it wouldn't be the last. The thought of returning to Earth was a frightening one, but the contract said if she didn't find a mate within four weeks, she could return home.

Taking off her dress and heels, she pulled on a comfortable pair of pajamas and pulled out the small tablet-like device she'd purchased the other day. It hadn't taken her long to realize it was boring sitting in her suite all alone. The shop owner had showed her how to download books from their Earth library to her device and she'd spent hours reading ever since. Brielle had always enjoyed reading, but now it was a lifeline during a time she'd have died of boredom without it.

A knock sounded at the door, making her frown. She rose and went to answer it, more than a little surprised to see Ryoku and Kel on the other side.

"I thought I was clear that things were finished between us," she said.

Kel held out a container of food. "You left without your dinner. We thought you might be hungry."

She accepted it grudgingly. "Thank you, but I meant what I said. Maybe we can be friends, but I won't see the two of you romantically."

Ryoku and Kel shared a look.

"What will it take to change your mind?" Kel asked.

"I don't know that you can." She shrugged. "Wait for the other brides to arrive and see if any of them appeal to you. You may find I'm not what you really want. Like I told you earlier, you don't know me well enough to make the decision that you want me for a mate. We haven't even known each other twenty-four hours. That's just moving way too fast for me."

A shadow fell across the door. "Problem?"

Brielle smiled at the one male she'd wanted to see for days. "Everything is fine, Syl. I believe these two were just leaving."

Syl might not be a warrior, but his muscles bulged as he folded his arms over his chest and stared at Ryoku and Kel, obviously waiting on them to take their leave. She'd found him charming and possibly the nicest Terran she'd met, even nicer than Reyvor. Too bad he didn't seem interested in her as a mate.

Chapter Six

Syl glowered at the two warriors outside Brielle's door. He'd heard her say she wasn't interested, and yet they remained. He knew some Terrans could be hardheaded, but he hoped he could make these two see reason without using his fists. He wasn't sure he would fare well in a fight with them.

"She told you to leave," he said. "Why are you still here?"

The two shared a look and then the Bentares spoke. "We were just bringing her dinner. We'll leave if that's what she truly wants."

"It is," Brielle said with her arms now crossed over her chest. A chest Syl was doing his damnedest not to notice. Her breasts were pushed up in the most enticing manner.

"We're going," the Terran said.

After the two warriors left, Syl moved closer to Brielle.

"Are you all right?" he asked.

"I'm fine." She bit her lip. "Thank you for rescuing me. I think they would have gone away eventually, but I think your presence urged them to leave a little sooner."

"They brought you dinner?"

"I was going to eat with them, but then I found out they were assholes."

Syl frowned. "I'm going to assume that's a human way of putting them down?"

"Something like that." Her lips twitched as she fought a smile. "Have you eaten yet?"

"I was actually on my way here to see if you wanted to join me. I've been caught up in a special project, but I realized it's been several days since we spoke."

She motioned to her clothes. "I'm already dressed for bed, but if you want to go pick something up and bring it back here, you're welcome to join me."

"Why don't we eat at my place? I have a rather large Vid-Comm and we could watch a movie while we eat."

She looked down at herself. "I won't have to change?"

"Not unless you want to."

"Then I would love to join you."

"Take the lift to the top floor and press in code 2-4-1 when it stops. I'll return as quickly as I can."

She picked up the container of food she had set down at some point and stepped out into the hall, drawing his attention to her feet and the white fluffy rabbits she wore. He couldn't help but smile and thought she was sexier than any woman he'd ever seen. He gently placed his hand at her lower back and escorted her down the hall to the waiting lifts. She took one and he claimed the other.

It didn't take him long to order food and return to the building, the lift doors sliding open on his floor. He found Brielle seated at the small table in his dining area, and he quickly scooped up her container and urged her to follow him. When they entered his main sitting area, he heard her indrawn breath.

"Everything all right?" he asked.

"Your place is just so… large. Your Vid-Comm is easily the size of the ones at the doctor's office, and all those windows! I bet you can see all of Terran Prime from here."

"Not quite, but the view is rather spectacular." *Especially right now.*

They sat and began eating, Syl stealing glances at her. He'd been fascinated by her since the first moment he laid eyes on her, and he felt much the same now. He'd been around other females, so he knew it wasn't the novelty of having one in his living space, it was just *her*. The way she moved, the way she smelled and the sound of her voice. He was spellbound by her, and she didn't even seem to notice.

He put one of her Earth movies on and after they were finished eating, they settled back to enjoy the show. He caught her looking his way once or twice and he wondered what she was thinking. Syl had never been tempted to reach for a woman before, but he found himself curious as to what she would feel like in his arms. Was she as soft as she looked?

On the floating brothel, he'd learned a little about kissing, and he hoped, how to please a woman. But other than going once or twice a year to find some satisfaction, he'd never once been tempted to be intimate with someone. None of the brides had appealed to him over the past two years, so he knew that it had to be something about Brielle that called to him, something about her that pulled him in and made him never want to let her go.

"Have you talked to your family since you arrived?" he asked.

She shook her head. "They're too far away from a Vid-Comm for me to contact them. Reyvor said once I was mated to someone, that perhaps my new mate would purchase a Vid-Comm for my parents so I could talk to them."

If he thought she'd accept such a gift, Syl would offer to purchase one now. He might not have been close to his family, but he got the feeling Brielle loved hers and that it pained her to be separated from them.

The few times she'd mentioned them the other day, her face had lit up and he'd seen the love shining in her eyes. He wished someone would look at him like that one day.

Brielle sighed and shifted.

"Everything all right?" he asked.

She looked his way, indecision in her eyes. "Why am I here?"

"Here as in Terran or here as in my quarters?"

"Here as in here with you. You vanished after my first day here. I thought you weren't interested. I mean, you mentioned an experiment or something, but…"

Not interested? He felt his heart kick in his chest.

"I'm very much interested, Brielle, but I don't think I'm the right fit for you. Wouldn't you rather have a strong warrior by your side?"

She gave his biceps a pointed look. "You aren't exactly weak."

"Compared to our seasoned warriors I am. I'd lose a fight against them within seconds. I'm a scientist and my life is in the lab. If you want a cure for something, call on me. If someone is trying to abduct you, I don't know that I would be much good to you."

Her cheeks burned and his eyes narrowed.

"Someone tried to abduct you?" he asked, his tone harsher than he'd meant.

"It was earlier today. Some Tourmalanes tried to grab me when I was by the pool. The two warriors you just chased off came to my rescue. I thought I owed it to them to have dinner and see if there was a spark there, but then I found out they were assholes."

His lips tipped up. "You didn't like them?"

"They want a strong woman. All the qualities they liked about me could be found in any number of women. Meaning they don't really want *me*."

"Then they're fools. Anyone would be lucky to have you, and not because you're a strong, fierce woman, but because you're beautiful, sweet, and your smile lights up a room. You're intelligent and yes, strong, but I have a feeling there's more to you than any male could discover in just one meeting. I think it would take years to learn everything there is to know about you, and some male is going to be lucky enough to do just that."

She scooted closer. "You think I'm smart?"

"Well, you were smart enough to punch your ex-fiancé in the face when you found out he was cheating on you. And you were smart in realizing those two warriors weren't the right males for you. I don't know much about what you did on Earth, but I have a feeling it was a job that required a lot of thinking."

She snorted. "Not hardly. I was an executive assistant, and while yes, there were tasks that required more brain power than most, I set up appointments, took meeting minutes, scheduled trips and other mundane tasks for the majority of the time. Every now and then someone would ask my opinion on something, or I'd have to set up a gala for the company. But I lost my job before I came here. It was one of the deciding factors in my accepting to become a bride for a Terran male."

"Would you want to work while you're on Terran, even after you find a mate?"

"It would be nice to have something to do with my time. I can only read so many books, and I know nothing about the upkeep of a Terran household."

Syl knew just how he could spend more time with her, and give her a job. He only hoped she would accept his offer.

"What if you came to work with me?" he asked.

Her brow furrowed. "As what? I don't know anything about working in a lab."

"You could be my assistant. You could help organize my office area and help with communications." He smiled. "Make sure I remember to stop long enough to eat."

"Are you serious? You'd give me a job?"

"Well, I've never had an assistant before and I could certainly use one. I'm sure you're more than qualified for the job."

Her eyes brightened and a sweet smile curved her lips. "I'd love to work with you. Do I have to fill out an application or something?"

"Things are handled a little differently on Terran than on Earth. I need to notify the council that I'm hiring you. Once we figure out your duties, I'll have to give them a comprehensive list of your tasks. You'll earn credits that you can use at the stores and restaurants in the area. Your housing is taken care of by the council until you find a mate and then you'll move into your mate's quarters. Because your don't have to pay for housing, your credits earned will be lower, but it doesn't that doesn't mean we don't appreciate you."

"It will just be nice not to run up a high bill for my future mate. I worry that he won't be able to afford my expenses."

"Warriors earn a lot of credits because they put their lives at risk to defend our planet."

"And scientists?"

He felt his cheeks warm. "We come in at a lower rate than the warriors and councilmen. Healers make more than scientists as well, even though they use our serums to vaccinate their patients or cure them."

"That doesn't seem fair." She frowned. "You'd think the council would appreciate your efforts more."

"There are some planets that pay their scientists and inventors more than their warriors, but I can't imagine ever leaving Terran Prime. This city has everything I'll ever need."

She tilted her head to the side. "It's a lot like Earth. I had expected something different, with it being an alien planet, but the sights are rather comforting."

"Terran Prime used to look different than it does today. We studied Earth before reaching out to humans. Long before the first human was invited, our city was revamped to mirror the big cities on Earth. When we first had the idea to bring Earth brides to Terran, we wanted them to feel comfortable, like they belonged. Every year, something new is added to the city."

"What did it look like before?" Brielle asked.

"There were no parks, no swimming pools. We hadn't heard of such things, but now that we have them, we enjoy them. There were fewer shops, fewer Earth-like items. You've seen the toga-style dresses our Terran women wear, and the leathers the males wear. Those were the only forms of clothing we had, until the brides began arriving. In order to make the women of Earth more comfortable, we opened shops that sold clothes like you would find on Earth, as well as shoes and other items."

"Are the other Terran cities set up the way Terran Prime once was? Or have they adapted as well?"

"They have adapted to some extent, but not as much as Terran Prime. There are a few human mates in the outlying areas, and their Terran -- husbands? Is that the word? -- wanted them to feel at ease in their new homes."

Brielle nodded. "Yes, when humans marry, they call each other husband and wife. We have a ceremony, either with a justice of the peace or a religious figure. The marriage is recorded with the state and they are given a piece of paper showing they are now joined."

"Fascinating."

"Is there a ceremony here?" she asked.

"No." Syl shook his head. "A petition is filed with the council, and as long as the woman's family does not object to the union, which isn't an issue with Earth brides, then they approve the request and the couple is considered mated from that moment on."

A frown marred her lovely face. "Why does it not matter if the woman is from Earth? Is her family not just as important as a Terran family?"

Syl pondered her words. "I'm not sure anyone has considered it before. Your family was paid for the privilege of you becoming a bride on Terran, so it is reasonable to assume they would agree to a mating you have chosen. Terrans do not marry for love. It's usually an alliance, or a woman trying to better her situation by marrying a male who receives more credits than her family."

"So they are business transactions?"

"Yes, that's the best way to put it."

"That's rather sad, Syl. Do they at least grow to love one another?"

His eyebrows slanted over his eyes. "I'm not sure. I can't remember my parents acting as if they loved one another in the last thirty years. They respect each other, but I know that isn't the same thing."

"I always thought love would grow over time." She nibbled her lower lip, her brow wrinkled. "What if I'm wrong? What if I agree to be mated to someone and we never come to love one another?"

He reached over and smoothed her lip with his thumb, pulling it from between her teeth and then reached down and took her hand. "I think some male is going to be really lucky to have you as his mate, Brielle, and he would be a fool if he didn't fall in love with you."

"Some male," she murmured, her eyes cast down. "But not you."

Syl felt his heart give another kick. "You wish to mate with me?"

"It's okay. I know you aren't interested, not in a romantic way."

He squeezed her hand. "Brielle, what made you think I wasn't interested in you?"

"You didn't kiss me at the end of our first date, and you didn't ask for a second one. I just figured I wasn't smart enough for someone like you. Or that maybe you didn't really think I was all that pretty, despite what you'd said."

He was a fool -- that much was certain. She'd hesitated that night because she wanted something more from him, and imbecile that he was, he hadn't given it to her. And now, she believed he didn't want her.

"I'm uncertain how males act when they are courting a female of their choosing," Syl said. "It isn't something I've ever done before. But I can assure you, I never meant to make you feel like you were unwanted.

That couldn't be further from the truth. I want you so much I ache with it."

Her lips parted and her eyes widened slightly, a sense of wonder in their beautiful depths, and yet there was an uncertainty to her, as if she were afraid he was merely jesting. How to tell her that he was sincere? He had never been very good with words, always fumbling along. He dealt in facts, not emotions. And right at that moment, the only fact pulsing in his brain was that he very much wanted to kiss her.

Cupping her cheek with his hand, he leaned forward, moving slowly so as to give her time to pull away if she desired to, his eyes sliding shut when he was a mere breath away from those luscious lips he'd thought of rather often over the past few days. The first brush of his lips against hers was soft, almost hesitant and then he grew bolder, his lips moving against hers with firm, decisive strokes. He felt her respond, her body softening, her mouth opening to invite him in. He thrust his tongue inside, her taste nearly stealing his breath it was that good. Brielle placed her hand on his shoulder, then wrapped her fingers around his braid, pulling him closer still.

As she kissed him back, his pants began to tighten as his cock strained against the fastenings. It had been more than his usual six months since the last time he was with a woman, but he knew this was different. He didn't merely feel the urge to relieve some sexual tension and frustration, he wanted to taste her skin, feel the softness of it against his fingertips as he explored her curvy body. He didn't want just any female; he wanted Brielle.

She pulled away first, her breath fanning his face. "That was…"

"The best experience of my life," he admitted, knowing a warrior would never show such weakness, but then Syl would never be considered a warrior. And he hadn't been flattering her. He'd merely stated a fact.

Brielle licked her lower lip. "If a kiss is that perfect between us, wouldn't it stand to reason that other things would be perfect between us as well?"

His cock jerked with the implication that they should become more intimate. Did she realize what she was saying? No, it didn't necessarily mean a mating, but he didn't want to dishonor her by taking what he wanted so desperately and yet giving her nothing in return.

Her fingers caressed his braid, her other hand gripping his shoulder. "Do you want more than kisses from me, Syl?"

"You know I do, but I don't want to take advantage of you, Brielle. You should wait until you're mated."

A smile spread across her lips, laughter dancing in her eyes. "Are you under the misconception that I'm a virgin? Because I'm not. I haven't slept with a lot of men, but I have been intimate with three of them. I'll admit, I was in a serious relationship with each of them at the time, but I want to feel closer to you, Syl. I want to share this with you."

"It's not right, Brielle. It shouldn't be something casual. Being with you will just make me want you even more."

"What's wrong with that?" she asked, her lips brushing his softly. "What if I want you to want me more? What if I want you to keep me?"

Syl's heart crashed wildly within his chest. "Are you saying you wish to mate with me? To become mine?"

"I did come here to find a mate, and I've found it very hard to get you off my mind. I would imagine that being intimate with you will only make it more difficult."

"You deserve someone better than me, Brielle. I'm not poor, but there are still things I will never be able to give you. Warriors live in large homes with beautiful gardens. If you were to mate with the two warriors who were outside your door earlier, you would live in a place that is the equivalent of the castles on your world. Kel is very well connected."

"I don't want Kel. I want someone who makes me feel special." Her lips brushed his again before she lightly nipped him on the jaw. "You make me feel special, Syl."

He felt his resolve crumbling, felt himself weakening and tightening his hold on her waist. Never before had he been tempted the way Brielle tempted him. He should do the right thing and back away, allow her to mate with a more deserving male, and yet, he found that he couldn't release her, didn't want to.

"If we do this," he said, "I will petition the council in the morning to claim you as my mate. Do you agree to become mine?"

"Yes." She smiled. "I can't think of anything I'd like more than to be yours."

"There is very little you know about me, Brielle. I don't presume that things will always go smoothly between us. There is fire in your veins and there will be times we disagree; there will be times I work long hours and you will feel neglected. This mating will not be an easy one. Are you certain this is what you wish to do?"

"I've been on several dates since being on Terran, been exposed to countless males, and none have made me feel the way you do, Syl. It's your touch I crave. No man, human or Terran, has ever made me want them as much as I want you."

"Then you shall have me."

He claimed her lips in a searing kiss once more, rising with her in his arms. He strode quickly through his living space to the bedroom he had claimed as his own. The door slid open upon his approach and he prowled inside, moving with purpose toward the bed.

Syl let her slide down his body until her feet touched the floor, then he released her only long enough to slowly peel her clothes from her body. As each delicious inch was exposed, his cock hardened even more, jerking in his pants in time with his heartbeat. He'd never experienced this throbbing ache before and he knew that it was something he would only feel with Brielle. She was special, and she was his. Or she would be.

When she was bare before him, he drank in her beauty, his fingers exploring every dip and curve. She was every bit as soft as he'd thought she would be, if not more so, her pale skin a beautiful contrast to his lilac-toned hand. She was built differently from the women he'd used on the floating brothel, but she was absolutely stunning. Heat flared inside of him and he felt pre-cum leak from the double slits in his cock as his fingers brushed the damp curls between her legs.

She unfastened his pants and let them slide to the floor. Her small hands reached for him, her fingers skimming along his chest, down his abdomen, and then cupping his balls. "No hair," she said with a hint of wonder in her voice.

Syl felt his cheeks warm. "Is that a bad thing? I know your human males are hairier than Terrans."

She smiled. "I like it."

He felt some of the tension ease inside of him. Syl couldn't help but thread his fingers through her long hair, the silky strands wrapping around the digits, as he pulled her in for another kiss. Her beautiful swollen lips parted as he sipped at them, his tongue flicking against her full lower lip before dipping inside. His tongue found hers, darting, dancing, twining with hers.

Brielle let out a low hum in her throat and he gave her a gentle nip before pulling away. Her eyes were glazed with passion, her lips red and moist. Syl led her over to the bed and toppled her onto the soft blankets. She let out a squeak of surprise before he fell to his knees in front of her.

Syl parted her thighs, exposing her to his hungry gaze. He knew he would never get enough of her, and hoped this would be the first of many times they would be together. Her aroma teased his nose, tart and spicy, and he couldn't wait to taste her. He'd watched videos of humans having sex and knew this was something their females enjoyed. Syl only hoped he did it right.

His hands slid up her thighs, spreading them wider as he settled between them. With his gaze fastened on hers, he leaned forward, his breath stirring the curls at the junction of her thighs. Syl used his thumbs to part her delicate lips, exposing the bundle of nerves that he knew would bring her great pleasure. His tongue laved her soft folds, her taste exploding on his tongue. She was far sweeter than he'd have ever thought possible.

His tongue speared her, diving between the moist lips and seeking the heat within. Brielle gasped and wriggled her hips, trying to get closer. Syl loved her heat, his tongue delving into her petal-smooth center, the slick wetness of her excitement coating his lips. She was tight, wet, warm... his cock throbbed, aching to be inside her, to feel her wrapped around him in the most intimate of ways.

"More," she begged softly.

His tongue found the little bundle of nerves and he flicked it. Once. Twice. Then sucked it into his mouth, drawing on it long and hard. He watched as she gripped the bedding, twisting the blankets in her hands, her hips rising so that she pressed against him, seeking more.

Syl eased a finger inside of her, her silken walls clamping down on the digit, sucking him further into her body. He pumped in and out of her, his hips flexing as his body mimicked the motion, his cock rubbing against the soft blankets. The friction against his sensitive head made him growl as he reveled in her taste, reveled in the feel of her.

He moved faster, pushing her toward orgasm. When she exploded around him, it took an extreme amount of effort not to allow himself to follow her, her expression one of complete bliss. Syl kissed her inner thigh, tracing the line of her leg to her hip with his tongue.

"Syl. I need you," she mumbled, reaching for him.

He settled over her, his cock brushing against the silky hair between her legs. "Are you sure you still want me?"

"More than anything."

Despite how tight she'd felt around his finger, he knew she could accommodate him. Her body was made for his and he couldn't wait to join with her. His cock slid between her slippery lips as he slowly pressed inside of her. Her sweet pussy encased him, hot and tight, and so damn perfect. He couldn't hold back the groan that spilled from his lips as his hips came to rest against hers, his cock filling her to the point that he brushed against her cervix.

Brielle didn't complain about his size. She actually shifted, lifting her hips, as if asking for more. Syl threaded their fingers together, planting her hands by her head. He took up a slow, steady rhythm, wanting the moment to last as long as possible. His shaft ached and jerked inside her, eager to rush to the finish line, but Syl held back. He was rock hard as he began to move inside her, Brielle's body arching to meet each and every possessive thrust, as he tried to brand her body with his.

He rocked against her and Brielle brought her knees up, feet flat on the bed, opening herself to him further. Her pussy clenched and shuddered as he delved deeper, his movements became frenzied as he felt himself drawing near the end. Brielle became wild beneath him, lifting her hips to his thrusting body.

Syl felt her tighten around him, then felt the warm rush of her release as she cried out, his name on her lips. He let go, abandoning himself to pleasure, as he spilled his seed inside of her, forever marking her as his. He slowed, then stilled, buried deep within her, and wishing they could stay like that.

"Syl, that was…" She panted. "I've never experienced anything like that before."

"Neither have I," he admitted.

"We're mates, right?"

He nodded. "I'll submit the papers tonight and by morning we should know something. Knowing we've been intimate, I can't imagine them denying our request. None of the human brides have met with resistance when they've found their mates."

She unraveled his braid and buried her fingers in his hair. "Then we should get cleaned up and get those papers filed. The sooner I'm yours, the better."

Syl smiled and pressed a kiss to her lips. "It shall be as you wish."

Chapter Seven

Brielle woke with a start, listening intently. Something didn't feel right. The bed space beside her was cold and she wondered where Syl had gone. Tossing aside the blankets, she quickly pulled on her clothes and searched room by room. There was a dense blue smoke in the lab area, so thick she could barely see through it. Opening the door, she called out.

"Syl! Are you in here?"

There was a groan and Brielle began to wade through the thick mass, searching for her soon-to-be mate. When her bare foot touched something warm, she dropped to her hands and knees; broken shards of glass cut into her legs through her thin pajama pants; her eyes stung from the smoke. Syl lay on his side, an arm flung across his face.

Gently, she rolled him to his back and gasped at the gray stain across the chest of his lab coat. She nearly ripped the buttons off in her haste to part the material. There was a ragged hole in the center of his chest, nearly to the bone. Brielle, with tears falling down her cheeks, made her way to the Vid-Comm. She wasn't certain how to use it, but pressed buttons until someone appeared on the screen.

"Where's Syl?" the man demanded, his tone harsh. "You shouldn't be using the Vid-Comm without him."

"He's hurt. Please. Send help! There's so much blood."

"Where is he?"

"The lab." She coughed. "There's a lot of smoke and he was hard to find. I found broken glass around him. I think something exploded."

"Go back to Syl and wait for assistance. Don't try to move him."

"Do the windows here open? I could try to get rid of the smoke."

The man frowned. "There should be a release switch on the bottom right of the window. It won't lift all the way, not that high up, but it will crack open enough for the smoke to dissipate."

Brielle didn't even stay long enough to end communications, just ran back toward the lab. When she entered the space, she dropped to her hands and knees and crawled along the tile, remembering that there would be more oxygen closer to the floor. She went to the windows first and opened two, then returned to Syl's side, pressing a piece of torn cloth against his wound to slow the bleeding. He looked pale and had yet to open his eyes.

"I'm here, Syl," she said softly, stroking his cheek. Her fingers twined with his as she tried to calm her racing heart. He would be fine. He had to be!

Brielle heard voices coming and called out.

"We're in here!"

The smoke had thinned and she could make out three figures heading toward her. One she recognized as Xonos, the doctor. The other two looked like warriors, but she hadn't met them before.

Xonos gently moved her out of the way as he examined his patient. "I think it's safe to move him. Kril. Myro. Lift him gently and carry him to my office. If we're lucky, we arrived in time to save him."

Brielle bit back a sob at the thought of losing Syl. They might not know each other as well as she'd like, but she wanted a future with him. Had he filed for a mating yet? Would they get the chance to share a life together? Or would he be taken from her all too soon?

She followed the men toward the lift, but Xonos stopped her.

"You can't come to the clinic looking like that, Brielle. Go home. Shower and change, then you can come to the clinic and check on him. I swear I will do everything in my power to save him."

She gave a jerky nod, waited until they left and then called the lift back up so she could return to her apartment. She showered and changed, but didn't pay much attention to what she was doing, her thoughts consumed by Syl and worry for him. Brielle exited her building, pushing past her would-be suitors, and nearly ran to the clinic. When she entered the office, she wasn't certain where to go.

"Xonos!" she called out.

One of the warriors from Syl's appeared in the doorway. "The doctor is operating right now. It would be best if you waited out here. Someone will fetch you when you can sit with Syl."

She swallowed hard and nodded her understanding, collapsing into a chair and clasping her hands together between her knees. With her shoulders hunched and her head bowed, she prayed harder than she'd ever prayed before. She didn't know if God could hear her on Terran, but she felt the need to do something, anything, to help save him.

It felt like hours had passed before Xonos came out to the waiting area, gray smears on his coat that Brielle knew to be Syl's blood. The doctor looked worried, his lips thinned and his face tight. She felt her heart drop as she prepared herself for bad news.

"How is he?" she croaked, her throat raw from holding her tears at bay.

"I have him stable for the moment, but we'll have to watch him carefully for a few days. If he makes it through the next seventy-two hours, we'll be in the clear and he'll make a full recovery. The next twenty-four hours will be the most critical."

She nodded and rose unsteadily to her feet. "May I see him?"

"Maybe hearing your voice will be soothing for him. There's a chair beside his bed. You can sit with him for a while. I can't let you remain for more than an hour at a time because you aren't mated."

"He was going to submit the paperwork this morning. I don't know if he did or not."

Xonos' gaze softened. "If you'd like, I can check with the council and see if he filed the proper paperwork. If he did, I'll explain the situation and ask them to put a rush on it."

"Thank you," she said softly.

Brielle followed Xonos toward the back of the clinic and a small room that held a bed, Vid-Comm, chair and nothing else. The walls were stark white and there was a window over the bed, letting sunlight into an otherwise depressing room. There was a steady beep and she looked at the Vid-Comm. It was set up to show Syl's vital signs and she watched the steady thump of his heartbeat.

Claiming the chair, she gripped his hand, afraid that if she let go he might give up his will to live. Their relationship might be brand-new, but she knew she needed him as much as he needed her, if not more.

"Don't give up," she whispered into the quiet room as she fought back tears. "Don't leave me now that I've found you."

A heavy hand landed on her shoulder and she looked up at Xonos. "I'll go contact the council. If they haven't made a decision in two hours, you'll have to go home for a while."

She hoped the council would make a hasty decision, in their favor, once they learned of Syl's condition. Brielle wasn't sure she would be able to stand being parted from him while he was like this. Not knowing what the future held had never been this scary before.

Time passed more quickly than she'd anticipated and Xonos stepped into the room a few hours later. He gave her a sympathetic look and she knew what he had to say wasn't good news.

"I spoke with the council, Brielle. I'm afraid they have denied your request for a mating with Syl."

He looked like he wanted to say more and she wondered what else he knew about the situation.

"I shouldn't say anything," he said, "but I think you were denied because of Kelvyk. He's most favored by the council and has probably told his uncle of his wish to mate with you."

She released Syl's hand and rose swiftly to her feet. "Well, if they think I'm going to mate with men like Kel and Ryoku, they are sadly mistaken. Denying my mating to Syl isn't going to change my feelings toward those two."

Xonos nodded. "Then maybe they need to hear that."

"What do you mean?"

"Speak with Kelvyk. He'll be able to help you talk to the council. It's unheard of for them to listen to a female, especially one who isn't Terran, but perhaps they need to hear your side of things. They want to make the humans here comfortable, and have altered Terran Prime for that purpose, but I think their sympathies toward the females only goes so far." Xonos frowned. "I can't think of any other reason they would have denied your mating. Unless someone protested."

She looked at Syl, reaching out to smooth his hair back from his face. "Do I really have to leave now?"

"I'm afraid so."

Brielle stood, reluctantly letting go of Syl's hand. Leaning down, she pressed her lips to his, not knowing if he could feel it or not. Was he even aware that she was there?

"When can I come back?" she asked, turning to face Xonos.

"Tomorrow. I know it seems like a long time from now, but I can't bend the rules for you, no matter how much I'd like to do so."

Tomorrow felt like forever. What if something happened overnight? What if Syl took a turn for the worse? If he died and she wasn't here with him, it would haunt her for the rest of her life. Even if he wasn't aware she was present, she felt that, by being there, she could somehow will him to live.

Resigned to her fate, she followed Xonos out of the clinic and stepped into the sunlight outside. She turned to face him, not wanting to see the pity in his eyes, but unable to look away.

"You'll call me on the Vid-Comm if there's a change?"

"I promise. If something bad happens, you'll be the first call I make. I'll escort you back here myself."

"Thank you, Xonos."

Brielle trudged back to her quarters, her heart feeling as if it were breaking with every step she took. She didn't know Syl well enough to be in love with him, but she knew that she didn't want to live without him. He was important to her and she wanted the opportunity to see where things would go with their relationship. Was it asking too much to be given a chance at happiness?

***

Ryoku and Kel frowned.

Chief Councillor Borgoz stared at his nephew, making Kel squirm. "I did this for you."

"I didn't ask you to deny Brielle's mating, Uncle. She made her choice, and it wasn't us. It isn't like there won't be other brides coming to Terran."

"You want her, do you not?" Borgoz asked.

"She's physically appealing, if that's what you mean," Kel said. "But I don't really know much about her. I know she's fierce, and that's what drew me to her, but she was right when she became angry with us. We wanted her, but only knew of one small part of her. Had we taken the time to get to know her before pushing, maybe things would have turned out differently."

"We heard what happened to Syl," Ryoku said. "By denying their mating, you've condemned her to only seeing him two hours a day and being unable to sit with him during the rest of his stay in the clinic. What if he dies, Chief Councillor?"

"So the two of you want to cater to her? Give in and not fight for the right to have her at your sides?" Borgoz asked. "You would give up so easily, just because she fancies herself in love with the scientist?"

"Syl is brilliant," Kel said. "And if things were fair, he would be paid just as well as Ryoku and I are. Without him, we wouldn't have the weapons we use daily. And think of the lives he's saved with his serums? And you want to deny him the only thing he's ever asked of you?"

His uncle's eyes flashed. "I did it for *you*. Little did I know you would be so ungrateful."

"It isn't that we don't appreciate what you tried to do," Ryoku said. "But we don't want to win her that way. It's obvious she chose Syl and we will honor her decision. Isn't that what being a warrior is all about? Honor?"

Borgoz seemed to deflate a bit. "I will put the matter before the council again and see if I can get the decision reversed. But I make no promises."

Kel and Ryoku nodded.

"That's all we can ask of you, Uncle."

They bowed before the Chief Councillor and made their way back outside. Ryoku placed his hand on Kel's arm to draw him to a halt.

"You think he'll get it overturned? I would hate to think Brielle lost her chance to be happy just because we'd shown an interest in her."

"I'm certain it will be."

Ryoku tipped his head toward the building where Brielle lived, the top of it showing above the other buildings in the area. "Should we give her the news?"

"No, let's wait and let her be surprised. Besides, there is a slight chance my uncle won't be successful. I would hate to give her hope and then have Syl taken from her once more."

Ryoku slapped him on the back. "Let's go check out the docking station. I heard new brides are arriving this morning. If we hurry, we may get there in time to see them land."

Kel smiled. "New brides? That may be just what we need to prove to my uncle that we aren't interested in Brielle any longer. Let's go find a lucky lady to claim for our own."

"If they'll have us," Ryoku said quietly. "Since Brielle turned us away, I have to wonder if we aren't as charming as we thought."

Kel frowned. "You think we need to learn more about seducing a woman? We've never had problems before."

Ryoku snorted. "We *pay* those women to like us."

Kel grunted. "Perhaps you're right. We'll keep an eye on this batch of brides and watch how the males interact with them. Maybe we haven't been paying close enough attention to those who are victorious in claiming a woman for their own. For instance, what did Syl do that we didn't?"

"I'm sure if we asked Brielle, she would tell us how to go about winning a woman."

Kel stared at him. "The same Brielle who probably blames us for her mating request being rejected? I think we'd better try to figure this one out on our own."

Ryoku shrugged. "If that's what you want. But I still say Brielle would help."

Kel shoved Ryoku in the direction of the landing dock. Despite what his brother-in-arms said, Kel knew it would be best to give Brielle some room. She might have contacted them on the Vid-Comm to ask for their help with her mating, but that didn't mean she had forgiven them for their blunder.

Chapter Eight

Brielle had visited Syl as often as she was allowed over the next week. He'd improved, opening his eyes on the third day. Xonos claimed Syl would be well enough to go home today. She'd tried to contact Kel and Ryoku a few times to find out the status of her pending mating with Syl, but so far, she hadn't been able to reach them. She'd mentioned it to Xonos, but either he hadn't heard any news or it was bad news and he wasn't sharing.

There was a knock at her door and she flung her wet hair over her shoulder before opening it. Her jaw dropped and her eyes widened when she saw who stood on the other side.

"Syl! What are you doing here?"

He gave her a tired smile. "The good physician released me this morning and I wanted to come see you. I'm supposed to stay out of my lab and try not to overdo it, so I was hoping I could convince you to come upstairs with me and maybe watch a movie."

"I'd love to." She fingered her hair. "Can I meet you up there? I need to dry my hair."

He reached out and rubbed a silky strand between his fingers. "Leave it. I've been apart from you long enough."

She wrapped her hand around his. "You know our mating wasn't approved. I want to spend time with you, more than anything, but I agreed to mate with someone when I came here."

His hand fell to his side. "So you're going to choose someone else?"

"No. I'm going to ask them to return me to Earth. I can't imagine choosing anyone else, and seeing you around town would be painful, knowing that we couldn't be together."

His jaw set. "I won't give you up."

Brielle moved closer to him. "How can we fight them, Syl? The council made their decision. I asked the Chief Councillor's nephew to speak with him about the matter, but the decision to deny our mating hasn't been reversed. That was a week ago. I don't think they're going to change their minds."

"I'll bargain with them. There has to be something I've refused to make at some point in the past that I can barter with. Maybe a new weapon?"

"I don't want you to bend your morals just so we can be together. I've come to care for you a great deal this past week, Syl. I know I didn't do much other than sit in the chair by your bed a few hours a day, but when I thought I'd lost you…" She shook her head. "I don't ever want to feel like that again."

"You let me worry about that. What I need you to do is agree to help me fight them. I won't rest until I know you can stay by my side. In fact, I want you to stay the night at my place."

She gave him a small smile. "I thought you were supposed to rest."

His lips tipped up on one corner. "If I lie back and let you do all the work, then I'm resting."

Brielle warmed at his words. She'd never been very good at being on top, but with Syl, she was willing to give it another try. She'd been so worried about him this past week that sex had been the last thing on her mind, but knowing he was well enough to be home changed things. If he thought he could withstand a round of lovemaking, then he'd have it.

Lovemaking? It had always been just sex to Brielle before, even with Aaron. Had she become closer to Syl than she'd thought?

Syl tugged on her hand. "Come on, love. Come upstairs with me."

"Love?"

He smiled. "Is that not right? I thought it was a term of endearment on Earth."

"It is, but I've only heard it used once, and the two people were in love with each other."

Syl placed his other hand at her waist and pulled her closer, until their bodies were touching. "And who says I'm not in love with you?"

"Syl, you don't know me well enough for that. Love grows over time."

"All right. Then I like you very, very much, and I want to have you in my life long enough to grow to love you. I've never wanted a mate before, Brielle, and now that I've spent time with you, I know that no other female will do."

Brielle went up on tiptoe to kiss Syl, a gentle brushing of her lips against his, before she moved away and began leading him toward the lift. They rode up to his floor in silence and when the lift doors opened, she followed him into the sitting area. He put on a movie that she'd seen countless times before, but it was one of her favorites so she didn't mind. Curled up beside him, her body curving into his, she realized she felt more at peace in this moment than she had all week.

The woman on the screen dropped to her knees in front of the man she was seducing and began to unfasten his pants. A glance at Syl showed that he was most interested in the scene and Brielle wondered if he'd ever experienced a blowjob.

"You told me before that you'd used the services of a nearby brothel," Brielle said. "But you never said what exactly they did for you."

His cheeks warmed as he looked at her. "You want me to discuss what I did with other females?"

"Not in any detail, but if we're going to have a limited amount of time together, I want to make it count. We should do something you've never done before."

He glanced at the screen then back at her. "I've never… I mean, a female has never… That is to say…"

She arched a brow. "You've never had your cock sucked?"

His cheeks flushed a dark purple and she fought not to smile at how adorable he was. He gave a quick shake of his head before meeting her gaze again. "I've never, um… The females at the brothel… they never let me…"

She ran her fingers across his smooth jaw. "They never let you what?"

"I've only ever taken a woman the one way. With me on top."

"Then we have a bit of exploring to do, don't we?" She smiled. "Are you watching the movie or do you want to play?"

"Maybe I should clear it with Xonos first?"

She walked her fingers down his chest to the laces on his leather pants. "If that's what you want."

He audibly gulped as her fingers brushed across his straining erection. "Or we can just assume that he wouldn't release me from the clinic unless I was all right."

Her fingers traced the dark purple line that ran down his chest, where Xonos had put him back together after the explosion. Perhaps he was right to worry and they *should* call the physician. Brielle wouldn't be able to live with herself if she caused harm to Syl. He was too important to her.

Taking the remote from him, she dialed Xonos, a number she had memorized over the past week. When the physician appeared on the screen, he smiled at them.

"I see he found you after I released him," Xonos said.

"He did," Brielle said. "But he was a little unclear on just how much rest he needed to get."

Xonos' eyebrows shot up. "I see. If you're worried his chest is going to pop open, it won't. It may cause him some pain, but he'll know when enough is enough. So if you're asking if the two of you can mate, the answer is yes."

Syl scowled. "Don't bring up that word. I still have to speak to the council about reversing their decision."

Xonos nodded. "I'm sure you will make them see the error of their ways. If I know you, you'll just threaten to withhold services from them until you get what you want."

"I would never do anything that would jeopardize our warriors, but yes, I am thinking of using my services as a bartering tool."

Xonos nodded. "Good. If you experience any problems during your…" He cleared his throat. "Well, let me know if you overdo it and need assistance."

"Thank you," Brielle said and then she disconnected the call and focused on her adorable alien geek once more. "Now, where were we?"

Syl fisted her hair. "I think you were about to show me what I've been missing."

With a wicked grin, Brielle sank to her knees between his sprawled legs and began undoing the laces on his pants. He lifted his hips and she tugged the pants down his thighs, watching hungrily as his cock sprang free. She hadn't explored him much during their one brief night together and now she eyed him in fascination. His cock was long with a slight curve downward; pre-cum leaked from two slits in the head, and dark purple veins were visible through the thin skin of his shaft.

"You're beautiful," she said, stroking him reverently.

He stammered and stuttered, but didn't seem capable of actually forming words.

With a smile, Brie licked her lips before flicking her tongue across the tip of his cock, gathering the pre-cum on her tongue. A sweet taste exploded on her tongue and she went back for more. He tasted almost like… taffy? She took another taste. Yes, definitely taffy. Her favorite sweet treat.

Fitting her lips around his shaft, she bobbed her head up and down, her lips and tongue gliding along his length. Syl groaned and shifted beneath her. She looked up and noticed his eyes were squeezed shut, his teeth bit into his bottom lip, and his hands were fisted at his sides. She pulled away for a moment.

"Let go, Syl. Don't hold back."

"But I'll…" His eyes popped open and his cheeks flushed even more. "You know, in your mouth."

Brielle tried not to smile. He was so damn cute. "It's okay. I want you to."

His eyes widened and she went back to bringing him as much pleasure as she could. He seemed more relaxed as she deep-throated him. After only a few strokes, the first sweet splash hit her tongue before bathing the back of her throat. She swallowed down every drop and then licked him clean before rising and settling on the seat next to him.

"I never imagined... I mean, that was..."

"Awesome?" she supplied. "Fantastic? Wonderful?"

He smiled. "All of those things."

"Why don't we get you cleaned up and into something more comfortable? Then we can relax the rest of the night. When it's time for dinner, I can run out to grab us something."

"I'll call ahead so they will bill me for it," Syl said. "I don't like the idea of your roaming the city on your own, though. What if some warriors corner you?"

"They've left me alone lately. I think the council refusing our mating has made me less desirable in their eyes. Either they worry they would be denied as well, or they realize that you're who I want and no one else will measure up."

Syl ran his fingers through her hair. "I'm going to fight for us, Brielle. I may not do it with weapons the way a warrior would, and I know you deserve so much better than me, but I want you in my life and I'm not going to give you up easily."

"If I can't have you, I'll leave Terran and go back to Earth. I can't imagine being mated to anyone else," she said. "Too bad you can't come to Earth to live with me. No one would deny our mating there. I don't know that we could have a human wedding, since you wouldn't be a citizen of Earth, but no one would stop us from living together."

Syl smiled and kissed her softly. "I don't think Earth is ready for my kind to live there. But if that was the only way for us to be together, I'd take it. I don't know how I would provide for us down there, but I would find a way."

"You're brilliant, Syl. Any lab would be honored to have you, I'm sure."

"Let's see what kind of headway I can make with the council before we take drastic measures. Terrans may go to Earth for short trips, but we've never tried to live there. Most of your humans have never seen a Terran, much less had to live beside one or work with one."

"Then maybe it's time."

He nodded. "Maybe so."

His stomach rumbled and she ran her fingers over the ridges of his abdominal muscles. "Why don't you call in our food and I'll run to pick it up?" she suggested.

"While you're gone, I'll call Larimar. He's on the council and is someone I've dealt with a few times. Maybe he can tell me whether or not a fight would do us any good."

Brielle kissed him. "Make the call and then let me know what he says, good or bad. We'll face this together, Syl."

He laced their fingers tight. "Together."

Chapter Nine

Syl waited until Brielle had gone down in the lift before dialing Larimar. The councilman came on screen and smiled when he saw it was Syl on the other end.

"How are you faring?" Larimar asked. "I heard about the explosion."

"Did you hear about it before or after you denied my mate claim?" Syl raised an eyebrow.

Larimar had the grace to wince. "If it's any consolation, I was for the mating, along with two other council members. But you know Borgoz. What he wants, he gets, and he claimed you weren't deserving of the mating, that she should go to a warrior."

"In other words, he wants her to mate with his nephew. It won't happen."

"I know that and you know that, and I think Borgoz knows it, but he'd never admit it. Are you going to reapply?"

Syl shrugged. "I thought about it. Even thought about withholding my services until the mating was approved."

"I wouldn't go that route. You know Borgoz. He'll have you locked up immediately and you won't see the light of day for many years. You're going to have to find another way."

"Nothing I say or do will convince him that I'm deserving of a mate and I'm a lower rank than his exalted nephew."

Larimar tipped his head. "So what are you going to do?"

"Brielle mentioned something. She said she wished I could go to Earth with her. I realize it's never been done, but are there any laws stating I can't live on Earth?"

Larimar's mouth opened and shut a few times. "You would seriously think of living on such a primitive world? You wouldn't have access to our healing centers and scientific advancements."

"Then maybe it's time we change that. Our people travel to Earth all the time. What if one of them was harmed or became ill while they were there? Wouldn't it make sense to have a clinic on Earth? And maybe a lab?"

Larimar scratched his chin. "You mean set up a proper station on Earth, with Terran amenities and necessities, and yet you would have the freedom of living in the outworld and not having to follow all of the Terran rules?"

"Exactly. I know something like that would take time to set up, but don't you think it makes sense?"

"Yes, I do. And I'm going to call a council meeting in the morning to discuss it." He cleared his throat. "But I may… what's that human term? Stack the deck? I'll call my council friends and try to assure that we get a positive ruling tomorrow. No way am I letting Borgoz shoot down anything else that will impact your future. They don't realize just how much you've sacrificed for us."

"So I can move to Earth with Brielle?"

Larimar nodded. "When you reach Earth, you'll be able to transfer some of your Terran credits to Earth dollars. I don't know the exchange rate, but I'm sure you'll have enough to get the two of you set up."

Syl sighed. "That would be nice. Now, if I could only marry her, an Earth mating custom, but I won't be a citizen of Earth."

"One thing at a time," Larimar said. "If we set up a more permanent presence on Earth, then maybe we can get them to waive the citizenship requirement and you will one day be able to marry your mate. You may not be mated by our laws, but I can tell the two of you are meant to be together. I came to the clinic to check on you and your Brielle was leaving. She looked devastated and when I asked Xonos about it, he said it was wearing on her to have to leave you after such a short time each day."

"She means so much to me," Syl admitted. "I know there will be other brides, are even some here now, but no one will ever be like Brielle. She's warm and funny, and beautiful. While she may not have had the most glamorous job on Earth, I can tell she's smart. I couldn't find a better mate if I tried. She's everything I want and everything I need."

"Then I wish you both every happiness," Larimar said. "Get clearance from Xonos to travel, and get her to Earth as soon as you can. Since she did attempt a mating, she has met the terms of the contract she signed. She's free to leave at any time."

"Thank you, Larimar."

Syl disconnected the call and went to rinse off quickly before Brielle returned. He knew if she was in the room when he was completely naked, he'd want to do much more than get clean, and he probably shouldn't push it too much today. Syl quickly stripped out of his boots and pants and stepped into the cleaning unit, not much different from the showers he'd seen from Earth, except their cleansing agent was mixed in with the water. After he was clean, he dried off and pulled on a loose pair of pants. He'd never used them before, even though he'd purchased them months ago after seeing a video from Earth where the men wore them around the house. He had to admit, they were rather comfortable and he could see the attraction.

He looked around his quarters, moving to stand in the doorway of his damaged lab. Was he really thinking of giving all of this up? He knew very little of Earth, other than what he'd seen in movies. He didn't think it was going to be an easy transition, and not just because he was the first Terran to live among them, but because of how much he would be giving up.

"But look at what I'm getting in return," he said softly. Brielle was worth it; he knew that, but it didn't make the task any less terrifying.

He heard the lift come to a stop and went to help Brielle. He took the containers of food from her and took them into his dining area, setting them on the table. He got out drinks for them and then motioned for her to sit.

"We aren't going to watch the Vid-Comm while we eat?" she asked.

"We have some things to discuss. I thought this might be a better setting."

Brielle nodded. "You talked to your councilman friend, didn't you?"

"Yes, I spoke with Larimar. He pointed out that if I try to fight the council by withholding services, I will only end up imprisoned for who knows how many years. I won't lie, the idea of living on Earth scares me; it's an unknown and people may not react well to having me as a neighbor, but I'm willing to do anything to be with you."

Brielle placed her hand over his. "We can find a place close to the Terran station. I'm sure the neighborhoods there are more likely to accept you than one in the heart of the city. I don't care where we live, as long as we're together."

"There are Terran stations in every country, and in yours, there are several. We could live anywhere, but perhaps we should start out close to your home, a place you're familiar with. I'm sure you'll want to have your friends around you, assuming they don't turn their backs on you when you tell them we're living together."

She chewed on her lip. "I don't really have any friends. I stayed too busy. When I did go out, it was with people from work, and I lost my last job so I doubt any of them want to hang out."

"Is there a station near your family?"

"A few hours away. It would put us within driving distance so we could visit maybe once or twice a month, if our schedule allowed it."

"Then let's move there," Syl suggested. "I want you to be able to see your family. You're going to need their support if we do this. *When* we do this. I have to make an appointment with Xonos to find out when I'll be able to travel. My worry is that you won't be able to stay here until that time comes, not if you aren't actively seeking a mate. But I've thought about that already and decided I would settle some credits on you that you could cash out when you got back to Earth and then you could find us a place to live and get everything set up."

"We're really doing this?" she asked and blew out a breath. "I'm nervous, mostly for you, but I can't wait for us to be able to live together."

"Yes, we're really going to do this. Start making arrangements tomorrow for your trip home. I'll go to the clinic tomorrow and see how soon I can travel. Xonos will probably want to make sure I'm one hundred percent before letting me go since there isn't a Terran clinic on Earth."

Brielle chewed on her lip. "What are we going to do if you get sick?"

"Larimar is moving to have a clinic and lab opened on Earth. I doubt I'll be able to work in the lab, or they will impose their mating rules on me once more, but maybe I can freelance with them every now and then."

"Do you know what I need to do in order to return to Earth?"

"You'll have to notify the council, that since they rejected your chosen mating, you are returning to your world. They will have no choice but to let you. Then you'll be given twenty-four hours to pack and return to Earth."

"So this is our final night together?"

He cupped her cheek. "Only for a little while. Which Terran station will you be travelling to?"

"The one outside of Lexington, Kentucky. As much as I hate to move home, I'll stay with my parents while I find a place for us to live. Do you have any preferences?"

He shook his head. "Someplace spacious would be nice. I'll check in the morning for the exchange rate on Terran credits to your U.S. dollars."

"A nice place is probably going to cost us quite a bit. Do you want to rent or buy?"

"If I can give you enough, let's buy a place. I would imagine with neither of us having a job already, we would have to pay for it outright. I'm not wealthy by Terran standards, but maybe by Earth standards I'm well-off enough to buy us a home. It will have to be in your name since I won't be a citizen of Earth."

"We'll figure it out. Since I'll be near a Terran station, I can always call you on the Vid-Comm there."

He shook his head. "It's best if you don't. The council isn't going to take my leaving very well and I don't want them to retaliate against you. It's best if you stay away from the station. Leave word with the front desk there about where you'll be staying and I'll find transportation there."

"I don't want to be parted from you."

He leaned forward and kissed her softly. "I don't either. But in the end, it will be for the best."

She nodded. "If you're finished eating, can we cuddle and watch a movie? If this is our last night together, I want to make the most of it. I know you can't do anything but sleep beside me tonight, but I'm not leaving your side until morning."

Syl rose and pulled her to her feet. "Come on, love. Let's enjoy what time we have left together."

They snuggled in front of the Vid-Comm, sitting as close as they could, their fingers entwined. It was a moment Syl would have to remember in the upcoming days, days that he would be without Brielle. After speaking with Larimar, he doubted that the council would stop him from leaving, but until his feet touched the ground on Earth, he would be a little tense.

Chapter Ten

Three weeks had passed since Brielle and Syl had been able to spend time together. She'd only been on Earth for two weeks when she'd discovered something rather amazing. She was pregnant. And without a way to contact Syl, he had no idea he was going to be a father. Was it even remotely sane for them to live on Earth while she was carrying a half-Terran baby? She didn't know if the birth would be normal or not. What if the baby needed something human doctors couldn't give him? Or her.

"Everything all right?" her mom asked as she wiped her hands on a dishrag.

"I'm fine, Mom. Just not sure what I should do."

"Well, if you go back to Terran, what are the chances you'll be paired with Syl?"

"Since I'm carrying his child, I'm not sure. I don't know how Terrans feel about such things. It's possible they could still force me to choose another mate."

Her mom nodded. "And if he comes here, you're worried about our doctors being able to handle the birth."

"Right."

"So why don't you use the Vid-Comm in Lexington to contact that doctor you've talked about? Surely he could answer your questions. You could always ask him not to tell Syl about the baby."

Sometimes her mother was the smartest woman on Earth. Brie grabbed her purse and keys. "If I hurry, I can make it there just after lunch."

"Drive safe," her mom said, giving her a one-armed hug.

"I will, Mom."

Brielle hurried to her car and made the three-hour drive to the Terran station. When she stepped through the door, the woman at the front desk smiled and waved to her. Brielle remembered her from the trip back home.

"Casey, right?" Brielle said as she approached.

"Right. What can I do for you, Brielle?"

"I need to contact Xonos on Terran Prime about a medical issue. Would that be possible? Preferably a private viewing?"

Casey nodded. "I'll get Tyril to show you the way."

She pushed a button and spoke to the invisible Tyril and a few minutes later a large Terran headed their way. He smiled when he saw Brielle and introduced himself.

"I'm Brielle," she said.

Casey explained that Brie needed a private Vid-Comm set up and Tyril escorted her further into the station and into a private room.

"Do you know the number you need to call?" he asked.

Brielle nodded.

"Then I'll leave you to it. I'll be waiting outside the door to show you back to the front of the station when you're finished."

Brielle blew out a breath as the door closed and she dialed Xonos. The physician appeared on the screen a moment later, his smile dazzling when he saw who was calling.

"To what do I owe the honor, Brielle? Is everything going well for you on Earth?"

"Everything is great, Xonos, but I have a rather delicate question to ask you. But before I tell you my news, you have to swear you won't say anything to Syl. I want to tell him myself."

He frowned. "I couldn't tell Syl if I wanted to. He left this morning on a shuttle to Earth. I would imagine he'll be landing in about two hours."

Her mouth dropped open. "Really?"

Xonos nodded.

"Then I'll wait here for him."

"If that isn't what you wanted to talk about, what can I do for you, Brielle?"

She leaned her hip against the table in the center of the room and folded her arms across her breasts. "It's personal."

"I'm in my office," he assured her. "No one can see or hear this conversation except me."

"I'm pregnant," she blurted. "Can human doctors handle the pregnancy?"

His eyes widened and his mouth opened and closed a few times. "Pregnant? You're sure?"

"I took three tests and they all came back positive."

"No one knows this, but we're working on opening a clinic at the station you're in now. Since Syl will be living in that area, it made sense to open one there. But it won't open for another month. If you need medical assistance between now and then, have your doctor contact me immediately."

"Yes, Xonos. I will; I promise."

"A baby." He smiled. "Syl is going to be thrilled."

"I hope so. We didn't discuss having children this early so I know it's going to be a surprise. I mean, the entire purpose of a mating is to have children; I realize that, but we were only intimate one night."

"Sometimes once is all it takes."

"Thank you for speaking with me, Xonos. I feel better, knowing that my baby will be all right."

"Contact me anytime, Brielle. Now that Syl is there, I'm sure you'll have a Vid-Comm installed in your home."

"Take care, Xonos. Hopefully, I will speak to you again soon."

"Get plenty of rest, Brielle. You're going to need it."

She smiled, ended the call and then stepped outside. Tyril gave her an assessing look and she wondered if he'd heard her conversation. The way he glanced at her stomach before meeting her gaze again told her that he had.

"Your mate is arriving today?" he asked.

"According to Xonos, Syl should be here in a few hours. I thought I'd wait for him."

Tyril nodded. "Come, I'll take you to an area where you can rest until your mate arrives. You shouldn't be standing for hours in your condition."

She felt her cheeks warm and followed the tall Terran through the station. When he pushed open a door, she stepped inside, surprised to find herself in what looked like a Terran break room. There were several groupings of comfortable chairs and a large sofa. There was an entire wall of windows that overlooked the docking area.

"When your mate arrives, someone will bring him to you," Tyril said. "We'll watch for him so you can rest."

"Thank you, Tyril. I appreciate it."

"Your home is nearby?" he asked.

"I've been staying with my parents a few hours from here."

Tyril frowned. "You shouldn't make such a long drive twice in one day. Let me make arrangements for you at the hotel we use when we're here. There's a boutique there where you can purchase more clothes since I doubt you brought any with you."

She chewed on her lip as she thought about the cost.

"This displeases you?" he asked.

"It's not that. I just don't know how many credits Syl has and I don't have a job. He left me some money, but I haven't been able to go house hunting yet and I don't want to spend it if we don't have to. We didn't really discuss money and I've been staying with my parents since I've been home."

"The Terran council will pay for the quarters. Your mate may be moving to Earth, but he is still Terran and they must take care of him. I'll call and make the arrangements."

"Thank you."

He nodded and excused himself.

Brielle wasn't sure what to do with herself while she waited. She'd purchased a new cell phone when she'd arrived back on Earth and scrolled through her apps until she found one for e-books. Opening a novella she'd started the other morning, she decided to read to pass the time.

***

Syl opened his eyes as he felt the shuttle touch down. He'd called ahead to ask that his luggage be delivered to whatever address Brielle had provided, only to be told she hadn't left one. His stomach was tied in knots as he pondered what that meant. Had she changed her mind about them? Or had she just not been able to find a place to live?

As he disembarked, his gaze scanned the area. Through a window not far away, he saw a woman who looked remarkably like Brielle, but he knew it couldn't be her. She had no idea that he was arriving today. He ambled up the walkway and into the building, where he was met by a Terran warrior who had been stationed here to keep the place secure.

"My name is Tyril," the Terran said. "Your mate is waiting for you."

Wait. What? "Brielle is here?"

"I put her in the employee lounge. I thought she would be more comfortable there, rather than standing around for a few hours waiting on you. She's been here for two hours."

Syl hastened his pace and followed Tyril into the lounge area. Brielle was sitting near the window, her head braced on one hand, her phone clutched in the other. And she was fast asleep. With quiet steps, Syl approached her, going to his knees in front of her. He gently ran his hand up and down her arm, trying to rouse her from sleep.

"Brielle?" He kept his voice low so he wouldn't startle her awake.

Her eyes fluttered and then opened. A sleepy smile adorned her face when she saw him.

"I was waiting for you," she said.

"I'm here now. I'm sorry you had to wait so long."

Brielle released her phone and reached out to lay her palm against his cheek. "It's okay. You're worth the wait."

"Come on, love. Let's go home, wherever that may be."

Tyril cleared his throat. "I've made arrangements for the two of you to stay at the hotel we use when we're on Earth. The council will cover the cost of the room and anything you order from room service. She'll need some clothes, though."

"Thank you, Tyril."

Brielle rose to her feet and Syl stood, wrapping an arm around her waist. "Tyril, could you see that Syl's bags are sent to the hotel? I'm sure we can fit them in the car tomorrow to take them home."

"Where *is* home?" Syl asked.

"I've been staying with my parents." She frowned. "But I've been sharing a room with two of my sisters, so that won't work. We may need to stay at the hotel until we find a place to stay. Would your council pay for such a lengthy stay?"

"They will," Syl said, "even if I did leave home permanently. Or until they come to their senses."

"Then I'll call my mom and ask her to bring my things to the hotel tomorrow."

"Let's get you settled into the hotel. You look like you need some rest."

"She should shop first," Tyril said. "Before she retires for the evening."

Syl nodded. "A sound idea. I take it there are shops at the hotel?"

"Yes," Tyril said. "Do you need to exchange some credits for dollars?"

"I need to change all of my money over and put it in a… what are those called? Banks?"

"There's one here," Tyril said. "Here in the station."

"Lead the way," Syl said. "The sooner I get this part out of the way, the sooner I can get my mate to our hotel room."

They followed Tyril through the station and Syl accessed his Terran accounts, exchanged his credits for

U.S dollars and then opened an account at the bank. If the poleaxed look on Brielle's face was anything to go by, he must be better off financially than he thought. He'd already exchanged some credits and had them put in her name, but since she hadn't bought a home yet, he wondered if he'd given her enough.

They exited the station after Syl pulled some cash from his new account. He knew little of how much things cost in this world so he withdrew a few thousand, hoping it would be enough to cover Brielle's shopping spree and anything else they might need for a few days.

Brielle led him to her car, which was rather large looking to Syl's way of thinking.

"Is this vehicle safe for you to drive?" he asked.

"It's an SUV, a highly recommended one. I know the money you gave me was for a house, but I knew we'd need a car too. I thought this one would accommodate your height better than a compact car."

He nodded, even though her words were foreign to him.

Brielle kept glancing at a piece of paper Tyril had given her, directions to the hotel, and before many minutes had passed they had reached their destination. He instructed the man at the door to have his things delivered to their room and Syl went inside to register. He was surprised to learn that Tyril had booked them one of the suites, and he hoped it didn't anger the council to pay for such lavish quarters for a male who had turned his back on them.

Before they went up to their quarters, Syl steered Brielle toward the shops. She seemed hesitant to purchase anything and he frowned.

"What's wrong?" he asked. "Nothing to your liking?"

"Do you understand American money?"

"Um, no. Not really. Do we not have enough?"

She gave a strangled laugh. "Syl, you're *very* wealthy. I thought you'd given me all of your money when I changed out the credits. The exchange rate was five hundred thousand dollars. But then, today, I find out that was only a pittance compared to what you have. Do you realize you're a billionaire?"

"I don't understand what that means."

"It means you're very much out of my realm of possibility. You should be with someone better than me. I grew up dirt poor, and my family still struggles day-to-day. They can't pay the mortgage half the time, and there are times we were without electricity because we couldn't afford it."

"Then we'll use some of the money to help your parents. How much does the house cost? Can we afford to pay off what they owe?"

She gave another laugh that sounded like someone was choking her. "Syl, you could buy my parents' house with your pocket change. I think they owe about twenty thousand on it, and that's only because they took out a second mortgage after the first was paid off."

"Then I'll go to the bank tomorrow and have it arranged."

She shook her head.

"That doesn't please you?" he asked, his brow furrowed.

"I just… I always felt Aaron was too far above me, as a doctor, but you? I know we're from different worlds, but this?"

"I don't understand. I thought having a lot of money was a good thing. It means I can provide for you better."

She fluttered her hands. "I'm just emotional."

"Love, tell me what's wrong. Something is bothering you."

"I don't want to tell you in the middle of a store."

Syl gripped her arms. "Tell me. Please?"

"We're... we're going to have a baby. I'm pregnant."

His eyes widened and he felt his heart kick in his chest. "A baby?"

She nodded, a smile gracing her full lips. "Is that okay?"

"It's more than okay. It's wonderful!" He felt his smile stretch so wide his face felt like it would split. He pulled her close and hugged her tight. "I can't believe we're going to be a true family."

"I've been so worried, not sure how you would feel about it. And then not being able to pick out a house because nothing felt right, but I was trying not to spend very much because I didn't want to use all of your money on a house."

"Brie, spend as much as you want on the house. We'll need something spacious so our son or daughter will have room to play."

"You'll need a laptop if you're going to work, but with as much money as you have, you really don't need to."

"So we'll buy one. I can get that here I think."

She nodded. "We passed an electronics store. If you get a laptop, I can pull up the website I've been using to house hunt and we can find a place together. We should have been looking together anyway. It isn't just my house, it's our home."

"Then we'll finish buying you some clothes, stop by the electronics store, and then go up to our room." He grinned at her. "The good Xonos gave me permission to celebrate our first night back together, in any way we see fit."

Brielle's cheeks flushed. "Then we'd better hurry, because I've missed you *very* much."

Properly motivated, Brielle was able to make her selections rather quickly, and she helped Syl select a laptop that he would be able to use for work, once he found a job. When they were finished and had paid for their purchases, they went up to their room, where Syl's bags were already waiting, along with a bucket of strawberries and a bottle of champagne. He figured the bottle was meant as a celebration, but from what he knew, scientifically, of the female body, Brielle wouldn't be able to have any.

Syl set their bags down and closed the door. He watched as Brielle poured him a glass of champagne and motioned for him to follow her. She led him to a bank of windows where sunlight spilled across the carpet. Before he could question her, she set the glass down and disappeared into what he assumed was the bedroom. She returned a moment later with a blanket in her hands.

Brielle spread the blanket on the ground and held out her hand. "Come join me."

Syl fell to his knees beside her, wrapping her hand in his. There was so much he should tell her before anything intimate happened between them, but his heart felt like it was going to beat right out of his chest and his tongue was stumbling over the right words to say. Brielle deserved to know that she was more than a convenience to him. During his time without her, he had come to realize that he more than cared for her. They may have been together such a short time, but it hadn't taken him long to realize that caring was actually love. For him anyway. He didn't know how she felt about him.

"I've felt so lost without you," she said. "Like I'd been cut in half and only part of me was here, while the other half of me remained on Terran with you."

"I've felt the same way. You mean so very much to me, Brielle. I more than care for you. I've never been in love before, but from what I've read and watched on the movies we imported to Terran, I think what I'm feeling is love."

Her eyes grew damp. "You love me?"

"Yes. I love you. And I love our child." He placed a hand over her still flat stomach.

Brielle threw her arms around him and hugged him tight. "I love you too, Syl. So very much. I didn't realize it until we were apart. And then it was too late for me to tell you, and the longer we were apart, the more I wondered if you would change your mind and decide I wasn't worth so much trouble."

He smoothed a hand down her hair. "Sweetheart, you aren't any trouble. I would move anywhere in the known universe for you, and even beyond that. No distance is too great, if it means we can be together."

"Make love to me." She pulled back and looked into his eyes. "I've missed feeling your hands on me, your lips against mine."

"I can't think of anything I'd like more."

Brielle stood and pulled Syl to his feet. He watched with rapt fascination as she shed her clothing, exposing her delectable body to his gaze. When she was finished and she reached for his pants, he realized he hadn't undressed yet and quickly stripped out of his boots and leather pants. When he was bare, his cock hard and aching, he pulled her into his arms and ravished her mouth, his tongue sweeping inside, searching, tasting and teasing. Brielle pulled away, panting for breath, and tugged him down onto the blanket.

The sun warmed his skin as he covered her body with his own. She gently fingered the scar that ran down his chest from the explosion and subsequent surgery. Xonos had said he would always have a scar because of how extensive the damage had been.

"Does it bother you?" he asked, feeling uncertain.

"Only in the way that it reminds me how I almost lost you. But it doesn't detract from how attractive I think you are, if that's what you're asking. Your body will always be beautiful to me."

He kissed her hungrily again, his hands stroking her body. His cock jerked in rhythm with his heart and he felt pre-cum dribble from the tip. Never before had he ever craved a woman as much as he craved Brielle, had never wanted to be inside of one so badly. Syl wanted to take his time, make the moment extraordinary for her, but he wasn't certain he could. It had been weeks since he'd had her taste on his tongue, the feel of her silky skin against his fingertips. Weeks that had felt like years.

"Syl, I need you," she murmured against his lips.

"I want to make this special," he growled back.

"Every time with you is, but I need to feel you inside of me."

Unable to deny her request when it was exactly what he wanted too, he settled between her splayed thighs, stroked her pussy and found her to be very wet and then positioned his cock against her. Reaching between their bodies, he parted the lips of her pussy as his cock stretched her, sinking in inch after inch.

She encased him like wet silk, her body molding to his, her walls squeezing him tight. "Brielle, I don't know that I can last," he said in a strangled voice.

"Then don't. We have all night, Syl. No one said you'd only get one shot."

He buried his face in her neck, breathing in her scent as he powered in and out of her body, his movements more frantic than smooth. He felt her hands on his back, her nails biting into his skin as she arched into him. Not wanting to leave her behind, he brushed his thumb over the sensitive bud at the top of her slit, wanting to take her over the edge with him.

The little nub was hard and standing at attention when he brushed his thumb over it and Brielle made the most delightful noise. He did it again, pressing lightly as he circled the bud. Her nails bit into him harder and her breath panted in his ear. Syl could feel her body tightening and knew she was close.

His balls drew up against his body and he felt a tingling in his lower back. No matter how much he wanted to hold on, he couldn't. With a shout, he was coming inside of her, his seed filling her as his world spun out of control. He worried that he'd disappointed her when he felt her channel grip his cock tightly, felt it ripple along his shaft, and then she was crying out her release, a gush of warmth coating his cock as he stilled inside of her.

"I promise, next time will be better," he said, kissing her lips.

"Syl, that was our first time together on my world. Nothing will ever be better than that."

"I love you, Brielle."

She leaned up and kissed him. "I love you too."

He withdrew from her body and lifted her into his arms as he rose to his feet. Carrying her into the adjoining bedroom, he pushed open another door and stepped inside the bathroom. He'd done some research before making the trip and knew how everything worked, so he started the shower and eased her under the warm water.

As his hands soaped her skin and hair, he reflected on their short time together and realized that his life had come to mean so much more since she'd come into it. Before Brielle, he'd coasted along, content but not really happy. Now that they were together, that they were going to be a family, Syl could honestly say he'd never been happier. Brielle was everything to him and he would spend the rest of his life making sure she never regretted choosing an alien geek for a mate.

Victoria and the Alien Doctor
Jessica Coulter Smith

Doctor. Hero. Alien.

Time is running out. Victoria Mathers has tried everything. Her daughter has a rare cancer that hasn't responded to any of the treatments human medicine has to offer. If she can't convince the sexy alien doctor to help her, she knows she'll watch her child die. Victoria will do anything to save her daughter, even if it means bonding with an alien for the rest of her life.

Per Earth's rules, Xonos isn't allowed to treat humans, unless they're one of the new human-alien pairs. However, looking at the small human child who is obviously suffering tears at his heart. It's been his life's work to save people, and he isn't sure he can stand by and watch an innocent child die when he might be able to help.

What starts as a simple arrangement quickly turns into something more as Xonos and Victoria grow closer. It isn't long before she realizes that she yearns for his touch and she wants so much more from him than he may be willing to give. Love was never mentioned when they struck their bargain, but now she'll settle for nothing less.

Chapter One

Xonos felt his frustration building. The entire situation was a mess, but it was out of his hands. When he'd asked to transfer to Earth, he hadn't realized his healing abilities would be restricted. Earth's government had been adamant that he only treat Terran patients. Terran. What a laugh. His planet had chosen the name to make them seem more human and less of a threat. His planet's true name was Zelthrane-3, but once lifeforms similar to his people had been discovered on Earth, a rather primitive planet, they had studied every aspect of Earth and its inhabitants. It was discovered through extensive research that Earth women would be viable for carrying Zelthranite babies, so his planet's ruling council had then changed Zelthrane-3 to Terran, in the hope it would put the humans at ease when contact was made.

"Please," the woman begged. "None of the treatments available on Earth have been able to cure her, or even slow down the progress of the disease. I know you can help her."

Xonos looked at the small child clutched in her arms. The little girl was deathly pale, as if she'd succumb to her disease at any moment. Her hair was thin and brittle, her body nearly skeletal. Xonos' heart ached when he looked at her, knowing it was within his power to ease her suffering even if he couldn't save her, yet being unable to because of diplomatic bullshit. It wasn't the first time Victoria Mathers had come to plead for his help, and definitely not the first time he'd noticed her, but it was the first time she'd brought her daughter. Eyes that should have been full of life stared at him with a tired acceptance that no child should feel.

"I wish I could help you, truly I do, but your government is adamant that I not treat human patients. If she was half-Terran, or even related to one of the human-Terran pairs, then I could do something."

"I applied to be a bride in the exchange program, but they turned me down." Victoria licked her lips and shifted the frail body in her arms. "They claimed none of your warriors would want to be saddled with a sick child."

"You need to understand that I can't cure everything. One of our captains recently lost his mate. Her cancer had spread too rapidly. As sick as your daughter is, it's possible I wouldn't be able to help her. Ease her suffering, yes. Cure her, I'm not certain. So if you tried to enter the bride program only as a way to help her, it might have been in vain. Then you would have been stuck on Terran with a mate you never wanted. That wouldn't be fair to you or the warrior who chose you."

Tears pooled in her eyes, but she blinked them back. He could tell she wanted to argue; it was shown in the stubborn tilt of her chin. Xonos truly wished he could give her good news. It had to break her heart, watching her child suffer, slowly getting worse, inching closer and closer to death's door. But unless Victoria convinced a Terran male to buck the authority of the council and bond with her, she was out of options. He supposed he could understand Earth's reasoning behind their decision. If he helped this child, thousands of humans would abandon their doctors to seek his aid. At the same time, however, he couldn't understand a world that would doom a child to die when help was available.

Victoria's breasts rose and fell in an enticing way when she huffed out a breath. She really was a rather attractive woman, despite the worry and fear in her eyes. She'd make some warrior a fine mate, if she could get someone to agree to bond with her. Despite the fact Xonos had to control his body every time she was near, he wasn't in the market for a mate. Not even one as pretty as Victoria.

"I believe you have an Earth expression," he said. "My hands are tied. Unless you mate with a Terran male, there isn't anything I can do for you."

"But no one would want me." Her lips trembled. "I have precious little time. Even if I were to apply for the program again, the time it would take…" She shook her head.

"Then you need to circumvent the program." Xonos crossed his arms. "I truly want to help your daughter and you, but we're at an impasse. You have to mate with a Terran for me to give you any assistance, so I would suggest that you dress in something other than that baggy outfit and try to snag yourself a warrior. We can be a compassionate lot, so your sick daughter may actually be to your advantage."

Her eyes sparked and her nostrils flared. Through pinched lips she hissed at him. "Do you honestly think I would just whore myself out?"

He shrugged. "I wouldn't think of it in those terms. The warrior would gain a mate and future children; you would gain the life of your daughter. Think of it as an agreement instead of a marriage if you wish. I've studied Earth enough to know that humans have married for less."

Like for sex. You could mate with her for sex. He gave himself a mental slap. He was *not* mating with her, for sex or otherwise. Xonos had seen the horror Reyvor went through when he lost his mate, and he wasn't in a hurry to put himself in that position. Not even for someone as tempting as Victoria. Not even if he had started dreaming of her and her creamy skin practically every night.

"You're an insensitive asshole." She cuddled her daughter closer.

Xonos sighed. "Give me some time. I might be able to find someone for you. There's a warrior here, Thrace, who has been eagerly seeking a mate. He may not mind that you already have a child and might want a mate bad enough to fight our government to keep you. But as I said, there's a chance I won't be able to save her."

Victoria smoothed her daughter's hair. "But you could take the pain away?"

He nodded. "That much I'm sure I could do."

"Then it will be worth it. I would give everything I have, even myself, just to give her a moment of peace." Tears streaked her cheeks. "She's the most precious thing in the world to me, and I would gladly die in her place if I could."

Xonos hoped it wouldn't come to that, that he could cure her daughter if given the chance and with a bit of help from Syl, but he didn't want to give her false hope. It would be cruel to promise her something he might not be able to deliver.

It pricked his conscience that she might not be a good mate if her daughter died, and he wouldn't wish that on any warrior, but he didn't know how else to help her. He'd thought, at one time, that he wanted a mate. Someone to share his life with, to love. And then he'd watched Reyvor's mate die. He didn't want to go through that pain, not now, not ever.

He watched the woman turn and walk away, her shoulders hunched as if she felt the weight of the world pressing down on her, and perhaps she did. He wasn't certain he could help her, but Thrace was a good place to start. He left the medical station in search of the warrior, finding him in the cafeteria.

"Thrace," he said, as he claimed the chair across from the warrior.

"Xonos." He took another bite of food and eyed the doctor as if wondering why he was there.

"I have a question for you. A rather important one. I know you've been seeking a mate but haven't been selected by any of the brides so far. And now that you're here on Earth, your chances are slim because all brides are being sent to our home world."

"Your point?"

"There's a woman who needs a Terran mate. She's been denied by the bride program and is out of options, but her situation is dire."

Thrace looked intrigued. "Dire how?"

"She has a daughter, a small girl who is deathly ill. I can't promise that I can cure her, but the Earth government won't even let me look at her unless her mother is mated to a Terran. Would you consider petitioning the council to become her mate?"

The corner of Thrace's mouth kicked up and humor lurked in his eyes. He wiped his mouth with a napkin, then steepled his hands in front of him. "So let me get this straight. There's a human female with a girl child who is ill, and I'm guessing the illness is hereditary, and you want me to mate with her? Why? So my future children could contract the disease as well?"

Xonos scowled at him. "There's no way to tell if future children would be affected. It's possible the child inherited the illness from her father's side of the family. As you know, all future brides are having a medical screening to determine if they have or carry the genetics for illnesses we can't cure. Victoria would have to go through the same tests."

"If you're so determined to help her, you should mate with her."

Xonos' mouth tightened. "I'm not taking a mate. Ever."

"And yet you want to saddle me with a defective one? Thanks, but no thanks."

Hell, this wasn't going the way he'd hoped. He'd thought surely Thrace would be agreeable to a match with Victoria. With that option off the table, he wasn't sure where else to turn. It wasn't like there were a ton of warriors who would be willing to take on a sick child, or any human child at all. Not that Terrans were speciests, they were willing to mate with humans after all, but there was a difference in asking a male to accept a half-breed child of his own and to accept a fully human child who would be a constant reminder their mate had loved someone before them. Even Xonos could agree that the Terran male ego could be a fragile thing.

He'd just have to come up with a different plan and be ready for the next time Victoria came to visit. He was certain he would be seeing her within a few days, if not sooner. The sicker her daughter became, the more frequently she showed up. And he couldn't blame her. If he had a daughter, he'd do anything in his power to save her.

* * *

You should mate with her.

The words played over and over in Xonos' mind. He didn't want a mate, not in the conventional sense, but what if they made a pact of sorts? He could claim Victoria as his mate. She would bear him future children, and in return, he would offer her a stable life and the opportunity to save her daughter. It didn't bother Xonos that the child was fully human. She was innocent, in all ways.

Maybe he should seek out Victoria, rather than wait for her to come to him again. Perhaps a trip to the bride agency desk was in order. They would have her information on file and could help him locate her.

And if his body seemed over eager to see her again, well that was a secret he'd just keep to himself.

Chapter Two

Victoria watched her daughter sleep. Evie had her hand tucked under her chin, her lips slightly parted. The poor girl had been through so much over the past year, and Victoria knew in her heart that her sweet baby was dying. The doctors had done all they could for her, and now it was just a matter of time before the little angel breathed her last. A tear slipped down her cheek and she hastily swiped it away. She'd cried so many nights, but she tried to never cry in front of Evie.

A knock sounded at the front door, startling Victoria. It was late, far too late for a visitor. Unease crept down her spine, and she rushed into her room to get the baseball bat she kept by her bed. Her neighborhood wasn't exactly safe, and it wouldn't surprise her if a thug tried to force his way into her home. Most of them left her alone, knowing about Evie's illness. But there was always a first.

Her heart hammered in her chest as she approached the door, another knock coming and this one firmer than before. She wanted to look and see who it was, but there wasn't a peephole. And she wasn't sure she would use it even if she had it. Victoria had seen too many movies where the person was shot through the peephole when there was a bad person on the other side.

"Get a grip," she mumbled to herself. She didn't know for sure there was someone bad on the other side of the door. What if it was the police?

Leaving the chain in place, she cracked the door and peered outside, more than a little surprised to see the alien doctor on her doorstep, sans white coat. He looked different, shirtless, wearing nothing but leather pants and boots. And far too mouthwatering for her own good. Had he been hiding all of those muscles under that drab coat?

"May I come in?" he asked.

She shut the door, removed the chain, then opened it and let him in. Xonos filled the space with his presence, making her small, ratty apartment feel even tinier than usual. She felt a moment of embarrassment as he looked around, taking in her stained sagging couch and threadbare carpet. He probably lived in a nice place, far nicer than anything she'd ever had.

In the dim lighting of her living room, he looked even better than he had in the dark. The muscles in his arms bulged. His shoulders were broad, his chest wide and firm. Other than his eyebrows and the hair on his head, she didn't see hair anywhere else. It made her wonder if he was hairless *everywhere*.

Victoria shut and locked the door, not wanting to invite trouble into her home, though something told her she just had. She couldn't imagine what the doctor could possibly have to say to her that couldn't have waited until morning. Her stomach bubbled and flipped as she thought the worst.

"I'm sorry to disturb you so late," he said, turning to face her. His gaze traced down her body, making Victoria more than a little aware of the tank top and skimpy shorts she had on. She'd intended to head to bed and had already changed for the night.

"Why are you here?" she asked.

"I spoke with Thrace about your situation, and I'm afraid he isn't interested. I can't think of another warrior who would be, not with your daughter in the equation. This leaves us with one option."

Her eyebrows arched. "Us?"

"I can't get your daughter out of my mind. I was worried about your situation before you brought her with you, but now…" He shook his head.

"This is my problem, not yours."

"What if it were my problem?"

Her lips turned down at the corners and her brow furrowed. "I don't understand."

Xonos sighed and looked around the room once more before settling his gaze on hers. "From the looks of things, you need my help for more than just medical assistance. I can't, in good conscience, leave a woman in a place like this. You should gather your things and come home with me."

"To the Terran station? They'd never allow us there." Not that they would be going with him. What had happened to the doctor since she'd last seen him? He seemed out of sorts, and she didn't understand his sudden need to take care of Evie and her.

"I have a suite of rooms at a nearby hotel. They've reserved the top three floors for Terran use and it's only a few blocks from the station. It's a two bedroom suite, so there's plenty of space."

"I can't just run off to your hotel with you. I don't even know you!"

He frowned. "You know a Terran male would never harm a female, and especially not a child. I only mean to help. Besides, if things go accordingly, you'll be living there before long anyway."

Her mouth opened and closed a few times before she shook her head. "You're not making any sense. Why would I be living there anyway?"

"Because." He smiled. "You're going to be my mate."

Her jaw dropped. "Excuse me? I'm going to be what?"

"My mate. I'd sworn to never take a mate, but I thought we could help each other out. I want children, and you need a way to ease your daughter's suffering. I realize I'm getting the better deal, since I don't know if I can save her or not. You may need some time to think it over, but while you do that, I think we should get to know one another."

She sank into her broken-down recliner. "Mate?"

He nodded, looking around again.

"But… why?"

"I can't sit back and do nothing when there's a chance I could help your daughter."

"Evie."

"Pardon?" he asked.

"Evie. Her name is Evie. And how is it we're having this conversation outside of the station? Don't I need a translator to understand you?"

His smile broadened. "I wasn't using the translator systems at the station, either. I learned your language when I realized I would be stationed here."

"So you're doing this for Evie?" she clarified. "And because you want children? What happens if I can't have any more children? I had a difficult pregnancy with Evie. The doctor said it might be better if I didn't have another baby."

He frowned. "I hadn't counted on that. There are medical tests you'll have to undergo before you could be approved as a mate. If you carry the cancer gene, or the genes for any illness we might not be able to cure, the request will be denied. If you are unable to have more children, you will also be denied. What kind of complications did you have?"

"I was put on bed rest the last three months of my pregnancy because of preeclampsia. I know it's a common enough condition, but I was severely underweight during my pregnancy and that just added to the problem. I wasn't really in a good situation and couldn't afford to eat more than twice a day, and even those meals weren't as nutritious as they should have been. Evie arrived early with underdeveloped lungs and had to stay at the hospital for a few weeks after she was born."

He rubbed his chin and began to pace. "But it's possible, if you were in a home where food was plentiful and healthy, that if the stresses in your life were removed, that you could carry a baby full-term without issue and have a healthy child. I think the problems you faced were due to your circumstances and not because you're unable to have a normal pregnancy. Tests would give me decisive answers, but you'd have to agree to be my mate first."

"And if I'm your mate, you'll heal Evie? Or at least try to?" she asked.

Xonos nodded. "I give you my word. She'll become my daughter the moment we're mated, and I'll do everything in my power to save her life."

Victoria bit her bottom lip to stop its quivering. "She's never had a father before," she said softly. "Maybe knowing that someone else cares about her would give her the strength to keep fighting."

"What type of cancer does she have? Perhaps if I did some research…"

"Osteosarcoma. It affects children. Usually it doesn't show until they are around ten or older, but Evie's showed up when she was two. It's practically unheard of for it to happen so soon. And hers has spread like wildfire, starting in her right leg and now it's in her arms and the last tests she had done showed it had moved into her lungs. She has maybe a month, two tops, to live."

Xonos studied her with a grim expression. "I hadn't realized it had progressed so far. I'll see what I can do, but it isn't likely I'll be able to cure her. There's a scientist here from my world. His name is Syl. I'll call him tonight to get his help with this. I know I won't be able to do it alone."

Her heart sank, but she tried to stay optimistic. Just because Xonos hadn't been able to cure the mate who had died from cancer, it didn't mean he didn't have the power to cure Evie. Miracles happened all the time, and Victoria had been praying hard for one for Evie. Her little girl was due for some good news, and maybe telling her she would have a daddy would be enough for the moment.

"What happened to Evie's father?" Xonos asked. "If he's still around, he might protest my claiming her."

"I don't know who Evie's father is," she admitted. "I was at a party and was quite drunk. I remember I walked off with two men and by morning I could tell we'd had sex, but I never got their names and if I've seen them since, I didn't recognize them."

He scowled. "And do you make it a habit to be so reckless?"

"No. Not since Evie. I was young, only twenty, and I was trying to escape from my life. I had a father who beat me and a mother who whored herself out for drugs. I've lived in neighborhoods like this, or worse, all my life. I don't want that for my daughter. Especially not if she doesn't have much longer to live. I want her to see the good things in life and get a chance to experience them." She twisted her hands. "I haven't had a drink since the moment I discovered I was pregnant with Evie. And I don't do drugs or smoke. I try to live a peaceful life, and most of my time and energy goes toward Evie. I had a job up until a month ago. I'm on unemployment right now, but it isn't really enough to pay the bills."

"Just how dire is your situation?"

"We'll lose this place next week if I can't come up with the rent money. The utilities are scheduled to be shut off in four days. I can't afford them either. Evie's medicine is expensive and takes up just about all of my money. I haven't been able to afford all of it, so I know I'm responsible for her current condition and the amount of pain she's in. I've done everything but solicit strangers for sex as a way to pay for everything she needs."

Xonos sighed. "I can't let you stay here. Even if the tests haven't been done yet, I can't leave you in this place, not knowing all of that. Pack your things. I'll carry Evie so we won't have to wake her. Take what you need for now and I'll send someone tomorrow to pack the rest of your belongings."

"We don't have much. Maybe two suitcases and one box worth of things I'd want to keep. And really, the clothes are more of a necessity. They're all second-hand and Evie's don't fit the best, but they've had to do for now."

"First thing tomorrow we're getting the blood samples I need from you and then we're going shopping. And don't even think of saying no. I'm not giving you an option. You're going to be my mate. You obviously need a protector more than I realized."

She wasn't sure if she should feel affronted that he thought she was doing such a poor job of taking care of Evie and herself, but she had to admit he had a point. They were on the verge of losing everything, and she couldn't afford to take care of her child. She was doing a horrible job as a mother and maybe it was time to accept some help.

"Just let me change out of my pajamas and I'll start packing."

"Tell me where Evie's suitcase is and I'll start packing her things. I promise to be quiet and not wake her."

"In the top of her closet. Most of her clothes are hanging up but there are a few things in the dresser drawers."

Xonos nodded and followed her down the hall. She pointed to Evie's room before dashing into her own. Pushing the door shut, she quickly changed into jeans and a tee, and then began shoving her clothes into her suitcase. When she was finished, she took the box out of her closet and began packing the few pictures and knickknacks she wanted to keep. The furniture and dishes could stay behind. If she was moving in with Xonos, she wouldn't need them. And if things didn't work out, maybe he'd let them stay at least long enough for to save for another apartment or find a new job.

He was waiting in the living room when she came out of her room. Her daughter was in his arms and the suitcase at his feet. There was a knock at the door and she hesitantly opened it only to discover a human male in a chauffeur's outfit standing on her stoop. She ushered him inside, and he promptly picked up the box and one of the suitcases.

"I'll return in a moment for the other bag, Mr. Xonos. Is there anything else you need?"

"I believe that will be all, Ned."

The man nodded and carried their meager belongings outside. Victoria held up her key. "I need to return this to the manager and let them know I'm not staying."

"I'll have someone take care of it for you tomorrow. Tonight, we're going home and getting Evie settled. Then tomorrow starts your new life."

She shook her head. "We can't get used to a new life until the blood work comes back, and you determine whether or not I'm allowed to be a mate. I don't want to give her false hope that things are changing if they're only going to remain the same. I just ask that you let us remain with you long enough for me to find a place to live and another job."

Xonos smiled. "Have a little faith, Victoria. Things will work out the way they're supposed to. If we're destined to be a family, then that's what will happen."

She nodded. Ned returned and took the other bag. They followed him down, Victoria pausing only long enough to lock the apartment. She handed the key to Xonos and they walked out to the limo that waited for them. Victoria had never ridden in one before and wasn't sure what to expect. There was enough space for Evie to stretch out and lay her head on Victoria's lap, while Xonos sat on her other side. She found his presence comforting and hoped for the best.

When they arrived at the hotel, he took Evie from her and led the way to his suite on the top floor. The view outside his living room window was breathtaking, unlike anything Victoria had seen before. She followed him into the second bedroom, where he gently tucked Evie into bed. The bed would be plenty big enough for her, but she didn't dare sleep with her daughter for fear of hurting her if she accidentally bumped Evie's leg or arms. It wouldn't take much to fracture a bone and Victoria was a restless sleeper.

"I'll have Ned bring your things up," he said as they backed out of the room.

"I'll take the couch," Victoria said.

Xonos frowned. "Why the couch?"

"If I sleep with Evie, I might hurt her. I've slept in worse places than your couch. It won't be a hardship. I bet it's more comfortable than any of the beds I've slept in before."

"You'll be sharing a bed with me soon enough. You might as well sleep there. I promise to keep my hands to myself, if it will ease your mind. I'll not expect anything of you."

"Until we're mated?" Her heart fluttered in her chest at the thought of sharing a bed with him, whether sex was involved or not. What would it be like to wake up in those muscular arms?

He nodded. "Even then, I don't expect you to just jump right in. I know we need to get to know one another before things progress between us. I'm willing to give you the time you need, as long as I have your assurance that we will be intimate at some point in the future."

"Thank you," she said softly. *Please don't embarrass yourself and try to cuddle him in the middle of the night.*

Ned returned a few minutes later with their belongings and Xonos carried Evie's to her room and Victoria's to his, leaving the box in the living room. She reached inside and pulled out the few pictures she had of Evie and her and placed them around the room, putting one in her daughter's room on the dresser. She wanted Evie to feel at home when she woke in a strange place.

The rooms were spacious, with furnishings nicer than anything she'd seen before, except for in shop windows when she'd gone uptown. When everything was put away, and Evie's clothes had been placed in the dresser, she returned to the living room where Xonos was staring out the window.

"You should get some rest," he said. "We have a big day ahead of us tomorrow. Evie can come with you to the clinic in the morning and we'll take your blood. I'll need several vials; the tests are extensive. You'll also need a wellness exam, but if you'd prefer, I can ask my assistant to handle it. I don't want things to be awkward between us."

She felt her cheeks warm. "If I have to remove my clothes, I'd rather you do it."

He nodded.

"Are you coming to bed?" she asked.

"In a little while. I need to contact Syl. Even though the hour grows late, I want to discuss the situation with him, see if he'll do some research tomorrow and start working on a cure for Evie. It may take him some time, but since time isn't on our side, I'll see what I can do to prolong her life while he works in his lab."

"I seem to be saying *thank you* an awful lot, but thank you, Xonos. You're the answer to my prayers."

He gave her another nod with a small smile and she hurried into the bedroom, where she closed the door and changed back into her pajamas. After putting her clothes in the dresser, she pulled down the covers and slipped into bed, not even bothering to turn out the light. She wasn't sure how well Xonos could see in the dark and didn't want him to bump into the furniture when he finally came to bed.

Closing her eyes, she breathed a heavy sigh and settled into the softest bed she'd ever slept in. Yes, she was pledging herself to a man she didn't know, but it was a small price to pay if it meant her daughter would live and would get to experience things Victoria would never be able to give her. And he wasn't exactly hard on the eyes. If just one look made her warm from the inside out, what would happen when he kissed her?

Maybe things were finally turning around for them.

Chapter Three

A cry pierced the air and Xonos leapt to his feet, his future mate bolting upright in bed. She scrambled out from under the covers and went running through the suite before he could stop her. Following, he realized she was going to Evie's room, having recognized her daughter's cry. He quickly made sure his loose sleep pants were still sitting at his waist, and hiding his semi-erect state, before stepping inside the little girl's room.

She clung to her mother, tears streaking her cheeks. "I thought you'd left me," Evie cried.

"Never, precious," Victoria assured her. "You remember Mr. Xonos, don't you? From the Terran station?"

Xonos cleared his throat. "Just Xonos is fine."

"Why are we here?" Evie asked in a small voice, eyeing him over her mother's shoulder.

"We're going to live with Xonos for a while, maybe forever. Would you like that? To keep this room for your own?"

The little girl nodded, slowly extracted herself from her mother's arms and came to stand in front of Xonos. She reached up with her little arms, and he bent to pick her up. Immediately, she hugged him tight and he returned her affectionate embrace, careful not to hurt her fragile body.

"What do you say we order breakfast before we start our day?" he asked.

Evie nodded and he carried her out of the room, picked up the phone, and ordered one of everything on the menu. He wanted to start the day off right, and his new family needed to eat a nice, big, healthy meal. Especially if they were going to keep up with him today. He'd just have to keep an eye on Evie and make sure she didn't tire too quickly.

When breakfast arrived, Evie helped lift the silver domes, her eyes going wide at the variety of foods available to her. He wondered if she'd ever had an omelet before, or when the last time was she'd gotten to indulge in a sweet, syrupy waffle. She seemed hesitant to reach for anything, so he piled several things on her plate with the assurance she could have more if she finished everything.

There were tears in Victoria's eyes as she watched him serve her daughter, and he wondered if it hurt her pride that she hadn't been the one to provide such bounty for her daughter. He could tell she was an independent woman, someone used to standing on her own two feet and having to fight for everything they had. He admired her for it, but those times were about to change. She had him now, at least, as long as the blood work came back okay.

"This is really all for me?" Evie asked as she picked up her fork and poked at the omelet on her plate.

"It's all for you," Xonos assured her. "And I can promise there will be just as much food at lunch today. Maybe we'll stop at a restaurant and you can pick anything you want from the menu."

Her eyes lit up. "Even dessert?"

He couldn't help but smile at her enthusiasm. "Yes, even dessert."

"Mommy, you should try this," Evie said, shoveling a bite of the ham and cheese omelet into her mouth.

Victoria had yet to fill her plate and Xonos took over the task. She tried to protest as the plate overflowed with food, but he didn't stop until she had nearly one of everything to choose from. He set the plate down in front of her and then took to the task of filling his own. But he kept an eye on his two girls, making sure both were eating well.

It was strange. He was single yesterday and had planned to stay that way, but when he'd woken in the middle of the night with Victoria wrapped in his arms, something inside of him had shifted. He'd never held a woman before, not like that. Sure, he'd been with women at the floating brothel near Terran, but those were quick encounters meant to alleviate some stress and lacked intimacy. There was something almost sweet about having her snuggle close to his chest, giving him her trust.

When he'd previously contemplated having a mate, he'd thought it would be nice to have a woman in his bed every night and someone to share his days with. He'd never stopped to think how having a woman in his life would make him feel. Sure, he'd thought about the physical aspect of it but not about the emotions involved. After just one night, he wasn't sure he could keep their deal strictly that. If what he'd felt stirring inside of him when he'd woken to her soft body pressed to his, her breath caressing his bare chest, was a hint of things to come, then he could guarantee that feelings would definitely be involved, and probably sooner than he'd ever thought possible. He already admired her for her strength and the care she gave her daughter. It wouldn't take much for him to grow to love her.

Love. He nearly snorted. He'd seen the mates on Terran and knew the Terran males were capable of such an emotion, but he'd never thought he'd be one of them, not even when he'd wanted a mate before. He'd just wanted companionship and a warm body at night.

No more trips to the brothel. But he had a feeling that with Victoria in his life, he was getting so much more.

Evie finished her food and popped up from the table. "May I be excused?"

"Of course." Xonos fought a smile at how adorable and well-mannered she was. He hadn't expected such a thing of someone so small. "And where are you off to?"

"I want to get ready so we can go shopping."

Shopping? Victoria must have mentioned it to her while Xonos was lost in thought. Even though her skin was ashen and her bones poked through, the light in her eyes at that moment made her truly beautiful. He gave her a nod and she dashed back into her room, pushing the door shut. He could hear her opening drawers and then heard the shower start in her connected bathroom.

He gave Victoria a surprised look. "She can bathe herself?"

"She's five, Xonos. Of course, she can bathe herself."

It seemed there was a lot he needed to learn about children, particularly small ones. He knew about the anatomy of small humans, but he'd never bothered to study their mannerisms. It seemed he'd been missing out. If he was going to be a father to Evie, there was a lot he needed to absorb from books and observation. He wanted to be a good father, someone she could look up to, someone she could one day love. Victoria had said the child had never had a father, and he wanted to make up for all that she had missed in the first five years of her life.

Victoria pushed her still half full plate away.

"You aren't done, are you?" he asked.

"I'm not used to eating a lot. Small stomach."

He nodded but wasn't pleased with her answer. If he had any say in the matter, within the next few weeks, she'd be cleaning her plate. She wasn't frail looking like her daughter, but Victoria could certainly stand to gain a little weight. At least now he understood why she was so small. It wasn't because she was on some fad diet, but because she hadn't been able to afford to feed her child and herself. He didn't like the thought of the two of them starving or living in that awful place he'd found them in last night. They deserved so much better, and he intended to see that they had it.

"I'm going to go shower," she said, pushing back her chair. "Give me a half hour to get ready and then I'll watch Evie while you get ready. Not that she would do anything but watch TV. We only had the basic channels, but I'm sure you have much more to offer her. She loves cartoons."

"Then I'll find something for her to watch while you get ready."

Xonos finished his meal and turned on the TV. As he surfed through the channels, he called room service to have their leftover food taken away. When he found some cartoons that looked age appropriate, he set down the remote and went to knock on Evie's door. But before his fist could connect with the wood, it swung open and she bounced into the living room, wearing pink from head to toe.

"You seem to have a lot of energy this morning. Did you sleep well?" he asked, remembering how sickly she'd appeared yesterday.

"I have good days and bad ones. I don't feel as tired as usual, not right now."

This meant she could feel that way later. He'd have to ask Victoria about the medicine she said the child needed. Even if they weren't mated yet, he could ensure she had the proper pills. Getting medication for the child was different from healing her. There was no sense in him watching her waste away if he could do something about it. He'd spoken to Syl for an hour last night and they had agreed that even before the mating papers were done, the scientist would begin researching Evie's disease to see if they could at least slow it down while he found a cure. If anyone could cure Evie, it was Syl. The man was beyond brilliant.

Syl... He still had Terran connections and was allowed to work for the Terran station, even though at first he'd been told he would be completely cut off. What were the chances that the same would happen for Xonos if he decided to stay on Earth and assimilate? Would the council turn their backs on him if he pulled away in order to mate with Victoria? He'd go through the proper channels first, but if things didn't work out... it was something to think about.

Victoria opened the bedroom door and stepped into the living room wearing another pair of jeans and a T-shirt. Did the woman not own anything else? He'd have to make sure she bought plenty of clothes today, not just for Evie but for herself as well. If they'd been shopping in secondhand stores all this time, he would imagine the local boutiques would be a treat, and Xonos could certainly afford it. Doctors were very well paid on his planet, since their skills were required to keep the warriors in top shape.

"We need to stop by the clinic before we go shopping," he reminded Victoria. "We can get your bloodwork and exam out of the way. My assistant can run the tests on your blood. We won't have to wait around for the results."

"You don't want to know if I'm allowed to be your mate before you spend money on us?" Victoria asked.

Xonos shook his head. "It isn't important. Making sure the two of you have everything you need is more pressing. And I mean everything. If you have outstanding prescriptions for Evie, give them to my assistant."

Color flooded her cheeks and she tightened her lips, but he knew she wouldn't argue, not when it was for her daughter. Victoria was a good mom, doing the best she could, but the best wasn't good enough anymore. She needed help, even if she didn't want to admit it. She'd made the first step, agreeing to move in with him, so he had no doubt that she would accept whatever help he offered. At least, when it came to her daughter. Accepting things for herself might be another matter.

Xonos ushered them out of the room and down to the waiting limo. When they arrived at the station, Evie clung to her mother's hand, eyeing the surrounding aliens with wide eyes. Thanks to Brielle, negotiations were being made with other races to take part in the bride program, and several dignitaries were at the station, checking things out. Gray aliens, blue aliens, aliens with tattoos, some with fangs. There were a wide variety residing on the station.

They entered the lab, and Xonos led them back to his office. Pulling up some cartoons on his large Vid-Comm, he settled Evie in the chair behind his desk. She looked at everything in curiosity but didn't reach for the items on his desk. He gave her a few instructions, mostly not to mess with his papers, and then led Victoria to an exam room. He pulled out a hospital gown and gave her orders to strip and put it on.

While she was changing, he stepped out of the room to find his assistant and let him know what was going on. The male was in training to be a doctor, but hadn't finished his studies yet. He had several years left but knew enough to handle the blood samples that came through the lab, and could even give basic exams now. Xonos had to admit the male was brilliant, if a bit young still.

Zaylon gave him a knowing smirk and Xonos scowled back. "What?"

"You're acting out of character. I think you have feelings for this woman."

Xonos shook his head. "It isn't like that. She needs my help."

Zaylon kept smiling, but wisely kept his mouth shut. Thinking Victoria had had plenty of time to change he went to check on her, stopping long enough to pick up the tools he'd need to do a scan and draw her blood. He knocked before entering and found her sitting on the edge of the exam table.

Was that disappointment that he felt? He had to admit he wouldn't have been disappointed if she hadn't put on the gown yet. After feeling her curves against him last night, he was more than ready to get a look at her without her clothes, and maybe do a little exploring of the non-medical kind.

"You'll need to lie back."

While she complied, he washed his hands with a special cleanser that would kill any bacteria on his hands, far stronger than Earth's version of anti-bacterial soap. He moved to stand beside her once more and held up the Terran version of a syringe.

"I need to get the blood samples first. This needle is similar to the ones you use on Earth, but it will compartmentalize the samples inside the barrel, based on the programming I entered. It saves me from filling many vials, as they're all part of the needle."

She frowned at the gadget. "It doesn't look like it holds very much."

"More than you think." He smiled. "Now take a deep breath and relax."

After she complied, he stuck the needle in her arm and withdrew the amount of blood needed, then put a small bandage over the pinprick. Next, he picked up his scanner, explained how it worked, and did a scan of her from head to toe, paying special attention to her reproductive organs. Everything looked to be in good shape.

Xonos set the machine aside and proceeded with the physical part of the exam. His pulse raced at the thought of touching his potential mate. He gave her a brief exam, checking her lymph nodes, her throat, and her eyes. Then he stepped back to give her some space.

"All done?" she asked. "I have to admit, when you told me to put on a gown, I thought your exam would be a bit more invasive."

He smiled. "Nothing like the yearly exams human women go through. My scan and the blood work will tell me most of what I need to know. I'll go type up my notes while you change back into your clothes and then we can head out for a day of shopping."

She sighed. "You don't have to spend a lot of money on us, Xonos. If the council denies our mating, I'll just have to find a way to pay you back and I'd rather not have to go through that."

"You won't owe me anything, Victoria. Let me make your life, and your daughter's life, comfortable for a while. Like you said, she deserves a chance to get to see a different side of life. I can't very well spend money on her and not her mother. How do you think that would make her feel?"

Victoria chewed on her lower lip. "She's rather observant."

Xonos nodded. "I've noticed."

"Very well, but keep the spending to a minimum. It won't take much to make her happy. If it weren't for charity, she wouldn't have had a Christmas -- ever. And I'm a horrible mother because I didn't think to pack the few toys she did own. They weren't much, mostly things I'd found at the dollar store, but at least she had something to play with. Now she has nothing."

"Then the first place we're stopping is a toy store."

"Xonos…"

He held up a hand. "It's not negotiable, Victoria. I will treat her as if she is mine, and you're going to let me. It's important that Evie and I bond, and if you're always undermining me and telling me I can't do things for her, then Evie will think you don't want the two of us to become close and she'll hold back."

"You're right." Victoria sighed. "I don't like it, though."

"Do you remember the way to my office?"

She nodded.

"Get dressed and head in that direction. I'll be waiting with Evie."

He closed the door behind him and entered his office with a smile on his face. Evie was curled in his chair, her chin propped on her fist, as she watched the cartoon on the screen with rapt fascination. Xonos settled on the leather sofa, not wanting to disturb her, as he typed up his notes and created a file for Victoria. If all went according to plan, he'd know by end of the day whether or not the council would accept her as a mate. At least, as far as the physical aspect went. Convincing them to let him bond to a mate with a human child was another matter, especially one who had already been rejected for the bride program.

Victoria entered the room a few minutes later, and he set aside his work and stood. When she came closer, there was a look in her eyes that he didn't like. He wasn't sure how he knew, but something had happened since she'd left to change clothes, and whatever it was had obviously upset her.

"What happened?" he asked.

She shook her head.

"Don't lie to me, Victoria. I know something happened."

"Your assistant barged in while I was changing. He caught me in my bra and panties." Her cheeks flushed. "He... he said he didn't understand why you would want an exam and bloodwork on me when I was obviously not woman enough for a male of your intellect."

Anger built slowly and steadily, traveling through his veins like hot lava, until he was certain steam was coming out of his ears. Someone had dared see his mate in a state of undress? And then made disparaging comments about her?

With a command for Victoria and Evie to stay in his office, he charged out into the clinic to find his assistant. His soon to be *ex*-assistant. The male might be intelligent when it came to medical matters, but obviously he was lacking in other areas. Insults to Xonos' mate would not be tolerated for any reason.

"Zaylon," he roared as he stormed down the halls.

His assistant popped out of an exam room, a look of curiosity on his face. "Is something wrong?"

"Did you or did you not insult my intended?"

Zaylon couldn't stop the sneer from spreading across his face. "Mate," he spat. "She's not your mate and she's not fit to lick your boots. Do you honestly think the council will approve a match to someone like her?"

Xonos stalked closer, wrapping his hand around Zaylon's throat. "Let me make something perfectly clear. That woman *will* be my mate, whether the council approves or not, and you *will* treat her with respect. As of now, your position is terminated. I want you on the next shuttle back to Terran."

"Terran." The male growled. "If it weren't for these useless humans, we wouldn't have had to change the name of our beloved Zelthrane-3. They're inferior to us in all ways, and it's insulting that we should breed with them."

His hand tightened on Zaylon's throat. "Out. Now."

He dropped the male back to his feet, not even realizing he'd lifted him off the floor, then watched as Zaylon scurried out of the clinic. Heading to the nearest Vid-Comm, he called security to inform them that Zaylon was to be on the next shuttle home and then called the council to inform them of what had happened.

"So you're taking a mate?" Larimar asked. "I thought you'd decided against it."

"Victoria needs me, and I'm starting to realize that perhaps I need her as well. I'll have the lab results and my exam notes to the council before nightfall. I had intended for someone impartial to run the results, but with Zaylon out of the picture, there's no one left but me. I can't wait for the labs to be sent home."

"If she was previously denied, why do you think we would accept her now?" Larimar asked.

"Because you denied her on the premise that no one would want a sick child. I'm willing to claim Evie as my own, regardless of her illness. You and I both know that this is the best chance that little girl has to have a normal life, even if it's only for a short while. But Syl and I are going to do everything in our power to ensure she lives a long time."

"Get me your results and I'll speak with the council. If anyone deserves to have a mate of their choosing, it's you. I have to tell you though, there's been talk of bringing you back to Terran. Your replacement is not adequate as far as the council is concerned. How much longer do you intend to remain on Earth?"

"Until Syl's child is born. No one on Earth has more experience delivering Terran-Human babies than I do. I'm glad the council reconsidered and has allowed Syl to work for the Terrans once more. Now I need them to agree to allow me to remain until his child is born."

"Very well." Larimar smiled. "I'll see what I can do."

Xonos ended the call and then went back to his office where he found Victoria and Evie curled up on his sofa watching the Vid-Comm. He leaned against the doorframe, just drinking in the scene, before making his presence known. Victoria looked his way, but Evie kept watching the cartoon.

"I'm going to have to stay long enough to process your bloodwork and then put together a report to send to the council. We can go shopping once I'm done. So, maybe an hour? Do you want to hang out here in my office, or would you prefer to go back to the hotel?"

"Here is fine. If we aren't in your way?"

He shook his head. "If you're going to sit there, I can work at the desk. The cartoon won't bother me. I'll be in the labs for a little while. Take a right down this hall, then a left at the T and I'll be in the second lab on the right. I'm going to lock up the front and put up a notice that we're closed today."

Victoria turned away from him so he wandered off, leaving them to the show they were watching. In the labs, he ran all the necessary tests, made some notes, then gathered what he needed for his report. He cleaned up the lab and then went back to his office. Neither Victoria nor Evie looked up when he walked in. When he stepped in front of them, he realized they'd both fallen asleep. A glance at his watch showed he'd been busy a little longer than he'd anticipated.

Sitting at his desk, he began to type up his report, giving all his findings and trying to stay clinical in his observations. It was hard since this was a personal matter for him, but he tried to keep his emotions out of the equation. When he was done, he cleaned off his desk and gently woke Victoria and Evie.

"Are you finished?" Victoria said, blinking at him sleepily.

"I am. Are the two of you ready for some shopping? Or would you prefer to return to the hotel for a nap?"

Evie's eye widened. "We can go shopping now? In real stores?"

Real stores? He must have looked puzzled because Victoria gave him a sheepish look. "She means stores that aren't thrift stores. She's never owned anything new before, except for a few things from the dollar store."

He wasn't surprised, not after having seen where they lived and hearing a little more about Victoria's background. Xonos was anxious to buy as much as Victoria would allow. He wanted them to have the best of everything and hoped he could convince her to get rid of their old belongings. Neither of the girls needed a reminder of their past, not when their future was going to be so much better. At least, if he had anything to say about it. One way or another, he was taking Victoria as his mate, and he would do all he could to cure Evie.

Chapter Four

Evie was wilting like a flower after too much sun, but the little girl just refused to quit. Victoria knew it had been an exciting day, for both of them, but she worried her little girl was going to overdo it. Evie needed lots of rest, even if her energy levels had been high today. Victoria knew tomorrow could be the complete opposite, with Evie staying in bed the entire day, barely able to walk herself to the bathroom.

Xonos removed something from his pocket. A green laser slid across Evie's forehead, and he frowned down at the device before eying the little girl once more. He knelt in front of Evie, taking her small hand in his much larger one.

"Today has been fun, hasn't it?" he asked.

Evie nodded enthusiastically.

"But we have lots of days ahead of us to have more fun. We don't have to squeeze everything into just one day. What do you say we go back home, order some room service, and watch a movie?" Xonos asked.

Evie wavered.

"You can pick any movie you want. I had someone at the Terran station set up several of those streaming accounts for me, so you'll have lots to choose from. It can be something you've seen a hundred times or something you've never watched before."

"I want to see that new movie at the theater about the princess who gets lost." Evie gave him a pleading look.

Xonos smiled. "Why don't we save that one for another day? I'll have to go into the office tomorrow to work for a little bit, but if you're up for it, maybe we can go see it tomorrow night. Or we can wait until another day when you're feeling not quite so tired."

"We aren't going back to the apartment tomorrow?" Evie asked softly, scuffing her toe along the ground.

"No, Evie." Xonos squeezed her hand. "You're never going back to that apartment. You're going to live with me from now on. Do you think you'd like that?"

"Like a family?"

"Just like a family." He smiled.

Evie seemed to contemplate his words before speaking again. "If we're going to be a family, does that make you my daddy?"

Tears gathered in Victoria's eyes as she looked at her daughter's hopeful expression. They'd discussed daddies more than once over the years, the little girl asking for one every Christmas. Victoria had finally explained that Santa couldn't bring a daddy to Evie because a dad was someone special and she would find him when the time was right.

Xonos' gaze never wavered from Evie's, but even Victoria could see the emotion welling inside of him. He nodded and pulled Evie in for a hug, just tight enough to show that he cared but not so tight he would hurt her fragile bones.

"Okay, Daddy," Evie said, pulling away and taking his hand. "We can go home."

Xonos reached for Victoria with his other hand and led them to the waiting limo. Once inside, Evie cuddled up next to Xonos and rested her head against him, falling asleep before they reached the hotel. He carefully carried her up to their suite, with several hotel employees following with armfuls of shopping bags.

Victoria pushed Evie's door open and watched as the large alien placed her daughter on the bed. Their daughter, she supposed. It seemed he was going to claim them even if the paperwork hadn't gone through yet. It warmed her heart that Xonos was willing to play the role of daddy to a little girl who wasn't his own. He'd been wonderful with her all day, listening to everything Evie had to say and taking her into the shops she seemed most interested in. If she could have handpicked a father for Evie, she couldn't have found a better one than Xonos. After spending the day with him, she'd discovered that he was a kind, caring, very considerate male who seemed to want only the best for them.

She'd balked at the expensive clothing stores, insisting she didn't need anything, but somehow he'd talked her into a new wardrobe, complete with shoes and matching purses. Matching *purses*! It still boggled Victoria's mind. She'd never owned such pretty things before. Part of her said not to get used to it, that it could all be a dream and she'd wake up at any moment. The other half wanted to embrace this new life wholeheartedly.

It had seemed Xonos looked for an excuse to touch her throughout the day. Little touches, or hand holding, but it had been enough that by the time they were climbing in the limo she was more than ready to discuss the more intimate aspects of their relationship. With every touch, her heart raced and heat pooled low in her belly. He'd told her she could have as much time as she wanted, and she was truly grateful for that, but it had been a long time since she'd had a man in her life or her bed. She hadn't slept with anyone since discovering she was pregnant with Evie, and that was five long years ago. More like six if you added the pregnancy to Evie's age. It might be a good way for them to grow closer together.

Xonos eased out of the room while Victoria finished tucking in Evie, kissing her goodnight and then closing the door quietly. Xonos faced her, arms folded, looking pensive. She moved closer to him, placing a hand on his arm.

"Thank you for today," she said.

"I'm worried it was too much for Evie. I should have paid closer attention and called a halt to our activities long ago. She was just so happy that for a moment I forgot she was a very sick little girl who needed her rest. It won't happen again."

Victoria's lips tipped up on one corner. "Xonos, she's fine. Yes, she probably overdid it today, but you gave her a magical day unlike anything she's ever experienced. She may be tired and need to stay home tomorrow, but once her energy is back, she'll be begging you to take her out again. You may regret all of those impulsive buys today because she's going to think you can buy her whatever she wants whenever she wants. Evie isn't used to getting things, and I'm worried it may become too much for her to handle. She wouldn't mean to take advantage of you, but I don't know that there's a way to end her spending spree. You may have created a monster by giving her everything she's ever wanted. She's used to limits and you've blown right through them all."

"If you're worried about making a dent in my accounts, you can't. I'm not the richest man on my planet, but the currency exchange rate for Terran money to Earth money is rather high. I changed out a few hundred thousand dollars. We didn't spend enough today for me to even notice any is missing."

Her jaw dropped. "A few hundred *thousand*?"

"I meant for us to stop long enough for me to transfer funds into your account. You do have one, don't you?"

"Well, yes, but... I may have fifty dollars in it right now."

Xonos frowned. "That won't do."

He pulled up someone on the Vid-Comm, giving instructions to transfer one hundred thousand Earth dollars into Victoria's account. Her head was spinning from the amount and the extravagance of Xonos' spending. To be able to move that much money around, simply because he wanted her to have funds, was beyond crazy. It was probably more than she would have earned in five years.

He ended the call and smiled at her. "Your funds will be available tomorrow. You can use them for whatever you want. Obviously, housing and transportation are taken care of, and any meals you eat here will be charged to the suite, but I don't want you to feel trapped because of a lack of money. If Evie and you want to go out and do something, go do it. Just call or leave me a note so I'll know where you are. Bad things happen on your planet, and I'd worry about you if I couldn't reach you."

"Maybe we should get cell phones."

His eyebrows shot up. "I'm familiar with your Earth phones. If you'd prefer reaching me through a phone and not the Vid-Comm, I can certainly procure some for us. I'll stop at a store in the morning before I go to work and have one delivered to you. I'll make sure they program in my number for you."

Her head spun from the way he handled things, but he was certainly efficient. She'd never been with someone like Xonos before, not even before Evie. Her boyfriends had been from the same neighborhood as

Victoria, all of them going nowhere fast. Several had dealt drugs to pay their bills; a few had been career criminals with a wide repertoire of offenses.

"You're unlike anyone I've ever met," she admitted. "And I don't just mean because you're a Terran and not from Earth. It's more than that. You genuinely care for people. You don't know me or Evie, and yet you took both of us under your protection, claiming us as your own."

He reached out and cupped her cheek, his palm hot against her skin. "I'd like to think any male would take care of you the way you deserve, but Thrace disillusioned me of that rather quickly. The males on my planet are far from perfect, Victoria, but I'd always thought they would behave better than your Earth males."

"I'm sure they do. You don't have crime where you live, do you?"

"Not like the crimes here on Earth. There are abductions and wars, but we do not steal from one another; we don't murder each other just because we like the other person's shoes."

"There are no drugs or alcohol on Terran, are there?"

"The only drugs are at the clinic and can only be administered by a physician. Our entire planet, comprised of Terran-Prime, the main city, and several smaller ones, is ruled by one council, unlike your Earth with its different countries and rulers. All Terrans speak the same language, though many have picked up several of your Earth languages to please their mates or to help them gain a mate. Although, we've had some trouble getting the other countries to agree to the bride program. We're currently in negotiations with China, but so far that isn't going very well."

"I know you're claiming me as a mate just so you can help Evie, and I can't tell you how much I appreciate that, but I feel like you're being cheated. Your assistant today wasn't wrong, even if his words were cruel. You *can* do so much better than me. I'm nothing, Xonos, less than nothing. I grew up in the gutter and that's probably where I should have stayed. You deserve someone with refined manners, a woman who knows which fork to use when you go to a fancy restaurant."

He placed his finger over her lips. "Not another word. Not if you're going to put yourself down. You're a vibrant, beautiful woman, Victoria. I don't care that you grew up poor. It may define your social status on this planet, but it doesn't define who you are. Just because you didn't have the same opportunities as, say, a woman who became a lawyer, it doesn't mean that you're nothing. You're a mother who was willing to do anything to save her little girl, including selling herself to an alien and giving up everything she's ever known."

Victoria snorted. "I didn't have much to give up. I figured whatever I faced on your world had to be better than what I had here."

"Most women wouldn't sign up for a loveless match, not with one of us. Every pairing I've seen since the bride exchange started has been a love match. But you were willing to give that up just so your daughter could live, or at least have a better life until…" He shook his head. "I already think of Evie as mine, and I'm going to do everything I can to save her. You have my word on that. And once she's healed, if you no longer wish to be with me, I'll petition the council to break our mating. It's never been done before, but I'm sure we could work something out."

"Xonos…" Tears gathered in her eyes. He really was the most selfless male she'd ever met. "I don't want to break the mating. You're a good, kind man, better than I could have ever hoped for in a partner. Do I love you? No, but I believe that love can grow in time."

He smiled and pulled her into his arms, holding her close. She felt the thump of his heart under her cheek and closed her eyes for a moment, savoring the feel of his arms around her. It had been so long since she'd been held, so long since she'd felt the comfort of being this close to another being, other than her daughter. She hadn't realized how much she'd given up by keeping people out of her life until this very moment.

"Let's order something to eat. We can set aside a plate for Evie in case she wakes up," Xonos suggested. "And if she sleeps through the night, we'll just have to make sure she gets a big breakfast."

Victoria smiled. "All right, but no more breakfasts where you order everything on the menu. That was a little much. Just eggs, bacon, and toast will be sufficient."

He raised an eyebrow. "No pancakes? No omelets? You'd give up grits, oatmeal, and whatever that fruit thing was?"

"Yes, I'd give that up." She laughed. "Oh, all right. *Maybe* we can have pancakes. Evie hasn't had them very often, but she seemed quite taken with them."

He snapped his fingers. "Muffins! We didn't have muffins this morning. I'll have to request some for tomorrow."

Victoria shook her head and led him over to the sofa. With a smile, she handed him the phone. "Keep dinner simple."

Xonos stared at the device a moment before lifting his gaze to hers. "Steak and potato? Maybe some pie on the side? I have to admit, I rather like Earth cuisine. I think I've tried one of everything on the hotel menu and requested some things they had to venture out to find."

She smiled wistfully. "I haven't ever had a steak. They were always too expensive for me to buy at the store, even when they went on sale."

"Then steak is what we're ordering. I'll make sure they send up a dish for Evie as well. Would she like the same thing?"

Victoria nodded.

"Pick a movie while I place our order, then we can spend the rest of the night getting to know one another."

As far as plans went, it sounded rather perfect to Victoria. There were lots of things she wanted to know about Xonos. Was he an only child? Were his parents alive? She knew there were some Terran females, had read the brochure on his species, but she wanted to know more about Xonos himself and not just Terran in general.

She had to admit that he fascinated her. And not just because he was an alien. The way he looked at her, the way it felt when he touched her… it made her want to explore more with him, made her wonder what it would feel like to have his hands on her intimately. Victoria couldn't deny her heart raced when he was near and she felt a flutter in her stomach. It had been a long time since she was drawn to anyone, and she didn't think she'd ever felt this way before. She felt more for Xonos than she had anyone.

Although... she'd love to know how an alien planet came to be known as Terran.

Chapter Five

Chief Counselor Borgoz glowered at Xonos. "What do you mean if I don't sanction your mating you'll leave Terran for good?"

Xonos glowered right back. "Exactly as I said. I'll not allow you to dictate who I can and cannot mate. I want Victoria and her daughter, Evie, to be mine. If you'll not allow it, I'll petition Earth to remain here. I have plenty of money to live on if you refuse to let me practice medicine at the station."

Borgoz blustered.

"Admit it, Counselor. You need me far more than I need any of you. I've played by your rules up to this point but, as the Earth people say, I'm putting my foot down. I won't be bullied by you or anyone else. If it weren't for me, you wouldn't even be breathing right now, and you know it."

Borgoz turned a really dark shade of purple, then blue, before letting lose a string of curses. He slammed his fist down on his desk, cussed some more, then turned a narrowed eye gaze back to Xonos.

"Very well. I'll approve the mating, allow you to claim Evie as your own, but know that this is forever. If you decide later you don't want them, or your mate wants out of the relationship, you're just going to have to figure out how to live with each other. You're making an unbreakable oath by taking the two of them into your home and it *will* be forever."

Xonos wasn't pleased to hear that, not after the promises he'd made Victoria, even if she had declared she didn't want to break the mating. Without an approved mating, he couldn't help Evie. He shouldn't have even allowed them to move in with him yet, but he'd broken that rule quick enough. Without a unanimous vote from the council, their bond would never be broken, and while there was a law that allowed for such a thing, it had never been used. It was just understood that all Terran matings were forever.

"Very well, Counselor. Approve the mating and I'll sign whatever you want. Just give Syl and me the freedom to treat Evie, possibly cure her. I already told my mate it may be an impossible task, but I'll do everything in my power to save the child."

"Don't say you weren't warned. It shall be as you wish. I only hope you don't come to realize later that you've made a mistake."

Not likely. Xonos bade him farewell and ended the call before returning to the mountain of files on his desk. He'd seen countless patients today as an unknown virus had swept through the station. Xonos still didn't have a name for the infection, but he'd found a way to cure it. Everyone had been treated, and he even inoculated himself to make sure he didn't take anything home to Evie.

Once he had made notes in all of the files, as well as their digital copies, he filed everything and went home for the day. It was growing late, well past dinner, and he worried that Victoria hadn't called all day. He'd had a phone delivered to her first thing in the morning, but she hadn't used it. At least, she hadn't used it to call him.

The hotel was quiet when he arrived, and he took the elevator to the top floor. Unlocking the suite door, the first thing he noticed was how still everything was. The lights were out; he couldn't hear the sound of a TV turned on in any of the rooms. He checked Evie's room first, but the lights were out and the bed was still made. Next he checked the other bedroom, finding it in the same state. Unease crept down his spine. It was too late for shops to still be open.

Pulling out the phone he'd purchased, he located Victoria's number in the directory and called. The phone rang several times before going to voicemail, which she hadn't set up yet. He was beginning to feel frantic when he remembered the salesman had told him the phone had GPS so he could track it from anywhere. Calling the phone company, he gave them Victoria's number and asked them to run a trace. Within minutes he had an answer, and it wasn't one he liked.

Taking the elevator back to the first floor, he hailed the limo before it could return to the Terran station. Ned popped out of the driver's side and ran around to hold the door open for Xonos. Once Ned was behind the wheel again, Xonos rolled down the connecting window and barked out his orders.

"Take me to the Shriner's Hospital. And get there as fast as you can."

Ned nodded and peeled away from the curb, tires squealing as he floored it. Xonos checked his phone several times, willing it to ring. Why hadn't Victoria brought Evie to him if she needed something? Had she taken a turn for the worse while he'd been at work? It bothered him that his daughter was ill and her mother had sought human medical assistance.

When they reached the hospital, Xonos ran through the emergency room doors, heading straight for the triage desk. He demanded to know where Evie was and they immediately ushered him through the locked doors and down a long hall. When he flung open the door on the room with her chart tacked to the outside clip, his heart was pounding so hard he thought surely Victoria would hear it.

His mate sat beside the hospital bed, her face streaked from her tears, as she held Evie's hand. The girl looked pale in the child-sized bed. Xonos let the door close behind him as he stepped fully into the room.

"What's wrong with her? Why didn't you bring her to me?" he asked.

"She wouldn't wake up from her nap. I tried everything, but she just kept sleeping. I listened to her heart and it seemed slow so I hailed a taxi and brought her here. You said we had to be mated before you could help her."

"We are mated. I had the Chief Counselor push through the papers tonight. Once he signs them, we're officially mated. There's a ceremony we can go through if you'd like, but it isn't necessary."

"So you can help her?"

"Yes, but I'd have to remove her from this hospital and take her to my clinic. Do you want me to do that? Or do you want to wait here and see what they say? They have a chart for her so they've obviously been treating her up to this point."

"I want you to help her."

Xonos nodded. "Give me a moment."

He went in search of the lead physician, explained the situation to the man and then signed the proper forms to have Evie's care transferred to him. An ambulance took Victoria and Evie to the Terran station while Xonos followed in the limo. The EMTs wheeled the small girl into the clinic. Xonos took her to one of the nicer rooms and eased her onto the bed.

Once he was left alone with Victoria and Evie, he went to get his gadgets, running a scan on her first. Other than the cancer being quite evident, there wasn't anything else affecting her that he could see. He drew some blood and ran it for everything he could think of, adding in the new virus as a last resort and then went to the lab to process everything.

Xonos returned to the room a short while later with a syringe in his hand. "It's my fault she's sick."

"How is it your fault?"

"A virus swept through here today, but I'm guessing the germs were present yesterday. I treated nearly every person that works in the station. The virus is curable, so once I administer this, Evie should be fine."

He injected the serum into his daughter, then sat back and waited for it to work. When Evie's eyes fluttered open a short while later, he breathed a sigh of relief. If she hadn't woken, he didn't know what he would have done. Syl wasn't anywhere near ready to treat Evie, even though he was working on a serum that would delay her disease and keep her alive for a while longer. Hopefully long enough for them to cure her.

"Where am I?" Evie asked in a hoarse voice.

"You're at the clinic, Evie." Xonos smiled. "But you're going to be all right. You had a nasty virus, but it will be gone by morning."

"Can I go home?" she asked.

"If that's what you want, I don't see why not."

Evie nodded and tried to sit up, but she was still weak. Xonos lifted her into his arms and carried her out to the waiting limo. When they reached the hotel, he tucked her into bed and turned on the TV for her. He handed her the remote and let her pick whatever she wanted. Something told Xonos that Victoria would remain by her side for much of the night. He'd enjoyed their time together the previous night and had hoped for a repeat.

Resigning himself to a meal alone, he ordered room service, enough for three, and then turned on the TV. As much as he'd like to be near Evie right now, he figured she needed her mother more. They would have plenty of time to spend together later, when she felt better and when he'd had some rest. He was exhausted, his adrenaline finally having dissipated. He'd never been more terrified than the moment he'd walked into the empty hotel room and hadn't been able to reach Victoria. He hoped he never had to experience that again.

The food arrived and he carried a plate to Victoria and Evie, but when he went to leave, the little girl patted the bed.

"Please stay, Daddy."

His heart warmed at her words and he smiled. "Just let me get my plate."

When he returned, he pulled a chair near the bed so he could be close without taking the chance of hurting her. He'd spent the morning talking to Syl about Evie's condition and had done a bit more research on it. Syl thought there was a chance he could cure the little girl, but he wasn't positive. It depended on how far the disease had spread. Victoria had mentioned that it had traveled from Evie's leg to her arms and lungs and from what Xonos had seen on the scan tonight, the damage was extensive.

They ate quietly, watching the program Evie had selected, and when they were finished, Xonos carried their plates into the living room and called room service to pick them up. He stretched and contemplated going back into Evie's room, but he thought she might like some time with her mother.

He called Syl on the Vid-Comm, wanting to discuss his latest findings.

"Are you calling about your daughter?" Syl asked.

"Yes. I ran a scan on Evie tonight. The damage is… I'm not sure we can reverse it. I took some of her blood today and there was a little left over. I saved it in case you needed it to study, or to help with the serum."

"Is the clinic code still the same?"

Xonos nodded.

"Then I'll swing by tonight and pick up the sample. I think I can have a serum ready in a few days that will delay the disease. Curing it though… that could take me a year or more."

"As long as you can prolong her life and keep her breathing until you find a cure, the timetable doesn't matter. I don't want her to feel pain and I don't want her to get worse. If we can take care of those two things, I think her mother will be pleased."

"I'm going to try to cure her, Xonos. You know I'll do anything I can. In fact, I called a scientist on Mirabar. He's traveling here to help with my research and to see if he can speed things along. It's Kronk. You know the male is brilliant, even more so than either of us. If anyone can help cure Evie, it's Kronk."

"Tell Kronk I'll pay for a suite at the hotel for him and make sure a driver is available to him. It's the least I can do."

Syl laughed. "I think the man can afford his own accommodations, but I'll let him know."

"Thanks, Syl. When I can pry Victoria away from Evie, I'll give her the good news. I'll let her decide how much she wants to tell Evie. I'd hate to give false hope."

"I'll contact you in a few days to pick up the serum."

Xonos nodded and ended the call. Giving the closed bedroom door a long look, he decided against intruding on them and went into his own room to take a shower and get ready for bed. The water was nice and hot, and he watched as steam billowed out from behind the curtain. Xonos stepped into the tub and let the heat ease his tense muscles. Bracing a hand against the wall, he bowed his head and let the water pour over him, washing away the hospital scent. He detested that scent. Like antiseptic and death. It was no place for a child and he vowed that Evie would never return there. She would have the best care possible, in Terran hands. And if they couldn't cure her, he'd scour the galaxies until he found a scientist who could. Hopefully, Kronk would be able to solve whatever piece was eluding Syl.

Xonos poured a healthy dose of shampoo into his hands and lathered his long hair. As the suds rinsed down the drain, he reached for the body wash, but something was slapped into his palm. Wiping the moisture from his eyes, he peered around the curtain at Victoria, his cock instantly going to attention at her nearness. He hoped to the gods she didn't look around the curtain and see his current state.

He examined the jar in his hand. "What's this?"

"I used my newfound money to do a little shopping today. I ordered a laptop and had someone at the hotel pick it up; then I shopped online and placed an order at one of those big box stores and had someone pick that up too."

Xonos brow furrowed. "But what's this jar?"

"It's for your hair. I noticed you had some split ends. It's repair cream, so you won't have to cut your hair. I haven't seen a Terran with short hair, so I figured it was taboo to cut it."

He stared at the jar. "You used your money to buy something for me?"

"It isn't anything big. I mean, it cost maybe five dollars, but I wanted to show you that I paid attention to your needs and not just Evie's. I guessed your size and bought you some more pajama pants too, since it looked like you only had one pair."

"You bought me clothes?" His eyebrows shot up into his hairline.

"Well, you wear those leather pants every day, and I saw that all Terrans seem to wear them, so I didn't buy you jeans or anything. Although..." She eyed him up and down. "I have to admit, you'd look rather spectacular in a pair of tight jeans and a black tee."

His jaw dropped and he nearly dropped the jar too. "Pardon?"

"I see you, Xonos. Not just as the man who saved us, but I see you as something more." She licked her lips. "I know you wanted to give me time to get to know you, and I'm grateful for that, but when the time is right, I want you to know that I look forward to being your mate in every way. And maybe, if we're blessed, we'll have more children so Evie will have brothers and sisters. I know the brochure said that Terrans are hoping for female children, but if there aren't male children too, who will the females mate?"

His jaw snapped shut. "You're ready to have children with me?"

"Well, not right this very moment, but... yes, in the future I want to have children with you. Would it be too much to ask for us to cure Evie first? I don't think it would be good for me to stress over Evie while I'm pregnant, and if she's cured, then I won't worry about her quite so much. She'll be able to have a normal childhood."

"Birth control doesn't work with Terrans. Are you saying you wish to wait and mate after Evie is cured?" Gods, he hoped not! Syl said that could be a year from now, and his aching cock was more than ready to get to know Victoria in a much more intimate way.

Victoria gnawed on her lower lip, her white teeth worrying at the pink skin. "Would you be upset if I asked you to wait that long?"

Yes! "No. Of course not. Take as much time as you need, Victoria. We have the rest of our lives together."

That much was true, but he didn't like the idea of having to wait a year or more to have sex with his mate. But then, he hadn't told her the latest news from Syl, and now he wasn't sure he should. It might disappoint her that she would have to wait so long to see her daughter healthy and behaving like a normal five year old. And the last thing he wanted to do was give her bad news. She'd had enough of that in her life.

Victoria left, leaving Xonos to read the instructions on the jar and finish his shower, painfully alone, and still painfully erect. A small part of him had hoped she'd strip down and get in the shower with him. All right, so it was the part of him that was currently waving around demanding attention, and he'd learned long ago to think with the head on his shoulders and not the smaller one, but the woman was just too tempting for words. The more he got to know her, the more he wanted her.

Chapter Six

Four days passed with Evie slowly regaining the energy she'd had during their shopping spree. Xonos hadn't told his family where they were going, only that they needed to leave first thing in the morning. He'd received a call from Syl after everyone had gone to bed and the serum was ready. Xonos had swung by his clinic first to pick up some syringes in case Syl wasn't prepared. Then he instructed Ned to take them to Syl's house.

Victoria's face when they pulled up out front was full of wonder. He had to admit the structure was rather impressive; two-stories with huge white columns across the front and a perfectly manicured lawn with blooming bushes along the walkway. If he remained on Earth, Xonos wouldn't mind a place like this one. They had large homes on Terran, but nothing like this. Would he be doing his family a disservice by taking them to Terran? It wasn't something he'd really thought about much, but maybe he should. There wasn't a reason he could think of as to why he couldn't ask to remain on Earth. They'd need someone in the clinic, so why should it matter if it was him? Yes, he was the best in his field, but surely he could come up with a bargaining chip of some sort, something to make them see it was better for him to remain.

Evie was practically vibrating with excitement when they reached the front door, and Xonos told her she could press the bell. An older gentleman answered the door and Xonos hid a smile at the looks on his mate's and daughter's faces when they realized Syl had a butler. He imagined they hadn't ever seen anything like it, except maybe on TV. They were ushered inside and the butler informed them Syl was waiting in the lab.

"You remember where it is?" the butler asked.

Xonos nodded and herded his family through the lower level and out into the backyard. There was a rather large building Syl had installed to use as his lab, and Xonos escorted his family inside. Syl looked up from a microscope and smiled before heading over to greet them.

"This must be your new family," Syl said, lowering himself to Evie's level. "It's an honor to meet you, Evie. I have something very special for you today."

The little girl's eyes widened. "For me?"

Syl nodded. "How would you like to feel as good as you do right now every day?"

"You can cure me?" she asked softly.

The light dimmed in Syl's eyes a moment before determination shone brightly. "Not yet, but I'm working on it. I can't tell you how long it will take, but I've asked a very special scientist to come to Earth to help me solve the riddle. Until then, I've made something that will arrest your cells and keep the cancer from spreading. You'll have to take it once a week until the cure is ready. Can you be brave and do that for me?"

Evie nodded and looked up at Xonos. "Will you give it to me, Daddy?"

"Of course I will," Xonos said, smoothing her hair back from her face. "As a matter of fact, I'm going to give you the first dose now. Then we'll come see Syl again in another week for your next dose."

Syl handed him the serum.

"Is this the exact dosage needed?" Xonos asked.

"Yes. I'll have to make more before next week, but now that I know how, it should be simple enough."

Xonos extracted the liquid then gave Evie an encouraging smile before he administered the dose. She didn't even wince as the needle went into her arm. Syl disposed of the syringe for Xonos and then welcomed them to explore the lab a bit. Evie was curious about the different gadgets around her and asked a ton of questions, but Syl never lost his patience with her.

The door opened and Brielle bustled in. Well, more like waddled in. Her pregnancy had progressed to the seventh month, but she was as beautiful as ever. Xonos glanced at Victoria, wondering what she would look like when she carried his child. The thought heated his blood and he had to control his body before he embarrassed himself.

"Xonos!" Brielle threw her arms around him and hugged him as tight as she could. "Syl mentioned you were coming today. This must be your new family."

"Brielle, this is my mate, Victoria, and my daughter, Evie."

Brielle shook hands with Victoria and Evie, a bright smile plastered on her face. If she noticed how pale Evie was, or how brittle and thin her hair was, she didn't show it. She treated the little girl just like she would any other, and it warmed Xonos' heart. He wanted everyone to treat Evie like a normal little girl, and one day she would be one. If he had to volunteer some of his time to Syl and Kronk, he would gladly do so.

"It's nice to meet you," Victoria said, eyeing Brielle's large stomach. "How far along are you?"

"Seven months. Xonos examined me last week and told us we're having a girl. I can't wait!"

"Congratulations."

Evie studied Brielle a moment before looking up at Victoria. "Mommy, are you and Daddy going to have a baby too? I've always wanted a brother or sister."

Victoria's mouth opened and shut a few times before she stammered out an answer. "Well, sweetheart, we thought we'd wait until you were better."

Evie's little chin jutted out and she balled up her fists, planting them on her hips, before glowering first at her mother, then Xonos, then looking at her mom again. "No. I want a baby *now*."

Victoria seemed to be at a loss so Xonos crouched down next to Evie. "You know, we can't just order one for you, Evie. Having a baby takes time, and it would take a lot of energy out of your mom. She wants to wait because she wants to be able to give you all of her attention until you're better."

"The medicine you gave me is supposed to keep me from getting sick, so you don't have a reason not to have a baby," Evie stated, still looking mutinous.

Xonos had to fight back a smile because he was ready to agree with Evie wholeheartedly. He wanted a baby with Victoria, and the sooner the better in his mind, but he'd honor her wishes to wait. However, if Evie wanted to get on his side and speed things along, he wasn't going to stand in her way. He'd like to say that he wanted to wait until he was sure Victoria wanted him, but after her comments during his shower the other day, he'd paid closer attention and caught her eyeing him appreciatively several times over the past few days. He didn't think it was a question of her wanting him, just that she wasn't going to allow herself to have the kind of fun that resulted in a baby until their daughter was well.

"You're right, Evie. The medicine is supposed to make you feel better, but your mother is still going to worry about you until you're cured."

Evie crossed her arms over her chest and poked her lower lip out. "I want a baby brother or sister. I don't care which one I get as long as I get a baby to play with."

Victoria knelt at Evie's side. "You really want us to have a baby?"

"Yes, I really do."

Victoria gave Xonos a helpless look and he winked at her before returning his attention to their daughter.

"I promise I will do my best to give you a brother or sister, Evie, but Mommy has to agree to it too."

Evie glared at Victoria, who visibly swallowed before looking at Xonos. He saw the uncertainty and helplessness there, but he wasn't going to throw her a lifeline. She was going to sink or swim on her own. Gods, but he loved Earth sayings!

"What's it to be, Victoria?" he asked.

"Can we talk about it more at home? Maybe after Evie's gone to bed?"

Xonos nodded and stood, noticing at once that Brielle and Syl had vanished during their discussion. He appreciated the time with his family but felt they had overstayed their welcome. Ushering Victoria and Evie out of the lab, he made their goodbyes to Syl and Brielle before climbing back into the limo and driving back to the hotel.

"Do we have to go home right now?" Evie asked.

She seldom asked for anything so Xonos was intrigued as to what she could want. "Did you have something else in mind?"

"Did you see the game room we passed in that big house?"

"Syl's room? With the video games and large screen TV?" Xonos asked.

Evie nodded. "I've always wanted to play a video game."

It reminded Xonos of everything she'd missed out on in her short lifetime and made him even more determined to give her everything she wanted. Victoria had already fussed at him about spoiling Evie, but as far as he was concerned, that was his job. To spoil both of his girls as much as he could. The money wasn't doing him any good just sitting in an account, and according to Victoria, he had more than enough of the stuff to go around, so why not make Evie happy by getting something she'd always wanted?

Xonos informed Ned to take them to the nearest store that sold video games, earning him a glare from Victoria, but he figured she could fuss at him later. When they pulled up, he had to grab Evie to stop her from launching herself out of the limo. He knew she was excited, but he worried she'd break something in her haste to get out of the vehicle.

They entered the store and Evie's eyes went wide in wonder. She slowly walked around, checking everything out and pointing out games she thought looked fun. Xonos had her try the display consoles to see which would be easiest for her to use. After she'd made a selection, he let her pick a handful of games to get her started, then paid for everything and ushered his family back out to the waiting limo.

Evie begged and pleaded to go home so she could play her new games, and Xonos didn't have the heart to deny her. At the hotel, he hooked everything up in her bedroom and handed the controller to Evie. Victoria seemed reluctant to leave her, but he drew her away and into the living room where he put on a movie for them to watch. Sitting on the sofa, he pulled her down beside him and wrapped an arm around her. It was the closest they'd gotten to cuddling since she'd moved in.

Victoria stiffened for a moment before relaxing against him. Xonos drew lazy circles on her arm and hid a smile when she shivered in response. He'd brought home several devices from work to make sure he could keep an eye on Evie without taking her into the clinic and one went off on the table beside him. With a frown, he lifted it and read the display, his frown quickly turning into a smile. A smile he had better control before Victoria saw it.

"Why is it going off?" she asked.

Lie or tell the truth?

"It was telling me the pheromones in the room just increased." He didn't want to tell her that her scent had changed with her arousal. He could smell things a little better than most humans, but she didn't need to know that.

A blush suffused her cheeks and she tried to draw away from him, but he held tight, refusing to let her go. It was cute that her arousal embarrassed her. She'd already told him about her lack of experience, and he found it refreshing since the only females he'd been with were whores. He'd come clean about his past and assured her he'd only gone when it had become absolutely necessary, maybe twice a year, if that much. He wasn't the most experienced male, but in studying the human anatomy, he'd stumbled across sex videos and had watched one after another, confused by the sexual experiences women seemed to crave on this primitive planet.

Would Victoria expect him to spank her? Or tie her up? None of that appealed to him, but if that's what she desired, he would strive to give it to her. They hadn't really discussed what they expected of one another in the bedroom, and he supposed they should have that talk soon, especially if they were going to fulfill Evie's request for a baby.

"You have nothing to be embarrassed about," he assured her. "I want you just as much as you want me. And we're mates. We're supposed to desire one another. What would be awkward would be no sexual attraction between us."

"I suppose you're right. I'm just not used to someone knowing I'm turned on unless I tell them or give them some indication."

"I'll make sure all of my work tools are put away before we spend time together from now on. I don't want to embarrass you. That was never my intention."

She smiled and settled against him once more, and Xonos felt the tension ease from his shoulders. He wasn't sure how she would react at first, and he was thankful that she'd chosen to overlook her embarrassment and cuddle with him some more, even if it was agony. The scent of her teased his nose; the plush suppleness of her body made him achingly hard. Thank the gods for leather pants! They mostly concealed his aroused state, and if she noticed, she didn't comment on it.

Xonos hoped like hell she'd be ready to take their relationship to the next level soon. He wasn't sure how many more nights he could sleep by her side, hold her in his arms, and not strip them both bare and have his wicked way with her. He nearly chuckled at the thought. *Wicked way*. Earth sayings were so much fun!

Chapter Seven

Victoria woke in the middle of the night, still in the grips of her nightmare. It took her a moment to orient herself and realize that the arm holding her down wasn't from an attacker but was her mate holding onto her. Sweat slicked her skin and her hair was plastered to her neck as she blew out a breath and tried to calm her racing heart. She knew that Xonos didn't intend to release her from their bond, but she'd dreamt that he'd given her away, and some non-Terran alien had claimed her and tried to force himself on her.

She shivered in revulsion just thinking about it. There was no reason for her to have had such a dream. Xonos had been attentive and caring. She hadn't missed the bulge in his pants earlier so she knew he desired her, but he hadn't acted on it yet. Did his chivalry run so deep that once he'd given his word, to give her whatever time she needed, he was just going to ignore his body's urges?

It wasn't fair of her to want him to make the first move, not after she'd asked him to wait until Evie was cured, but she had to admit she'd love being chased romantically. Xonos showed her he cared with everything he did for Evie and her, but she wanted more. The desire she saw in his eyes when she caught him unaware... she wanted him to unleash it, to throw her onto the bed and ravage her.

All right. Maybe she'd been reading too many romance novels in her spare time. Men didn't really do things like that, did they? She somehow doubted an alien would, unless he was a barbarian, and her alien doctor was definitely not that. He was refined, intelligent, and so far out of her league she kept waiting for him to realize he'd made a mistake when he'd claimed her.

Victoria lifted his arm and slid out of bed, padding quietly out of the bedroom. She pulled a bottle of water from the mini-fridge and took a long drink. A hand slid around the back of her neck and she dropped the bottle with a squeak.

"Easy," Xonos crooned, placing a kiss on top of her head. "I didn't mean to startle you."

"I'm sorry I woke you."

"I didn't hear you get up, but I felt your absence. Odd, since I've slept alone for so long, but within a week of being with you, the bed suddenly feels empty without you in it."

Victoria turned and wrapped her arms around his waist, resting her head on his chest. His deliciously *naked* chest. Her body burned at the thought that he was naked everywhere… if she just had the courage to strip those pajama pants off him. From what she'd seen and heard, Terrans didn't believe in underwear. He'd been teasing her every night since he first brought her here and probably didn't even know it.

"Xonos… you desire me, right?" She felt his cock pulse against her and smiled.

"You know I do, Victoria. Why are you asking?"

She leaned back enough to look up into his eyes. "What if I asked you to let that iron-like control snap for once?"

"You don't know what you're saying. Trust me. You want me in control of myself at all times." His eyes darkened and the bulge in his pants grew, far more than she'd thought possible.

Oh yeah, she definitely wanted him to lose control. Maybe she'd have to take things into her own hands. She'd never seduced someone before, but something told her it wouldn't take much to get him to break. At least, she hoped it wouldn't. The slight touch of his hands as they rested on her shoulders was enough to make her shiver. If something so innocent was enough to weaken her knees, what would happen when he had his hands elsewhere on her?

Victoria licked her lips, feeling a thrill run through her when he traced the movement. It made her wonder if he'd ever kissed anyone before. He'd told her that his encounters had merely been a way to expel some energy and frustration, but he'd left out all the details.

"Have you ever kissed before?" she asked. Was that her voice? That low, throaty, sultry sound?

"No." His gaze was fastened on her mouth, and she went up on tiptoe to press her lips to his.

Victoria felt him stiffen against her for a moment before wrapping his arms around her, lifting her so he could kiss her more thoroughly. For a man who'd never done it before, he sure seemed like an expert. His tongue swept into her mouth, drawing a moan from her. The kiss was deep and delicious, making her want even more. The seductive push and pull of his lips on hers made her nipples harden.

Xonos drew back, but only long enough to sweep her into his arms and carry her back to their bedroom where he used his hip to quietly shut the door, then set her down on her feet. His dark purple gaze was intense as it bore into her. Slowly, as if waiting for her to stop him, Xonos reached for her top and drew it over her head, letting it fall to the floor. He maintained eye contact as he stripped the rest of her before letting his gaze caress every inch of her.

Victoria shivered from both the chill and the unbanked passion blazing in his eyes. With shaking hands, she reached out tugged his pants down, letting them land around his ankles. She sucked in a breath at the impressive sight of him.

Oh lord! That's definitely more than a handful… or three.

"I won't hurt you," he said, mistaking her silence for unease.

"I trust you, Xonos. You're just… so big. I have to admit, I'm not entirely convinced you'll fit."

"I'll fit." He smiled. "All Terrans run a bit bigger than your human males. None of the other mates have had a problem, so I'm confident you won't either."

"I know you've been with… prostitutes before, but I don't know how much you've experienced in the bedroom," she said.

His smile broadened. "Not to worry, sweet mate. I've studied the Earth sex videos and know you may require things of me I haven't experienced before. But if you want to be tied up and spanked, I'll try to do it the right way."

Victoria choked and then burst out laughing.

Xonos frowned. "Is that not right?"

She wiped a tear from her eye. "You watched porn as a way to learn how to please a human woman?"

"If that's what it's called."

"Those videos are meant to entertain, not to be used as a how-to." She smiled and shook her head. "We don't have to do any of the things you saw. I don't want to dress up in outfits. I most certainly don't want your cock shoved in my ass, and there will be no paddles or whips."

"Then Earth women do things the same as the prostitutes?"

"Well, that depends... How do the prostitutes do it?"

His frown grew. "They lie still while the male gets on top."

Oh dear. "That's one way to do it, but I promise to never just lie there. You can take me on my side, on my knees, or I can ride you. We can do it standing up too, if that's what you prefer."

Now he looked curious. "Standing up?" He eyed her up and down. "But you're so much smaller than I am."

"You would pick me up, and I'd wrap my legs around your waist."

"Like this?" he asked, as he lifted her into his arms. Her legs folded around him and she grabbed at his shoulders.

"You might want to press me against the wall for extra support. Otherwise, your arms will get tired."

He snorted. "Not likely."

His cock brushed against the curls between her thighs, and she knew he could feel how wet and ready she was for him. And yet, he didn't move. Now it was her turn to frown.

"Are you just going to hold me?" she asked.

"What am I supposed to do now?"

Her cheeks burned at the thought of having to give him step by step instructions. She'd never been very vocal during sex before and all of this talking was... well, it wasn't exactly unpleasant, but it made her uncomfortable. "Now you have to enter me, then lift me up and down on your cock until both of us come."

Victoria felt the head of his cock press against her slick folds and then he was easing inside of her, taking his time and giving her body the chance to adjust to his size. When he was fully seated, she groaned at the fullness, but it was also the best feeling in the world.

She leaned forward and pressed her lips to his. "Now you move."

With his hands wrapped around her waist, he lifted her and then let her fall back on his cock again and again. Victoria tingled from head to toe, pleasure spiraling from her pussy throughout her body. Her nipples pebbled even more from the friction of rubbing against his chest as he slid her body up and down. The strokes became deeper and harder.

Victoria clawed at his shoulders as her orgasm flooded her, wave after wave of ecstasy bombarding her body. She could feel her pussy spasming around his cock as he gave a shout and stilled inside of her. Her channel warmed as his seed poured out of him. Knowing that her essence mingled with his made her feel even closer to him in that moment. He'd been there for her emotionally from the very first, but now they were tied together physically as well.

His breathing was faster than normal, but he hadn't even broken a sweat. "Was that the right way?"

She gave a weak laugh and leaned her head against the wall. "Xonos, if you did it any more right than that, I wouldn't be able to stand tomorrow. I think you turned my legs into Jell-O."

Xonos lifted her so they could separate, then he set her down on her feet. "We should shower."

"Together? I could scrub your back."

He looked intrigued. "I've never showered with someone before. I think I'd like to though. If you're sure you don't mind sharing the shower."

"Of course I don't mind. I almost joined you the other day, but I didn't feel like we'd reached that point yet."

"I was thankful you didn't look around the curtain that day. Just your presence was enough to arouse me. But then, I'm aroused every time I'm near you. Leather pants just make it a little easier to hide than not wearing pants at all."

Victoria laughed. "You don't have to hide your desire for me, and I promise I won't hide mine for you. I want us to have an open relationship, not open in the sense we see other people, but I want us to be able to talk to each other about anything. Don't hide your feelings for me, even if you think it will embarrass me or overwhelm me. I want to know what you're thinking and how you're feeling."

"I want the same thing, but you've seemed so reserved. I was worried I would push too hard and ask for too much from you. Trust is important to me, and I wanted you to trust me."

She placed her hand on his arm. "I do trust you, Xonos. I have from the very first, I think."

"Let's get you cleaned up and then we'll go back to bed. It won't be long before the sun rises, and our daughter seems to wake up early."

She smiled wistfully. "You really think of her as your daughter?"

Xonos wrapped his arms around her and drew her close. "I think of both of you as mine. We may not have known one another very long, but I've come to appreciate the strength and courage in both of you. Even when Evie has to be in a great deal of pain, she suffers in silence so she won't upset anyone. She has the spirit of a warrior, and I'm very proud to call her my daughter. We will cure her, Victoria. I won't settle for anything less than a full recovery. Syl has the best scientist in all of the galaxies coming to help."

"What will life be like for us on your world? Evie will be the only human child. I don't want the others to look down on her."

"A Terran would never make her feel like less because she's fully human. Just because they didn't want to become her father doesn't mean they don't care what happens to her. But you may not have to worry about it."

"What do you mean?"

"I'm going to ask the council if I can remain here and staff the clinic full time on a permanent basis. After seeing the things Syl has been able to give his mate, I want to do the same for you. On Terran, I'm not wealthy like I am here. Warriors are paid more than doctors and scientists, even though we're the ones keeping them alive so they can fight."

"Xonos, I don't need fancy things or lots of money. I can't miss what I've never had."

"But I want to give those things to you. You've lived such a hard life, Victoria. Let me spoil Evie and you for as long as I can. If I remain here, the council may cut my earnings."

"You said you cashed out several hundred thousand. If we don't go on wild spending sprees all the time, that money can last for years, Xonos."

"I want to buy you a house like Syl bought for his mate."

Victoria shook her head. "I don't need anything that big. I'd hate to clean it."

"We'll discuss it later." He swung her up into his arms. "For now, we're going to get you cleaned up and tucked back into bed."

Victoria sighed in contentment. She loved that he wanted to give her things, but it wasn't necessary. A small home in a nice neighborhood would be more than sufficient. She thought about the life that could very well have been created just moments ago and amended that to a medium sized house.

Regardless of the money, the one thing she'd learned tonight is that she wanted Xonos in her life always. She'd felt close to him before, but now she couldn't imagine going back to her lonely existence. He was kind, caring, and made her tingle in all the right places. She'd be a fool not to fall in love with him, and if she wasn't mistaken, she was already halfway there.

Chapter Eight

Xonos came awake suddenly, feeling as if he were being watched. Bolting upright in bed, he came nose to nose with Evie, who smiled and clambered onto the bed. He was rather thankful at the moment that he'd thought to put on more of those pajama pants Victoria had purchased for him, and insisted on his mate putting on the sexy nightgown he'd picked up the other day.

His daughter sat in his lap and leaned back against him. "I thought you'd never get up. I've been up forever and ever."

Xonos looked out the window at the pink streaks of the rising sun. "Did you get up when it was still dark?"

Evie nodded.

"Why couldn't you sleep? Are you hurting?"

"No, but…"

"Is there something you want to do today?"

"I've never been to an amusement park before. There was a commercial for Kentucky Kingdom and the roller coasters look like so much fun."

"Hmm. Well, you know, I've heard those roller coasters can jerk you around a lot. I think the amusement park would be better after you're well. What do you say we find something a little safer to do today?"

"No roller coasters?" she asked, her lip sticking out in an adorable pout.

"Not right now. What about a museum?"

"A horse-back ride?"

"Too dangerous right now. It's right up there with roller coasters. I don't want you to break something if you fall off. Your bones are still very brittle, but I promise we'll do lots of fun things. What about going swimming?"

She tilted her head and seemed to think about it. "I don't have a swimsuit. I've never been swimming before. Mommy said the pool where we lived was too dangerous, that bad people hung out there."

"Your mommy is very smart. But the pool here is very safe. Although if you don't know how to swim, it might be more dangerous than I think."

Evie looked up at him. "What if I had some of those arm floaty things? They'd keep me up in the water so I wouldn't drown."

"Hmm. I suppose that would work. What do you say we let your mommy sleep a little longer, and you and I can go out and find you a swimsuit and floaties?"

Her eyes lit up. "Just you and me?"

He nodded.

Evie squealed and scrambled off the bed, running back to her room. Xonos chuckled, checked on Victoria, and then quickly changed clothes. He tapped his fingers against his black leather pants and pondered what Victoria had said not too long ago. He'd seen the denim pants she'd claimed to want to purchase for him. They looked more comfortable than these were. Maybe he'd surprise her and buy a few human clothes while he was out. Guessing his size shouldn't be too hard. He knew his measurements so that should help.

Closing the bedroom door quietly, he left a note for Victoria on the sofa in case she woke and wondered where they were, then made sure he had his phone with him in case she called. Evie bounced out of her bedroom with a crooked ponytail and her purple unicorn shorts outfit on. It had been her favorite of the things he'd purchased for her that first day.

She clasped his hand and they softly walked to the door, closed it quietly, and then rode the elevator down to the lobby. He hadn't thought to call Ned, but Xonos figured there had to be someone who could give them a ride to the store. But as he exited the elevators, he was surprised to see not only Ned sitting on the couches nearby, but several other drivers.

"Is something going on I should know about?" he asked as he approached Ned.

"There are several dignitaries staying at the hotel right now. We just dropped off a new batch and were told to make sure drivers were available in case we're needed. But if you need to go somewhere, I can call the station and have them send another driver to take my place here."

"Evie wants a swimsuit and some of those float things for the pool. And I've decided it's time for me to change my wardrobe a bit. Do you know of any stores open this early?"

"There are two stores nearby that are open twenty-four hours. I can take you to one of them. The clothes won't be the quality you're used to though. You might want to wait on human clothes until you can go to the mall."

"I want to surprise Victoria so I'll grab at least one outfit while I'm there."

Ned looked at the boots on Xonos' feet. "Might want some sneakers too."

Xonos eyebrows rose.

Ned pointed to a young man across the lobby wearing clothes like Xonos wanted to purchase. "That guy is wearing sneakers."

"Ah. Yes, of course. I'll make sure I get some."

"And socks," Ned added. "You don't want to wear sneakers without socks."

Xonos nodded. "I'm sure I'll need some... what do you call it? Underwear?"

"If you're wearing jeans, I'd recommend it. The zipper can be painful if you get anything important caught in it."

Xonos laughed. "Yes, we definitely don't want that. All right, Ned. We're all yours. Take us to whichever store you think would be best."

Evie held tightly onto his hand as they approached the limo, then she cuddled up next to him when they had climbed inside. It didn't take long to reach the store and Xonos was impressed with the wide variety of inventory. They seemed to carry a little bit of everything, and while Ned claimed the quality of the clothes wasn't as good as some of the shops in the mall, he didn't see anything wrong with them.

He allowed Evie to pick out her bathing suit, grateful that he remembered her size. Then they shopped for the arm floaties, and she convinced him to get a blow up whale for the pool as well. She waited patiently as he browsed through the men's clothing and shoes, and on their way up front, she tugged him over to an aisle filled with small bottles and boxes.

"What's this?" he asked.

"Perfume and cologne. Mommy's never owned any perfume, but she's commented before on how nice a guy smelled. You should get some smell good stuff."

"I'll tell you what; you pick out something for me and I'll pick out some for your mommy so we can surprise her."

After they'd made their selections, they checked out up front and got back in the limo. Xonos checked his phone to make sure he hadn't missed any calls and wondered if Victoria was still asleep. He'd kept her up rather late and hoped he hadn't worn her out too much.

At the hotel, Xonos carried their bags in one hand and held Evie's with the other. The hotel room was still dark and quiet when they entered, and Xonos noted the bedroom door was still closed. He sent Evie to her room to change while he did the same, donning the swim trunks he'd picked up with the two outfits he'd purchased. His mate lay curled on her side, her mouth slightly open, and gave the softest snore he'd ever heard. With a smile, he left her to her sleep and rejoined Evie in the living room.

"We're going to leave mommy a note and then I'll take you down to the pool," Xonos said.

"Mommy doesn't have a bathing suit either."

"Then I'll leave her instructions to go purchase one and join us downstairs. How does that sound?"

Evie nodded, grabbed her floaty things and then waited while he left a note for Victoria. When he was finished, he took the things from Evie and led her downstairs. He hadn't been to the pool before, but he remembered where it was. It shouldn't have been a surprise to see Thrace lying beside the pool, not as much as the warrior had talked about it, but for some reason, Xonos had thought he would only see humans enjoying the water, especially so early in the morning.

Xonos did his best to ignore the warrior's curious looks and blew up Evie's things, helped her into the arm floats, and then got in the pool with her. The water was cool as it swirled around him.

"You're supposed to get your hair wet," Evie said.

Xonos smiled then dunked himself under the water. "Better?"

She nodded. "I can't get wet with these things on my arms though."

"That is a problem, isn't it? What if we took them off, and I could hold you while you tip your head back and get wet?"

Her eyes lit up. "Can I jump to you from the side of the pool?"

"I don't see why not."

Xonos helped her remove the floaties and then carried her over to the steps. She clambered up them, trotted around to the side of the pool, and gave him her biggest smile before launching herself into the air. Xonos caught her and dipped her down into the water, making her squeal.

She wrapped her legs around his waist and begged him to go deeper in the pool. He carried her until the water reached her shoulders and then decided that was far enough. His mate would kill him if he accidentally drowned their daughter.

"You should teach her to swim," Thrace said, joining them. "Then she won't need those things on her arms."

Xonos looked down at Evie. "Would you like to learn to swim?"

Her eyes went wide as she stared at something over his shoulder. "Don't look now, but I think we're in trouble, Daddy," she whispered.

Xonos whipped around, expecting danger, and instead finding his mate furiously tapping her foot, arms crossed over her chest. The dark look on her face didn't bode well, neither did the fact she wasn't dressed in a swimsuit.

"You." She growled. "You took my daughter swimming for the first time without me?"

"I thought you might want to sleep in."

Thrace snickered next to him, enjoying this far too much. Xonos waded closer to Victoria, Evie clutched in his arms.

"And where did she get a bathing suit?" Victoria asked. "Or you for that matter?"

"We went shopping this morning. I'd have purchased one for you, but I didn't know what you would like or what size to get. I thought you might enjoy purchasing your own. I'm sure Ned would be happy to take you shopping and then you can come back and join us."

"Don't be mad at Daddy," Evie said. "He was just trying to make me happy."

Victoria's expression softened as she looked at Evie. "Are you having fun?"

Evie nodded.

"Go purchase a swimsuit and join us," Xonos said. "We're not going anywhere anytime soon. Maybe tomorrow, while I'm in a meeting, the two of you can come down here together. Have some Mommy/daughter time."

Thrace cleared his throat. "I would be honored to watch over your family tomorrow."

"See, you'll even have a bodyguard while I'm gone."

He could see her relenting and finally she dropped her arms and sighed.

"All right. I'll go shopping and hurry back. You promise you won't leave the pool area?"

"We swear it, don't we, Evie?"

Evie nodded again.

Victoria shook her head, turned, and walked off. Xonos winked at Evie. "I think we dodged a bullet that time. Maybe in future, we should wait until mommy is awake to venture off."

"Can we go in the deep end again?"

Xonos chuckled and carried her back into the deeper water. She splashed and giggled, using her hands to spray water at Thrace, who gave her a mock glower, growled, and tickled her.

It made Xonos realize that Thrace would make a good father. He was lucky the warrior hadn't wanted to claim Victoria. If Thrace had said yes that morning, then he wouldn't have the blessings of a mate and child in his life. And would most likely still be living in the clinic, or damn close to it. He'd taken more time off this past week than he had in his entire life, and he knew the Terrans were getting upset with him for closing the clinic so much. As much as he hated to trust another assistant, he really did need one. He'd bring it up during his meeting tomorrow.

Chapter Nine

It had been nearly three weeks since Kronk had arrived on Earth to assist Syl with the cure for Evie, three long weeks. When Syl had called with the news, Xonos had rushed them to the lab to meet with the two scientists. Evie had been so excited; she'd barely been able to sit still while they administered the serum. And now, two days later, the little girl had shown so much improvement, if it weren't for her hair, it would be hard to tell she'd ever been sick.

Evie lay on Xonos examination table as he scanned her from head to toe. Victoria held Evie's hand, waiting for the news. The blood test Xonos had performed that morning proved that the serum had worked, but they weren't sure it would reset Evie's body completely. Xonos frowned as he scanned her arms and the affected leg. When he set his instrument aside, Victoria stared at him expectantly.

"Her bones haven't healed as much as I would like, but there is slight improvement. It's possible they will continue to improve over time, but I'd like her to start a special diet high in vitamins and nutrients that promote bone health." Xonos smiled. "Otherwise, we have a very healthy daughter."

Evie squealed and jumped off the table into Xonos' arms. As close as the two had become, it was hard for people to fathom that Evie wasn't Xonos' biological daughter. They'd been asked several times if she was his and just took after her mother in her looks. The questions always seemed to please Xonos, who never failed to respond with "she's my daughter in every way that counts."

"Does this mean I can go to the park now, Daddy?" Evie asked.

"Not quite yet. I don't want you tumbling with other children until we've strengthened your bones a bit more, but I don't think it will be much longer. Be patient for a few more weeks and then I think it will be safe for you to play with the other children." Xonos smoothed a hand down her hair, pressed a kiss to the crown of her head and then set her down.

"Will my hair get thicker?" Evie asked. "I want to have enough for pigtails."

Victoria ran her fingers through Evie's fine, thin hair. "I'm sure it will. And maybe Xonos knows of some vitamins that will help it grow faster."

Xonos nodded. "I'll do some research and see if there's something safe for her to take that might speed up the process."

Evie held her arms up to him and he picked her up again. As they left the clinic, Xonos locked up and placed his hand at Victoria's back, ushering her toward the limo waiting at the curb.

Thrace came up to them and paused, looking uncertain. Victoria had seen him several times at the pool when she'd taken Evie down to swim, and the big warrior always made time for her little girl. Xonos seemed to trust him, and that was good enough for Victoria.

"I heard Evie has been cured," Thrace said.

"She's on the road to recovery, but there are still things she's unable to do," Xonos said.

"I thought…" Thrace folded his arms over his chest. "I thought maybe I could take Evie for some ice cream and a movie. Give Victoria and you some time alone."

Xonos looked at Victoria and she shrugged. He knew the warrior better than she did, but she'd sensed no malice in Thrace. The warrior had always been kind and gentle when dealing with Evie. Truthfully, from what Victoria had seen and heard about the Terrans, she would trust her daughter with any of them. They seemed like a trustworthy lot, and seemed to have a soft spot for women and children.

Evie patted Xonos on the cheek. "Can I please go with Uncle Thrace?"

Uncle Thrace? That was a new one for Victoria, but as neither Xonos nor she had siblings, she supposed it was only natural for her daughter to adopt some uncles along the way.

"Do you have a phone?" Xonos asked.

Thrace nodded. "I'll give you the number if it'll make you feel more comfortable."

"Pleeeaassee," Evie begged.

Victoria couldn't help but smile. Her daughter had wrapped Xonos around her little finger, and she watched as her mate caved to the demands of their daughter. He sighed and nodded, handing her over to Thrace. They programmed the warrior's number into their phones, gave him theirs, and then watched as Thrace carried their daughter off to another waiting limo.

"So…" Victoria took Xonos' hand. "We have a few hours of time. Together. Alone. Whatever should we do?"

He gave her a wicked smile, picked her up, and carried her to the limo. Once inside, he tugged her into his lap and kissed her long and hard, his tongue darting into her mouth for a taste. She'd never admit it, but she liked it when he got a little rough and demanding with her. With any other man, it would make her feel threatened, but she knew Xonos would never harm her.

At the hotel, he carried her up to their suite, kicking the door shut behind him. He claimed her lips again, kissing her all the way through the living room to the bedroom where he toppled onto the bed with her, careful not to squish her. When he let her up for air, she smiled and ran her fingers through his hair.

"Every time we're together, we seem to rush through things, like it's a race to the finish line."

She smiled. "Been picking up more Earth sayings?"

He shrugged and grinned. "Maybe. But my point is that we never seem to take the time to enjoy one another. We have to stay quiet so we don't wake Evie in the other room, and I think part of you is only half-engaged because you're afraid we'll get caught."

"You might be right. But there's nothing to hinder me now. We have the suite to ourselves."

"Why don't we start off the right way? Think that tub is big enough for two?"

Her smile broadened. "I think we can certainly try it."

"You wait here." He pressed his lips to hers briefly. "I'm going to start the water."

She watched as he went into the bathroom and then heard the water running. Rising to her feet, she slowly undressed, savoring the moment. This was really happening. They had the suite to themselves, and he was going to love her long and slow… something she'd only dreamt of to this point. Not that every time with him wasn't amazing because it was, but he was right; they were always rushed. Maybe they could work out a babysitting arrangement with Brielle and Syl after their baby was born. Xonos and she could watch their baby one night, and then Syl and Brielle would watch Evie for a night.

She stepped into the bathroom and was greeted by steam rising from the tub. Xonos had already stripped out of his tee and was just wearing low-slung jeans. God, the man was sexy as hell! She didn't know what had prompted him to come for them that night, what had changed his mind about taking a mate, but she was glad it had happened. Victoria didn't want to imagine her life without him, and not just because he'd been instrumental in curing Evie. She knew without him, her daughter would have suffered and died. But there was more to it than that. She'd come to care for Xonos a great deal, perhaps she even loved him. No. She knew she loved him, but she hadn't said as much to him. What happened if he didn't love her back?

He tested the water before turning to her, his eyes lighting in appreciation of her currently naked state. She reached for his jeans, unsnapping and unzipping them and then shoved them to the floor. The boxer briefs he had on molded to him like a second skin, leaving nothing to the imagination. His cock, already hard, pressed against the material. She saw it give a kick against the material holding it hostage, and a smile ghosted her lips. It seemed her alien wanted her as much as she wanted him.

Feeling braver than usual, she stepped forward and cupped his hardness, her palm sliding along the length of him. Xonos groaned before swooping down and claiming her lips. He sipped from her. Feathery, gentle kisses that slowly built a flame inside of her. Her lips tingled as he deepened the kiss. A long, drugging, lingering kiss that both intoxicated and drove her passion higher. It was a thorough kiss, one meant to leave her mindless and wanting more.

Xonos pulled away, breathing heavily, and stripped out of his boxer briefs before lifting her into his arms and settling into the tub. Victoria straddled his lap, his cock bobbing in the water between them. There was something she'd been wanting to do, but had yet to feel brave enough to try. Sliding back in the tub, she bent over and pressed her lips to the crown of his cock.

Xonos took in a long, shuddering breath as her lips slipped around the tip and she sucked him into her mouth. His hard flesh throbbed against her tongue as she took him further, until he bumped the back of her throat. She relaxed and let him slide further until she'd taken all of him. Her tongue stroked him as she pulled back and then swallowed him again.

Through slitted eyes, she watched him grip the tub with such strength that she was surprised the porcelain didn't crack. His hands trembled, as did his body, while she pleasured him for as long as he could stand it. She felt him harden and lengthen even more and knew he was close to coming, but he gripped her shoulders and dragged her off his cock and up his body.

"Enough," he said, his voice dark and husky. "I'll not spill myself down your throat."

"Didn't you like it?"

He gave a strangled laugh. "How could you think I didn't like it? You had me about to come like some untried youth."

"Then why didn't you let me finish?"

He kissed her, his tongue delving inside before he pulled back. "Because I want to come inside this hot, curvy body of yours."

She skimmed her hands down her sides to her hips. "I do have a few curves now. Perhaps you've been feeding me a little too well. If I keep eating the way I have been, I'll be fat in no time."

"Not fat." He kissed her softly. "Pleasantly plump. And I'll love you no matter what you weigh."

Startled, she pulled away. "You love me?"

"I probably should have told you sooner. I've known since our first week together that I'd fallen in love with you. But it never felt like the right time to tell you."

Victoria felt tears gather in her eyes, and she flung her arms around him. "I love you too. I was too scared to tell you, for fear you couldn't love me in return. I know you said you didn't really want a mate…"

He shushed her. "That was before I met you and saw what a wonderful mother and mate you are. I'll admit, when I first came to you, it was with every intention of our mating being more of a business deal, but it only took one night of you sleeping in my arms for me to know that wasn't going to work. I liked the feel of you there far too much for my heart not to get involved."

"Make love to me, Xonos. I want it nice and slow, and hard and fast, until neither one of us can breathe."

"I'll give you anything your heart desires."

Rising with her in his arms, he stepped out of the tub, then set her down and grabbed a towel. As he dried her off, he explored her body with his hands and lips, kissing every inch of her from her lips to her toes. Victoria sank her fingers into his hair and held him close as he lavished her nipples with attention, first one and then the other, taking the hardened peaks into his mouth and lashing them with his tongue.

"Did I say slow?" she asked breathlessly. "I think I've changed my mind. I want to feel you inside of me. Now."

He chuckled. "Patience, my sweet mate. You'll get what you want in due time."

Backing her to the bathroom counter, he lifted her and set her on the marble surface, her legs splayed. He buried his face between her thighs and breathed in deeply, letting out a little moan before flicking his tongue out to taste her. Victoria gasped and wasn't sure if she wanted to pull away or shove her hips closer to his face. She didn't want him to stop, and yet no one had ever done something like that to her before. She wasn't sure how to act.

Xonos took his time, licking, sucking, and gently biting. He'd bring her right to the edge before backing off, then rebuilding the flames inside of her. Again and again he got her so close she nearly saw stars, then he'd stop to kiss her belly and thighs, and to stroke her calves. Then his mouth would fasten on her again and she'd rocket right back up to the breaking point.

When he finally let her come, she called out his name as she felt her insides heat as her womb clenched, and she felt as if she were flying. She panted for breath as she came back down and she was able to focus on her mate once more. He pressed kisses to her inner thighs before rising and helping her off the counter, but her legs wouldn't hold her and she had to grip him for support.

Xonos laughed and carried her into the bedroom where he tossed her onto the plush mattress and followed her down, his body settling between her legs. She welcomed him, wanting him to ease the ache that never really went away. As his cock stretched and filled her, she felt complete and loved. With his purple gaze fastened on hers, he began a slow thrust and retreat.

Victoria slid her feet up his calves before hooking her legs around his waist. She took everything he had to give her. Slow and easy. Fast and hard. The bed slammed into the wall with every plunge of his cock, but in that moment, she couldn't have cared less if the neighbors knew what they were doing. Xonos stopped suddenly and rolled to his back, taking her with him. She sat up, his cock still filling her, and before she could even stop to think of what to do, he'd gripped her hips and was surging up into her. All she could do was hold on for the ride of her life.

Her world came apart as he entered her one last time, filling her with his seed and crying out her name. She flew, and bright lights flashed behind her closed eyelids. Her nails dug into his chest as her climax spiraled out of control. She felt his hands caressing her hips and then rubbing up and down her back. Victoria opened her eyes and smiled down at him.

"That was different," she said.

"I thought, since we hadn't tried that position before, that we would do something different. I take it I pleased you?"

She laughed. "You couldn't tell? The neighbors have probably called downstairs to complain."

He shook his head. "A Terran warrior is on the other side of our bedroom wall. If anything, all of your passionate cries probably sent him running to the bridal registry to see if he could snag himself a mate. He'd be lucky if he found a woman half as good as you."

"Flatterer." She leaned and pressed her lips to his before rising off him and cuddling into his side. "How much time do you think we have before Evie comes home?"

He raised his head to look at the clock across the room. "It's been about two hours, and he said he was taking her for both ice cream and a movie. I'd say we have at least another half hour, maybe longer."

"Then what do you say I let you wash my back in the shower?"

His hands slid down her back to squeeze her ass. "And are you thinking there might be a bit of playing in this shower? Because just the thought of rubbing soap into your soft skin is enough to make me hard again."

She glanced down and smiled as she realized he spoke the truth. His somewhat flaccid cock was now rising to attention again. That was one thing she had to say for Terrans… they had wonderful stamina.

She climbed off the bed, gave him a saucy smile, then sashayed into the bathroom where she drained the tub and started the shower. She'd just soaked her hair when the curtain jerked open and Xonos joined her, a hungry look in his eyes. He helped Victoria wash her hair, then her body, paying special attention to all the important parts. But as he positioned her to wash her back, he pressed his hand to the middle of her back, bending her over.

Victoria braced her hands on the wall, ready and willing. She felt his cock slide into her, and she groaned at how wonderful it felt. Her fingers curled against the tiled wall as he pounded her from behind, taking her to dizzying heights before making her come with a loud, keening cry. She was still coming when he found his release, and she felt the evidence of their climaxes sliding down her thigh.

Xonos carefully washed her, being gentle and giving her sweet kisses.

"I didn't hurt you, did I?" he asked. "I know I was a little rough at the end."

She curled her hand around the back of his neck and kissed him again. "You were perfect. I absolutely loved it, in case you couldn't tell."

"I had an inkling."

Victoria laughed and wrapped her arms around him, hugging him tight, and then she took her time exploring his body and washing him, loving the feel of his hard muscles under her fingertips. She'd never grow tired of feeling his arms around her, of feeling his body pressed close to hers, having his lips on hers. No matter how long she lived, she would always love Xonos and everything he did to her and for her. She couldn't have found a better mate, even if one had been chosen for her by one of those dating sites.

"I don't know how I got so lucky to have you love me," she said, "but I'm going to spend the rest of my life showing you how much I love you too."

He kissed her hungrily. "Why don't you show me now?"

With a wicked grin, she shut off the water and dragged him back to the bedroom, where they both had another orgasm before Thrace brought their daughter back home.

Chapter Ten

Xonos sat at the table in the conference room. The Terran station was quiet this morning and he knew he'd have plenty of time for this call, even if the council members on the screen did look disgruntled at being called so early. Now was the time to get their agreement about him remaining on Earth. He had the love of his mate, his daughter was healthy, and once he ran the blood in the lab, he'd know for certain whether or not his mate was carrying his child. If Xonos was correct in his assumption, his little family of three was about to be a family of four.

"You wish to remain on Earth?" Larimar asked.

"Yes. I've done quite a bit of thinking about it. My daughter is human and quite a bit older than the children recently born to the human-Terran pairings on our world. The school isn't equipped to handle a fully human child. There are things Terrans are taught that would confuse Evie. While humans may be compatible with us, they are still a different species with different needs. Besides, I can do quite a bit of good here. Syl and Brielle will be having their child any day, and if any other mates decide to make their home on Earth, my services will be needed to deliver their children as well."

"But you're our best doctor!" Borgoz exclaimed. "What are we supposed to do in Terran Prime without your services?"

Xonos shrugged. "Train someone else? There are other healers on our world, men who are quite capable of stepping into my shoes. No, they may not be as good as I am, but given time, they could be."

"I see no reason not to accept his proposal," Faltz said. "We can put it to a vote if you wish, but I think you know which way the council will vote, Borgoz."

Borgoz looked like he was ready to blow, but he finally relented.

With his future secured, Xonos went to his lab to run the blood sample he'd taken from Victoria that morning. As he saw the results, he smiled. He'd been correct; their family was going to gain another member before too long. Xonos thought to rush home to tell Evie and Victoria the good news but then decided it was best told over a good meal.

He reached the hotel and went in search of his family. He found his girls sprawled on the sofa with popcorn and a movie playing. When the door shut behind him, they sprang up from the sofa and rushed to greet him, both of them wrapping their arms around him.

"I thought, if the two of you haven't filled up on popcorn, maybe we would go out to eat." He frowned. "Did the two of you really eat a bag of popcorn before having breakfast this morning?"

Victoria shrugged. "It seemed like a simple enough request."

"What do you say we get dressed up and go to a nice restaurant for breakfast?"

Evie bounced up and down. "A grown-up place?"

"A very grown-up place," Xonos said. "So be sure to put on your best dress. Mommy too."

Victoria kissed him then ushered Evie into her room. She emerged a few minutes later and hugged him tight. "Are you sure about this?"

"Very." He smiled. "Now get ready."

She nodded and followed him into the bedroom, where he changed into a pair of gray slacks and a pinstripe shirt he'd picked up the other day. He had a purple tie that matched, but it made him feel like he was strangling when he wore it. Victoria twirled in the fifties style halter dress she'd put on and he couldn't help but smile at her. While she put on her make-up and fixed her hair, he checked on Evie. His precious daughter was doing her best to braid her hair but wasn't having much luck.

"Would you like some help?" he asked.

Evie nodded eagerly and stood before him. Xonos, having studied videos on how to fix a little girl's hair, swiftly braided it. When they were finished, they joined Victoria in the living room and made their way down to the waiting limo.

At the restaurant, Xonos could barely contain his excitement. He wanted to shout his news from the rooftop but managed to refrain, if only for a little while. Once their breakfast was served and everyone seemed content, he couldn't hold back another moment. "I have to be honest. I wanted to bring my girls out to breakfast for a special occasion."

Victoria eyed him thoughtfully. "We get to stay here? We don't have to go to Terran?"

"That's a small part of it."

"Is it because we're having a baby?" Evie asked, with eyes wide and bright.

Xonos couldn't stop smiling. "Evie is correct. Smart little girl. I ran the tests this morning after my call and, Victoria, it confirmed my suspicions. You're pregnant."

Tears gathered in Victoria's eyes. "Really?"

He nodded.

"Oh, Xonos!" She scrambled out of her chair and threw herself into his lap, her arms winding around him. "I can't tell you how happy that makes me."

"Me too," Evie piped up. "I told you I wanted a baby brother or sister, and now I'm going to get one."

Xonos smiled at his daughter. "Yes, sweetheart. You're going to get your wish."

Victoria eased from his lap and sat in her chair once more. As Xonos went to take another bite of food, his cell phone chimed with a message. He'd put the ringer on silent so they wouldn't be disturbed, but it seemed someone wanted him regardless. He listened to the message and frowned.

"I have to return to the clinic. It seems there's an emergency."

Victoria stood and helped Evie up from her chair. "We'll go with you. We can always grab something on the way home."

"Hmm. Speaking of home, I think we should start looking for one. Maybe a big house with an even bigger yard. We could put in a play set for Evie, maybe even a tree house."

Evie chattered nonstop about the home she wanted all the way to the clinic. When they reached the Terran station, Xonos wasn't sure what to expect, but a pacing Thrace with a squalling infant wasn't it. By the black hair, red skin, and fangs, Xonos could tell the baby was a Drelthene. The question was how did one get to Earth?

"She won't stop crying." Thrace looked panicked.

Victoria rushed forward. "Give her to me."

Xonos' eyebrows shot up at how accepting his mate was of an alien baby as scary looking as the one in Thrace's arms. He watched as she cuddled the baby close and then wrinkled her nose.

"Did no one think to check her diaper?"

Thrace looked sheepish and handed her a bag. "She came with this and a note. It seems her mother couldn't handle raising an alien baby. She got 'knocked up' by a Drelthene when he captured her a year ago. Once she was pregnant, he returned her to Earth, which I still don't understand, but she had nowhere to go. It said she delivered the baby at a Terran station out west and then moved here for a job. She thought we'd be able to find the little girl a home."

Evie peeked at the baby. "Can we keep her?"

Xonos couldn't help but smile at her. "No, I'm afraid we can't. Your mommy is going to need her energy to take care of our baby and you. I'm afraid two babies at once might be too much for her."

"What are you going to do with her?" Victoria asked.

"We'll have to find her a home. I'm sure the intergalactic adoption agency can locate someone to care for her."

Thrace looked horrified. "You can't send her to that place!"

"Well, what else do you suggest?" Xonos raked a hand through his hair.

"I…" Thrace swallowed hard. "I could take her."

"Won't that make finding a mate a little difficult?"

Thrace shrugged. "I can't stand the thought of her going to that place. If it means I have to adopt her, then I'll do it. I always planned to have a large family. I'll just be going out of order."

Victoria finished changing the little girl and handed her back to Thrace. The gentle giant cradled her in his arms as if he'd been her father all along. Victoria walked him through changing a diaper and making a bottle of formula. According to the blanket the little girl was wrapped in, her name was Lily.

"Don't worry about Lily," Thrace said. "She and I will get along just fine. Won't we, little girl?"

The baby babbled at him.

"Looks like you're going to need the daycare center that just opened," Xonos said.

Thrace nodded thoughtfully and gathered the baby's bag. "I'll go talk to the lady now. See what needs to be done for Lily to start staying with her while I'm working."

Xonos watched Thrace walk off, a bemused expression on the warrior's face. Then he turned to Victoria. "You didn't really want to keep the baby, did you?"

"I wouldn't have minded." She shrugged. "But I'm not heartbroken that she isn't coming home with us. I think we're going to have a big enough family as it is."

Evie tugged on his shirt. "Can I have *two* baby brothers?"

Xonos laughed and gathered his daughter in one arm and his wife in the other. "You can have as many baby brothers and sisters as your mommy will allow." He winked at Victoria. "I'm more than happy to help her make them."

With his family held close, they ventured back outside into the sunshine. What had started as a good day turned into a *fantastic* day. Everything was turning out wonderfully for his small family, and Xonos would thank the gods every day for the blessings of Victoria and Evie, and now the little one growing inside of his mate. He didn't know that he deserved them, but he was going to do everything he could to make sure Victoria never regretted choosing him as her mate.

His smile broadened. Who'd have thought a quiet alien doctor would end up with one hot woman and the cutest daughter in all of the galaxies?

Avelyn and the Alien Daddy

Jessica Coulter Smith

Avelyn's life was turned upside down the day she lost her baby and realized her husband was a monster who couldn't be redeemed. Now that she's divorced and having to make it on her own, she knows she needs to make some major changes in her life. But when she enters the Terran Station in Las Vegas in search of a job, the last thing she expects is to find her arms full of a screaming alien baby, and faced with a very flustered daddy.

Thrace adopted sweet Lily to spare her from the Intergalactic Adoption Agency. Now that he's become a doting daddy overnight, he's feeling a bit overwhelmed. When Avelyn is dropped into his lap, he's more than grateful. A nanny is just what he needs!

There's only one problem. When Thrace looks at Avelyn, he doesn't see a caretaker for his daughter. He sees a vibrant, desirable woman who sets his blood on fire.

What's an alien daddy to do when what he wants most is to have the nanny in his bed?

Chapter One

Avelyn Murray clutched at her purse strap as she made her way through the Terran station of the Las Vegas strip. She was ready for a new chapter in her life, even if she wasn't sure what it would be. She was torn between looking for a job at the station and signing up for the bride program. It wasn't the first time it had crossed her mind, but it was the first time she'd found the courage to actually enter the station to put her plan in motion.

As she approached the reception desk, she argued with herself over which to ask for -- the employment station or the bride application counter. She'd only been divorced for six months, so Avelyn wasn't entirely certain she was ready for another relationship, even though she'd heard the Terrans made wonderful husbands. They were everything her ex was not, but the thought of signing her life over to another male made her a little nervous. Although, if the right male came along...

Avelyn waited in line to speak with the receptionist. She looked around, taking everything in. Aliens of all races rushed around, and reminded her that if she signed up for the bride program, it wouldn't just be Terrans who would be interested. In the last month, they had opened the program up to other races. Males of all types wandered through the station, some openly admiring her, and others bustling by without even realizing she was there. Maybe the bride program wasn't for her after all. Besides, she'd heard that having children was a requirement, and she wouldn't pass that test.

When it was her turn to speak with the receptionist, she smiled and waited for the woman to acknowledge her. It took a few minutes before the phone stopped ringing and the woman looked up.

"May I help you?" the receptionist asked.

"I wondered if the Terran station might be hiring humans? I'm looking for a job."

"I'm not privy to any openings for human females, but you can certainly ask the employment desk. It's through that archway," she said, pointing slightly behind her and to the right. "When you reach the next open area like this one, you'll see an employment sign on the far right wall. They'll be able to tell you if there are any openings and what you'll need to do in order to apply."

"Thank you."

Avelyn smiled at her once more and then hurried toward the archway. The hallway was brightly lit and very long. As she entered the next large room, the sound hit her and nearly knocked her off her feet. Somewhere in the midst of loud voices, a baby wailed. When it seemed that no one was going to quiet the poor child, Avelyn went in search of her, or him. What if it was a small child and not a baby? What if they were lost or hurt?

She pushed her way through the crowd and came to a stop in front of a large Terran warrior holding a squalling red baby. She'd never seen a baby quite like this one, with ruby red skin, sharp fangs, and coal black hair. But regardless of how the child looked, she was obviously in distress. The man holding her looked completely inept and her heart went out to him. He fumbled with the child making shushing noises and bouncing her in his arms.

Avelyn bit her lip and wondered if he would welcome her help, or feel insulted that she thought he couldn't handle the baby. She finally took a step closer and held her hands out.

"Mind if I try?" she asked.

He looked momentarily startled, hesitated a few seconds, and then handed her the baby.

"Her name is Lily," he said.

Avelyn held the baby closer and cooed at her. "Aren't you a pretty girl? What has Miss Lily so upset?"

The baby's cries stuttered and then stopped as she sucked in huge snotty breaths and looked up at Avelyn. She babbled at Avelyn and reached out to place her small, chubby hand against Avelyn's cheek.

"Well, aren't you a sweetheart?" Avelyn smiled at the girl with the pink bow in her hair.

"She likes you," the male said. "I sometimes think she doesn't like me very much. But then, Lily doesn't seem to like most people. The daycare where I work refuses to keep her because she screams the entire time she's there."

"What about hiring a nanny?" Avelyn asked and winced as the baby tugged on a strand of her hair. "You could hire someone to live with you and take care of Lily in your home."

"Who would accept such an offer from a Terran male? They would expect to become my bride, would they not? And how can I even think of getting into a relationship with someone when Lily clearly needs more from me than I'm able to give already?"

Avelyn looked at the sweet baby girl in her arms and then up at the Terran male. "I would."

"You would be willing to move to live with Lily and me?"

"Move?" She smiled. "You mean into your home?"

"No. I live near the station in Kentucky outside of Lexington. I merely came here in search of Lily's mother."

"Did you find her?"

The male nodded. "She signed away her rights to Lily. I've already adopted her, so I never have to worry about someone trying to take her away from me. Her father abandoned her before she was born and her mother left her at the station where I work with a note clipped to her diaper bag."

Avelyn brushed her cheek against the baby's soft curls. "I can't imagine anyone giving up their baby."

Tears misted her eyes as she thought about the child she'd lost. If things had gone a little differently, she'd be holding her own baby in her arms at this very moment. Of course, she'd also still be married to her abusive asshole of an ex-husband, and that would be truly horrifying. She couldn't imagine letting that monster anywhere near a child, but if she'd kept the baby, she had planned to stay with him. Now she realized just how foolish that was. The moment she'd found out she was pregnant, she should have packed a bag and taken off.

"It makes you sad to move elsewhere?" the alien asked, mistaking her tears.

"No. Moving away is actually a really good idea. I wanted a fresh start, and I can't think of a better way to do it. I don't have much to pack. When would we leave? Do you need me to fill out an application or complete a background check or something?"

He frowned. "I hadn't really thought about it. I've never hired a nanny before. I've only been Lily's father for a few short months. Let's go to the employment desk and see what they recommend. I want to make sure I do this the correct way so no one questions why you're staying with me."

"I'll follow you. Do you mind if I carry Lily?"

A smile spread across his face, making Avelyn go weak in the knees. Good lord, but the man was fine! He'd been handsome before, but now he was downright sexy. How he wasn't already mated to someone, she couldn't imagine. He seemed to truly care for his wee daughter, and from what she'd seen so far, he was a genuinely nice male. What woman wouldn't want him?

"You may carry Lily."

He led the way across the room to the employment station. At the desk, a Terran male looked up to greet them.

"How may I help you, Thrace?" the alien asked.

Thrace. So that was his name. She hadn't realized until just then that they had never introduced themselves, and here he was about to hire her. How crazy was that?

"I'd like to hire a nanny. I want this woman specifically," Thrace said. "What do we need to do?"

"Well, she'll need to complete some forms and sign a waiver for a background check, and then it will take around a week to process everything."

Thrace narrowed his eyes. "I need it done before morning. I'm due back home tomorrow and the jet leaves at nine o'clock. Do whatever you have to in order for her to be approved for work by that time."

The Terran frowned at Thrace. "It isn't that simple. Even after she's been vetted, there's still the matter of signing an employment contract. That means agreeing on a salary and negotiating benefits. You can't just pick up a random woman and decide to hire her."

"And yet if I wanted a bride, I bet your ass would be moving faster than this."

Avelyn watched them go back and forth and wondered what she could do to help things along. The longer they argued, the less likely she would be hired. If Thrace pissed off the Terran in charge of this process, no way would she be getting on that jet with him in the morning. And not only did she need this opportunity, she really wanted to help take care of the little girl in her arms. Already she could feel a bond forming between them.

Lily cooed up at her and yanked on her hair again. Avelyn smiled down at the baby and talked to her softly while the two Terran males discussed the issue of her employment. Hell, if it was going to be this much trouble, she'd work for free until they reached his home station and could get things arranged there. Maybe she should tell him that?

"What if I worked for free until we reach your home?" she asked Thrace. "I mean, I'd need my travel covered, and a hotel room once we reach our destination, but I wouldn't charge you for my time with Lily until you're able to get things settled with your home station. Would that work?"

Thrace smiled. "That would work nicely. I'll keep track of how much time you work between now and then so I can pay you accordingly once all of the forms have been completed and the contract signed."

Avelyn smiled. "Then I guess all that's left is to hand this precious bundle off to you so I can go home and pack. Where do you want to meet in the morning?"

"If you'll give me your address, I'll have a driver pick you up and bring you to the airstrip. We have our own so we don't have to go through the Las Vegas airport. It's less hassle when we have to travel between stations. There's been talk of one of the alien races who recently joined in the bride program letting us use their teleportation technology so a jet would not be necessary. I'm sure that won't be put into motion for a while though. Things move quickly once they are approved, but getting something like that going would take some time and a lot of alien species working together. I'm not sure we're to that point yet."

She nodded.

"Let Lily and me take you home. It's the least we can do."

"Thank you. I rode the bus here so I appreciate the offer."

Thrace guided her back through the station and out onto the walkway, where he hailed a waiting limo. Avelyn had never ridden in one before and handed Lily to Thrace before climbing inside. Once she was settled, Thrace handed the baby back to her. She cuddled Lily close, then buckled her into the car seat and gave the driver her address. She hoped Thrace wouldn't think badly of her when he saw where she lived. Once up on a time, she'd had nice things, expensive cars, a huge house… now she lived in an older neighborhood, where most of the homes were taken care of, but the one she'd been renting had not been. The driveway was cracked; the mailbox listed to one side, and the stucco was coming off in huge sections. She would imagine the Terran male lived in a nice home back in Kentucky.

When they pulled up to the curb, Thrace frowned. "This is where you live?"

"It's just been a temporary place the last six months. It's all I could afford after I divorced my husband. He'd made me sign a pre-nup agreement, so I didn't get a penny from him."

"What's that?" he asked.

"It's where someone wealthy asks the poorer person to sign away their rights to any money the rich person has or may gain during the time of the marriage. Otherwise, I probably would have gotten half his money, and he was worth millions."

"Having millions of dollars is important," Thrace asked, "in caring for a human mate?"

"No. Money is nice, and it's great to have a fancy car and large home, but those things aren't necessary. What's necessary is love and understanding. I didn't have those two things with my ex. I'd been blinded by his riches and was so swept away by a man like him paying attention to me that I ignored the signs that he was an abusive jerk."

The Terran's eyes darkened. "He hit you?"

"Sometimes." She bit her lip. "I don't want to be dishonest, so I'm going to tell you now, so you can change your mind if you want to. I was pregnant, about four months along. I got into an argument with my ex and he shoved me down a flight of stairs. I lost the baby, broke my wrist, and bruised my ribs. But it was the wake-up call I needed. Knowing that he'd taken something so precious from me gave me the courage to leave his sorry ass. I called a battered women's shelter. They picked me up from the hospital and helped me get a divorce attorney."

"I'm very sorry you went through that, and that you lost your child. Your husband should have been arrested, not allowed to go free and keep his millions. What kind of world is Earth if it allows women to be abused and their abusers to get off without jail time?"

Avelyn smiled. "My ex is cousins with the police chief and he played golf with the judges around here. No way was he going to get any jail time. When they questioned what happened to me, he told them I fell down the stairs. I tried to tell them I was pushed, but no one would listen to me. It was just my word against his, and he has a lot of connections in Las Vegas."

"Is he the reason you've agreed to move across the country without even knowing where you'll be living or how much you'll make? I promise I can pay you well. Since my job is security at the Terran station near my home, I'm allowed a housing expense and my transportation is covered. I need very little money to get by each month compared to what the Terran council pays me."

"I'm not greedy, Thrace. Whatever you can afford to pay me will be more than I'm making right now." She smiled. "You know, I learned your name inside, but not once have you asked mine."

"Avelyn."

Her eyes widened and he smiled.

"I heard you tell Lily your name when I was arguing with the Terran over at the employment department. Lily and I will walk you to your door."

She held up a hand. "That isn't necessary, but thank you. I only have one suitcase to pack so it won't take me long."

"Why don't we wait for you then? You could stay the night at the hotel where we've been staying and then we can leave tomorrow for the airstrip together. It would save time, unless you prefer to sleep in your own home one last night."

"I don't want to impose on you."

Thrace waved a hand. "It's no imposition. We'll wait while you pack and then we'll get you settled into a hotel room for the night. If you'd like, we could meet for dinner and you could get to know Lily a bit better. Although, it seems she's quite taken with you. She's never been this quiet for such a long stretch of time before."

"She's a sweet baby," Avelyn said. "And if you're sure it's no trouble, I would be delighted to go back to the hotel with you. Just give me fifteen minutes to pack everything. I'll need to drop the key off with leasing company though."

"We'll take care of it on the way."

She reached to place her hand over his. "Thank you, Thrace. I mean it. You're taking a chance on a complete stranger, giving me the opportunity to improve my life and put Las Vegas firmly in my past. Not everyone gets a fresh start in life."

"Well, they should."

With another smile, she got out of the limo and went to pack her things.

Chapter Two

Thrace spent a good portion of his morning watching Avelyn and Lily. Looking at the two of them, you'd think they were mother and child. His daughter had taken right to the human female, and he couldn't blame her. At least the child had good taste. Avelyn's golden blonde hair caught the sunlight and shone like spun gold, making Thrace wonder if it was as soft as it looked. He loved the way her blue eyes twinkled with merriment when she played with Lily. And he'd have to be blind not to notice her curves. He wondered what they would feel like pressed against him.

Maybe hiring her as a nanny wasn't such a great idea. She was a temptation that he might not be able to ignore, but he couldn't express his interest in her as a bride, not when he'd offered her a job. It wouldn't be right, and he would hate to chase her away, especially considering how good she was with Lily. His daughter adored her new nanny, and Thrace had to admit that he rather adored her as well. The more he knew about her, the better he liked her. She was strong to have escaped such a male as her ex, and yet despite what she'd been through, she always had a ready smile on her face.

The jet had touched down two hours ago and they were now safely ensconced in Thrace's suite. After he'd adopted Lily he'd thought of purchasing a home, but he hadn't found the right one just yet. He'd called from Las Vegas to have his suite at the hotel upgraded to a three bedroom so Lily wouldn't have to be with Avelyn all day every day. Their things had been moved while they were on the way to Kentucky. He figured his new nanny could use a break every now and then, which made him wonder about days off. He only worked four days a week, so he supposed Avelyn could have the other three days to herself. But how would that work if they lived in the same suite? Maybe he should have purchased a separate room for Avelyn and given her nights off too. There was no reason he couldn't get up to take care of his own child at night.

"You're thinking awfully hard over there," Avelyn said as she eased Lily down into the playpen across the room. "Are you having second thoughts about bringing me here? Lily is so well-behaved; I don't see why you needed a nanny."

"No. I'm not having second thoughts. She's so well-behaved because she loves her new nanny. She tolerates me. I'd thought after the last several months of us being together that she would have warmed to me, but she fusses with me more than anyone else. It's almost insulting."

Avelyn laughed. "She doesn't mean anything by it. Maybe she just missed having a woman's touch. You did say her mother abandoned her. Perhaps there wasn't a male in her life before you. She may just not know how to interact with you."

"I hadn't thought of that."

"Do you mind if I take a few minutes to unpack while she's occupied?"

"Not at all. Don't feel like you have to hover over her, Avelyn. She knows how to play with her toys. Besides, I'm right here if she needs anything. I don't expect you to jump every time she fusses, even when I'm not here. I read a book on babies that suggested it was good for them to comfort themselves sometimes."

Avelyn smiled. "Yes, it is. I'll try not to scoop her up every time she cries, but it won't be easy. I already can't stand to see her upset."

"At least when she's upset, you know it isn't because of you. I've questioned several times whether or not I should have adopted her, but I just couldn't bear the thought of her going to some intergalactic group home until they found a family for her, if they found one. Not everyone will take a Drelthene into their home. The males can be rather vicious when they get older, but little is known of their females. It's rare to see one away from their home planet."

"She's lucky to have you, Thrace. And I think she knows it, she's just confused. Maybe having a woman around will settle her enough that she'll start to bond with you like she should have done by now."

"Go take care of your unpacking. Lily and I will be fine on our own for now."

Avelyn nodded and stepped into her room, shutting the door behind her. Thrace blew out a breath and wondered how he was supposed to survive the upcoming months or years. Maybe if he had a mate he wouldn't feel the pull toward Avelyn, but at the moment, he couldn't conjure a single attractive female in his mind. Every time he closed his eyes, he saw blonde hair and blue eyes. She'd gotten to him, and in very little time. He wondered what she thought of him.

No, he wouldn't torture himself with those thoughts.

He got up and moved across the room to peer down at his babbling daughter. She'd pulled a foot up to her mouth and was nibbling on her toes. He winced when one of her fangs pricked the skin, but she didn't cry. Reaching into the playpen, he pulled her out and held her against his chest, smoothing her curls away from her face. She smiled up at him, a genuine smile, and the first ever to be directed at him. It lightened his heart and gave him hope that maybe their future wouldn't be so bleak after all. Well, not as long as Avelyn was with them. What would happen though, if she ever decided to remarry? What if one of the Terrans at the station caught sight of her and decided to woo her away from Thrace? He knew they wouldn't poach if they thought he was contemplating her as a bride, but as his nanny? She'd be fair game to them, and he didn't like it one bit.

"What are we going to do, little one?" he asked Lily. "I can't change the terms of her being here, and yet already we're dependent on her."

Lily babbled a reply and Thrace wished he could understand her.

"You like, Avelyn, don't you? I think you like her more than me, but that's okay. I don't blame you for liking Avelyn. She's sweet and funny, and she's very good with you."

Lily wrapped her fist in his hair and tugged as she babbled some more. Thrace carried her across the room and settled on the sofa with her in his arms. He loved holding her, especially when she was agreeable like this. Thrace had always enjoyed being around small children; he'd just despaired of ever having one of his own. He wanted more of them, a house full, but in order for that to happen he needed a mate, or a very understanding nanny, who wouldn't mind if he adopted a few more children of different alien races. It would make for an unusual household, but Thrace knew if he had more than Lily in his home, he'd never find a mate.

He flicked through the channels on the television until he found a program he thought Lily might like. It was one of those learning cartoons he'd heard about. There was a lot he still needed for Lily. She had some stuffed animals and baby toys, but he didn't know if he'd bought the right ones. From what he'd read, a baby's development was very important, and he wanted to make sure he gave her everything she needed. He hoped Avelyn could help with that.

He sighed. Avelyn. The more he saw her interact with his daughter, the more he wanted to keep her, and not just as a nanny. She would be a perfect mother. He wondered if she'd ever be open to the idea. What if she got attached to Lily? Would it be enough to make her agree to become his mate?

He brushed a kiss against Lily's head and leaned back, letting her rest on his chest. As his sweet daughter fell asleep in his arms, he closed his own eyes, hoping a short nap would put things into better perspective. If he didn't rein in his emotions where Avelyn was concerned, he was going to slip up and say or do something he shouldn't. If she left him, he wasn't sure what he'd do. Not only did he need her for Lily's sake, he was already getting attached to her as well. If he hated the thought of her leaving, after having only having known her for twenty-four hours, what was going to happen over the upcoming weeks? He was almost scared to ask.

Thrace wasn't sure how long he dozed on the sofa, but he felt Lily's weight shift and he tightened his embrace only to have small hands pry the baby out of his arms. He opened his eyes and found Avelyn leaning over them. She cradled Lily in her arms and pressed a finger to her lips.

"I'll go put her in her crib," she whispered.

He got up to follow and watched as she tucked his daughter in, tenderly brushing her fingers through Lily's curls. It was a touching scene, and one that he wanted to remember for a long time to come.

Avelyn tiptoed out of the room and Thrace followed her, pulling Lily's door shut. There was a baby monitor in there if she woke up. He watched his new nanny stretch, admiring the way her breasts strained against the material of her sleeveless top. He felt himself harden in his leather pants and willed his cock into submission. The last thing he needed was for her to see him with a raging hard-on. That was the surest way to run her off, and that was the last thing he wanted to do.

"If you want to go out for a while, explore the town, I'll arrange for a limo to take you wherever you wish to go," Thrace offered.

She sank onto the sofa and beckoned for him to join her. "I was hoping that maybe we could just relax around here today, and then if you don't have to work tomorrow, maybe Lily and you could show me around."

"I have to work in the morning, but I may be able to leave early. They want me to report at five o'clock, but Lily and you could come meet me for lunch if you'd like. You didn't get a chance to see the Terran station here. I could introduce you around. That way, if you ever need me and can't reach me, you'll have people you can turn to."

"That makes sense. We'd love to have lunch with you. Is there a certain limo I need to use?"

"There are always drivers waiting in the lounge area downstairs. Just tell them you'd like to be taken to the Terran station and one of them will gladly take you. And there are always limos at the station, waiting to return us to the hotel. We haven't been cleared by your government yet to drive cars ourselves, so we have to rely on the drivers. Since we tend to be rather large males, it made sense to hire a fleet of limos instead of relying on those small yellow cabs."

"I have a lot to learn, not just about Lily, but about how life works for Terrans on Earth. I don't want to say or do something that I shouldn't and have it reflect badly on you."

Thrace smiled. "You don't have to worry about that. I'm sure everyone at the Terran station will make allowances for you until you get the hang of things, especially since you're taking care of Lily. No one around here wanted that job, not even the daycare at the station. I took her for a few days and then they told me to never bring her back again."

"How horrible!" Avelyn narrowed her eyes. "They shouldn't be allowed to work with children if they can't handle one crying baby. Lily is sweet. She didn't mean to disrupt their day; she just wanted to communicate with them. It wasn't her fault they weren't listening."

Thrace thought his heart melted a little at her words. She sounded so fierce, protecting his child. Yes, she would make an excellent mother. He just wished he could make her Lily's mother, but he couldn't figure out how to dig himself out of the hole he'd dug. She'd become angry with him if he asked if he could court her, after bringing her here as a caregiver to his child. She might think he'd brought her here under false pretenses.

"Did I say something wrong?" she asked.

"No. I like that you're protective of Lily already."

"I can't imagine not wanting to hold her and love on her. I don't see how anyone could have called her a problem and told you not to bring her back."

"Well, it worked out for the best. If they'd agreed to keep Lily, then I wouldn't have brought you home with me." Thrace smiled. "And Lily seems to really like you. I think it will be good for her to be home with someone who obviously cares about her. I know they say it's good for a child to be around other children, and to learn how to socialize, but I think there's plenty of time for that."

"With the way things are going between the humans and alien races, I imagine it will only be a short amount of time before the human daycare and parents-day-out facilities begin accepting children like Lily. When that happens, you can send her to parents-day-out for a few hours a day twice a week so she can learn to play with other children, but still be home most of the time."

"You've thought of everything." Thrace fought the urge to reach for her. He wanted to touch her so badly he ached.

She smiled wistfully. "I did a lot of research when I found out I was pregnant. Now I can use that knowledge to help Lily."

"Until you have a child of your own."

She gave him a startled look. "I can't have children."

Thrace thought he'd misheard her. "What do you mean you can't have children? You said you were pregnant before."

"When my ex pushed me down the stairs, and I lost my baby, there was internal damage that couldn't be repaired. The doctor said it was very unlikely that I will ever carry another baby. Not impossible, but highly unlikely. And if I do get pregnant again, there's a good chance I won't carry to term."

"I'm sorry," he said softly. "You're so good with Lily. I can't imagine you not being a mother."

He watched as tears gathered in her eyes, but she quickly dashed them away.

"Thank you. That's the kindest thing someone has ever said to me." She gave him a weak smile. "Being a mother is all I'd ever dreamed about, and because I was too afraid to leave, I've lost that chance forever. Maybe it's for the best. What kind of mother keeps her child in an abusive situation?"

"You were doing what you thought was right, Avelyn. Don't be so hard on yourself. The important thing is that you did get out. You saved yourself and now you're here with Lily and me, and we're very glad you're a part of our lives."

"That's so sweet of you to say."

"I mean every word. Lily already is attached to you and it's only been a day. From the moment you took her in your arms, she's been fascinated with you. She loves your hair; I've watched her smile when you smile, and she's quieter for you than anyone else. It's almost like you belong together." *Just like I think you belong with me.*

"Lily is a very special, very sweet girl, and I'm honored that you've entrusted her care to me. I promise I won't let you down, Thrace. I know you didn't have to bring me here and give me a job, but I really appreciate it. And I know it's probably too soon to say it, but I think I love Lily already."

He smiled. "She loves you too, Avelyn. Anyone who sees the two of you together can't deny it."

And it was true. It was almost as if Avelyn was meant to be Lily's mother, and Thrace had screwed it all up by asking the woman to be a nanny. If they'd had more time, if he'd gotten to know her before employing her, then maybe he could have asked for a different situation. Maybe he could have found the courage to ask her to be his bride instead of his nanny.

What was he supposed to do now?

Chapter Three

Avelyn lifted Lily out of her car seat and set her down in the stroller. As much as she loved holding the little girl, she didn't want Lily to think she would be carried everywhere they went, especially as she grew. Once she was buckled in, she waved to the driver, who had promised to wait for them, and hurried inside. The station was set up a little differently from the one in Las Vegas, but the reception desk remained the same. She approached, pushing Lily in front of her.

"May I help you?" the woman asked, scanning her from head to toe.

It made Avelyn a little self-conscious; she smoothed her ponytail and pulled down the hem of her knit shirt. She'd dressed for comfort, but now she wondered if maybe she should have gone for style. Not that she had many nice outfits. She hadn't been able to scavenge anything her ex had bought her and had purchased most of her clothes at secondhand shops.

"We're here to see Thrace," Avelyn said.

The woman peered over the desk at Lily and her eyebrows shot up. "I don't believe I've ever seen her quiet before. Did you drug her?"

"Of course I didn't drug her!" Avelyn had never been more affronted. As if she couldn't handle one little baby without resorting to medication. The nerve of the woman! And to imply that Lily was a horrible baby. Avelyn wanted to reach across the desk and smack the woman. She clutched the stroller handle tighter so she wouldn't give in to the urge.

The woman shrugged and picked up a handset. "Thrace, please come to reception," she said over the loudspeaker.

Avelyn glared at the woman and pushed Lily off to the side in case anyone else needed assistance while they waited for Thrace. They didn't have to wait long, but she noticed that he had paused when he saw them. He had asked them to come, hadn't he? Had she misunderstood? No. She remembered clearly that he said they could meet him for lunch.

"What's that fierce expression for?" Thrace asked. "Did I do something wrong?"

"I'm contemplating murder."

His eyebrows climbed into his hairline.

She pointed her finger at the receptionist. "That… that *cow* insinuated that the only way Lily would behave is if I had drugged her! I just want to slap the crap out of her!"

Thrace bit his lip, but he couldn't hide his grin for long.

"Why are you smiling?" she demanded. "She insulted our… I mean, *your* daughter." Not much time had passed, but Avelyn couldn't deny the pull she'd felt toward Lily. From the first moment she'd held her, she felt like the baby was hers.

"Our daughter?"

Avelyn felt a blush rising to her cheeks and shrugged. "It was a slip of the tongue. I meant your daughter. She insulted your daughter and I think you should do something about it."

She couldn't afford to slip up like that again. What if Thrace became angry that she'd tried to claim his child? She hadn't meant the words to come out, but the more time she spent with Lily, the more she wished she was the precious girl's mother and not her nanny. And the fact Lily came attached to such a handsome daddy just made the darling girl even more tempting. Avelyn had spent a restless night with damp panties as she'd thought about her boss. At least, she assumed he was still considered her boss. They hadn't filled out any forms or contracts since arriving in Kentucky, and he hadn't mentioned any. What if he wasn't happy with the care she was giving Lily? It would break her heart to walk away from the little girl. From the first moment Lily had smiled at her, she'd had Avelyn wrapped around her tiny finger.

"What would you like me to do, Avelyn? The woman works here and has been witness to many of Lily's tantrums in the past few months. Everyone at this station knows that Lily usually screams her way through the place, regardless of who is holding her."

"I don't care what they've seen in the past. They should treat your daughter with more respect."

His smile broadened. "You are very fierce when protecting my daughter. I like that."

She felt her cheeks warm even more.

"Come with me and I'll introduce you around. We'll start with Lily's doctor, in case you ever need to bring her here for a check-up or if she's sick. You'll like Xonos. He's married to a human female and adopted the woman's human daughter as his own. They were with me the day I decided to adopt Lily."

Avelyn walked alongside of Thrace, and pushing the stroller, followed him inside the clinic. He rang a bell and a moment later a Terran doctor came out of the back. He smiled when he saw Thrace and immediately hunkered down in front of Lily to greet the baby. Avelyn decided she liked him on sight.

"And how are you today, Lily?" Xonos asked.

The baby babbled at him and waved her fists around.

He smiled and stood, holding out his hand to Avelyn. "I'm Xonos, the main doctor at the station. Are you Thrace's potential bride?"

She opened and shut her mouth a few times, but nothing came out. Bride? She rather liked the idea, but knew it would never happen. In order to be a bride, you needed to have the ability to give your mate a child, and she couldn't do that. As much as she'd like to keep Lily and Thrace for herself, she knew it would never happen.

"This is Avelyn," Thrace said. "She's going to be Lily's nanny. I found her in Las Vegas and brought her home with me."

Xonos shook her hand. "It's a pleasure to meet you, Avelyn. What do you think of the Lexington area so far?"

"Oh, well… I haven't really seen any of it. We went straight from the airstrip to the hotel, and I left the hotel to come straight here today. I haven't really had a chance to explore, but I'm hoping Thrace can show me around soon."

Thrace winced. "About that… I can't get off early today like I'd planned. There's going to be an influx of potential brides and mates this afternoon and they've asked me to stay over to help with security. And I work all day tomorrow, so that's out too."

She felt disappointed, but she understood that his job came first. "It's all right, Thrace. There will be other days to explore."

"I have an idea," Xonos said. "What if I called Victoria, my mate? She could show you around either before school lets out or after. Our daughter, Evie, loves Lily."

"Well… " She looked up at Thrace. "Would you mind if Lily and I went around with Xonos' mate?"

"Not at all. There will be plenty of outings for us in the future. We'll make plans for my next day off," Thrace said.

Avelyn smiled at Xonos. "Then Lily and I would be delighted to explore the city with your mate, but I'd... " She blushed. "I mean *we'd* like to have lunch with Thrace first, if that's all right?"

"Of course," Xonos said. "I'll call Victoria and have her call you at the hotel. You can discuss when would be a good time to explore. It doesn't even have to be today. You could always go in the morning after Evie is dropped off at school."

"Thank you. That's very kind of you. I look forward to meeting her." Avelyn smiled. "I don't have any friends here yet."

"I have a feeling Victoria and you will become the best of friends," Xonos said.

"Come along, Avelyn. There are other people I'd like for you to meet, but we'll save that for another day. I'm only given an hour for lunch."

Avelyn waved bye to Xonos and followed Thrace through the station and out into the sunshine. She walked toward the limo that she'd taken to get to the station and began unbuckling Lily. As she lifted the baby from the stroller, Thrace held out his hands. Avelyn passed Lily to Thrace and then climbed into the limo so she could help get the little girl settled into the car seat while the driver stowed the stroller.

Once Lily was situated, Thrace claimed the seat across from them and lowered the window to inform the driver of their destination. Avelyn used the time to study his profile. He wasn't classically handsome, but she was very drawn to him. When Thrace looked at her, she had the urge to strip off her clothes and beg him to make love to her. She'd been in lust with men before, but something was different this time. She didn't just want him for his body, or his daughter, she found him to be quite smart, funny, and very considerate. Avelyn truly enjoyed being around him and had looked forward to today's lunch all morning.

"I hope you don't mind, but I asked the driver to take us to an Italian restaurant nearby. The owners don't mind a fussy baby and I've found I rather like the cuisine. Some of your human foods aren't palatable to me -- who eats raw squid? -- but I've found I rather like Italian food and Mexican food. Are they to your liking?"

"I agree with you about the squid, but with the exception of sushi, I'll eat just about anything. Well, maybe not mushrooms. I've never developed a taste for them, not even on my pizza."

He nodded. "I'll endeavor to remember that."

Avelyn looked over at Lily and smiled when she saw the little darling had fallen asleep. She'd missed her morning nap because she'd been too excited. With any luck, she'd still go down for an afternoon nap after they reached the hotel. She didn't think Thrace would want to deal with a cranky baby when he came home from work later in the day.

The limo pulled to a stop and Thrace helped her out of the vehicle before reaching back inside for his daughter. He cradled Lily against chest and lightly placed a hand against Avelyn's back, escorting her into the restaurant. That slight touch was enough to warm her from the inside out. She only hoped he didn't realize how much his touch affected her, otherwise, she'd be highly embarrassed. It was definitely against the rules to lust after your boss.

Inside, they were ushered to a table, seated, and then each given a menu and a glass of water before the waitress made herself scarce. Lily still hadn't woken and was cradled in Thrace's arms, even though a high chair had been brought for her. The baby seemed content to sleep against her father's chest, and Avelyn had to admit they made a beautiful picture.

"Has she been good for you this morning?" Thrace asked. "Not too fussy?"

"She hasn't fussed a bit, barely even making a sound when she was hungry or needed to be changed. Lily is a wonderful baby, Thrace. You don't have to worry about her misbehaving. She's the sweetest thing."

He nodded. "You've brought this change in her, and I'm thankful for it. She's comfortable with you, more relaxed. I think I made her nervous."

"She just wasn't used to you. I told you my theory that she wasn't used to being around men. You're probably the first male she's lived with. It will just take her a little time to adjust. And I'm sure you were feeling frustrated when she cried non-stop, and that probably just fueled her irritation. I noticed last night that you seem more relaxed with her than you did when I first met you. When you're relaxed, it makes her feel safe. If you're stressed, then she senses that too. Babies are very perceptive."

"I have you to thank for that," he said.

"Do you believe in fate?" she asked.

"Fate?"

"You know, that some people are destined to meet one another? I believe it was fate that we met. I needed a job and had lost my baby; you needed someone to care for your daughter. We came into one another's lives at the perfect time."

"Yes, I do believe in fate."

The waitress came back and took their orders, then wandered off again.

There was tenderness in Thrace's eyes as he watched Avelyn take a sip of her water. Or was she imagining it? Was she seeing tenderness there because she wanted to? She couldn't deny her attraction to him, but it was probably too much to hope he'd feel the same about her. A male who looked like Thrace could have any woman he wanted, so why settle for a broken one who couldn't give him children? Of course, that didn't mean they couldn't fool around. It wasn't likely he'd get her pregnant. But something told her the alien wasn't the type to just scratch an itch. He seemed too responsible for that.

"How has work been today?" she asked.

Surprise flashed in his eyes. "No one has ever asked me about my day before."

"Never?"

He shook his head.

"Well… do you mind that I asked?"

His lips tipped up on one corner. "I like that you want to know how my day has been. And to answer your question, it has been fine. No disturbances at the station. There was a woman who became overly distraught when she found out she couldn't be a bride and she had a bit of a meltdown, but one of the human psychiatrists we keep on staff gave her a sedative."

"Poor woman. Why couldn't she be a bride?"

"The results showed that she can't have children."

It was like being doused in ice water. No matter how attractive she found Thrace, she would always be unsuitable for him. It was a good reminder that she couldn't have anything more from him than an employer-employee relationship, and to even dream of anything else would be heartbreaking.

His gaze softened. "I'm sorry, Avelyn. I didn't think before I spoke."

"It's fine. Really."

But it wasn't. And it never would be, not ever again. Who would want a broken woman? Even human males preferred women who could give them children. Was she doomed to spend the rest of her life alone? It was a depressing thought. Thankfully, their food arrived and distracted her from her morose thoughts.

She watched as Thrace held Lily with one arm and ate using the other. If she hadn't known better, she'd have thought he'd been doing it the baby's entire life. They were so natural together, so perfect... so not hers. She was merely borrowing the baby while Thrace was at work. Maybe she should start distancing herself at night, keep more to her room so she wouldn't become too attached to them. She'd only been with them for two nights, but it felt like longer. Although she feared it was too late already. Avelyn was already getting way too attached to the father-daughter duo.

By the time their meal ended, she had almost convinced herself that she could take a step back, that she could distance herself and pull away from the feeling that she belonged with them. Almost. Then Thrace had to ruin it by placing his hand against her back on the way out of the restaurant, the light touch wreaking havoc with her senses. For one brief moment, as she paused next to the limo, she'd thought he was going to lean down and kiss her. But she blinked and the moment was gone. Probably just as well. If the Terran ever kissed her, she had a feeling she wouldn't want to let go.

After dropping Thrace back off at the station, she returned to the hotel with a now awake Lily and spent the next hour pacing the living area as she pondered what she was going to do. When the phone rang, it was a welcome distraction.

"Hello?"

"Is this Avelyn?" a woman asked.

"Yes."

"This is Victoria. I believe you met my mate Xonos this afternoon? He asked that I call and set up a time to show you around the city."

"Oh! Of course. I don't think today is going to be a good day for an adventure, but perhaps tomorrow?"

"Tomorrow will be fine, but I have a favor to ask. I've just picked up Evie, our daughter, from school and she's been asking every day when she can see Lily again. I realize you may not be up for company, but would you mind if we came and picked up Lily for a little while?"

"Oh, well, I don't know… " Avelyn chewed on her lower lip. Would Thrace be upset if she let someone walk out the door with his daughter?

"I tell you what. I'll call Thrace, run it by him, and ask him to call you if he agrees. Sound fair?"

"Yes, all right."

"I look forward to meeting you."

Before she could respond, Victoria had hung up. It was only a few minutes later that Thrace called and said Victoria had permission to pick up Lily for a few hours, and that Avelyn should use the time to relax, do some exploring, or take a nap. He said the time was hers to use as she wished and that he would be home before Victoria returned Lily.

When Victoria came to pick up Lily, Avelyn was a little nervous. She greeted the woman with a smile, welcoming her into the hotel suite. Lily took notice right away and smiled, waving her hands around. The baby rolled onto her hands and knees and tried to scoot across the floor. It was the second time Avelyn had seen her try to crawl, but she thought Lily was still a little young to be crawling. But what did she know of alien babies?

"Has she been doing that often?" Victoria asked. "She's only five months old."

"This is the second time I've seen her attempt to crawl."

Victoria rubbed her slightly rounded belly. "I hope Terran children aren't so advanced that they crawl and walk before human children. I'm not quite ready to chase after this one yet."

"I already packed her diaper bag, just let me get it from her bedroom."

Avelyn left to retrieve the bag and heard Lily begin to fuss. Worried, she hurried back to the living room. Lily sat up, holding her arms out toward Avelyn with huge tears streaking her face.

"I've never seen her do that," Victoria said. "I mean, yes, I've seen her fussy plenty of times, but she's never gotten upset because someone left the room."

"Are you sure you want to take her?" Avelyn asked, lifting the baby into her arms.

"Positive. It will give you a bit of a break until Thrace comes home, and hopefully prepare Evie for what life will be like with a baby in the house."

Avelyn wasn't sure she wanted to let go of Lily, but eventually she handed her over to Victoria. The woman had already raised a child and had another on the way. That was way more experience than Avelyn had, so surely Lily would be all right. She doubted that Thrace would have given his permission for Victoria to take his daughter if he didn't trust that she would keep the baby safe.

"I'll bring her back after dinner. That will give you some alone time with Thrace."

"Alone time?" She felt her eyes widen. "Why do we need alone time?"

"Oh, I… " Victoria faltered. "I'm sorry; I just assumed you would want time alone with Thrace before you became his bride and a full-time mother. Xonos told me that you couldn't keep your eyes off one another, so I just… "

"It's all right. It was a simple misunderstanding." Thrace couldn't keep his eyes off her? She tingled all over at the thought of the big alien being half as infatuated with her as she was with him. "I'm not here to be Thrace's bride. I came here to be his nanny."

"I'm so embarrassed. Xonos never said anything about you being the nanny, and I know Thrace has wanted a mate for a long time. I just thought he'd found someone while he was out of town. None of the brides who have come through the station here have wanted anything to do with him, not after… " She glanced down at Lily.

"Not after they realize he's a father?"

"Right."

"Well, they're a bunch of idiots. Lily is the sweetest baby ever. Other than when we first met, I've never seen her truly upset about anything. She fusses a little when she needs her diaper changed or when she's hungry, but otherwise, she smiles all the time."

"You must be a miracle worker. I love Lily, don't get me wrong, but she has screamed the roof off every place she's been in since Thrace discovered her abandoned at the station. She'll quiet a little when I hold her, but for the most part, it doesn't matter whose arms she's in, she'll still scream."

Avelyn reached out and stroked Lily's baby soft cheek. "We get along just fine, don't we, Lily?"

The baby cooed at her and held out her arms.

"Uh oh. It looks like I'd better take off with her if I'm going to get out of here with a baby in my arms. My daughter fell asleep in the limo downstairs and the driver offered to sit with her. I don't want to abuse that kindness."

"I look forward to meeting your daughter. If you have any problems with Lily, please don't hesitate to bring her home. I really don't mind having her around."

Truth of the matter was that she didn't have the first clue what she was going to do without Lily in the suite with her. The little girl kept her entertained and made her smile.

"I'm sure we'll be fine." Victoria smiled. "Wave bye-bye, Lily."

The baby babbled and reached for Avelyn again. It wrenched her heart and she took the baby's hands in hers, leaned down and kissed the back of each fist, then took a step back. Avelyn watched as Lily's lower lip trembled and tears filled her eyes; a moment later, that sweet angel let loose with a wail so pitiful it almost made her snatch the baby out of Victoria's arms. The other woman gave her a reassuring smile, hitched the diaper bag over her shoulder, and left with the squalling baby.

As the door clicked shut behind them, Avelyn blew out a breath and looked around the suite. What the hell was she going to do now? She could only watch so much television, and she really didn't care to explore that much on her own. Thrace was busy at work, so she doubted he'd appreciate her popping in again. With no friends, and barely a penny left to her name, it wasn't like she could go to the movies with someone or go out shopping. She really needed to talk to Thrace about those forms so she could start earning a salary.

Avelyn flopped onto the sofa and began surfing channels. After a moment, she clicked the TV off and went to her room, where she tidied the already neat space, made the bed, and then fell onto the pristine surface, arms and legs spread like a starfish. Staring at the ceiling didn't give her any answers. She closed her eyes and tried to relax, ordering her muscles to go lax, focusing on one at a time. Her mind began to drift and as she floated, she conjured Thrace in her mind.

The long, hard lines of his body. The broad expanse of his chest. The rippling muscles in his arms that she loved to watch flex as he lifted and carried things. It was almost enough to make her find heavy things for him to move, just so she could stare and drool a little. His ebony hair hung long and straight, the mass so thick she wondered how he managed to brush it every morning.

His hands were large and strong, with just a hint of calluses on his fingertips. She'd felt those hands on her skin, even though the touches were brief. It was enough to make her want more, to make her wonder what it would feel like if he were to stroke her to climax. Avelyn doubted it would take much to get her there. Her nipples hardened and tingled in anticipation of feeling Thrace's hands and lips on them. She felt heat pool low in her belly and her panties dampen as she pondered what he was hiding behind those leather pants.

His clothing left little to the imagination, but if he'd ever had a hard-on around her, he'd hid it well. Pity. If she'd thought for one moment that he desired her as much as she desired him, she'd have offered to share her bed with him. It had been a while since she'd been touched intimately, and with her ex it had rarely been a pleasant experience, but she'd be willing to bet that Thrace had a gentle touch. She'd seen the way he cradled his daughter, and knew that if he ever took a mate, he'd treat her the same way. While Avelyn couldn't be his mate, she could warm his bed for however long he'd have her. Although, as Lily got older, that might be confusing for the little girl. Maybe it was best to leave things as they were.

Her hands roamed her body, skimming over her sensitive nipples and down her soft stomach... she slid a hand beneath the waistband of her yoga pants and inside her panties. Her curls were damp from her desire and she parted the lips of her pussy, seeking her clit. It throbbed in time with her heartbeat and just the slightest touch was enough to make her gasp. She lightly stroked the little nub, her flesh slippery and silky soft beneath her fingertips. Circling the sensitive bud, she spread her legs wider, pretending it was Thrace's hips that pushed them out as he stood between her legs, ready to pleasure her.

Avelyn tossed her head back and closed her eyes, imagining Thrace standing between her legs. His body was rock hard and she pictured his cock standing at attention, long and thick, and more than ready to pleasure her. She bit her lip and wondered what it would feel like to have his cock stretch her, fill her... would it be a tight fit? Would she feel him swell just before he came, or would he even do that? What would sex with the big, purple alien be like?

Faster. Harder. Her free hand reached for a breast and pinched her nipple, giving it a slight twist. Pleasure shot straight to her core, bringing her hips up off the bed. Her harsh breaths came out in pants as she slid her eyes shut once more, imagining the hand working her over wasn't hers but Thrace's. Her hips bucked, seeking the hard cock she still pictured was merely inches away, hard and ready for her.

Would he stroke in and out of her gently? Slowly? Or would he power in and out of her, pinning her to the bed with his frantic thrusts? Would Thrace be the kind of lover good girls dreamed about or would he be wild and savage, a beast who couldn't be tamed?

With a keening cry, she came, her pussy flooding her fingers as she called out Thrace's name. It was the best orgasm she'd ever had, and it made her wonder just how wonderful it would have been if Thrace had really been standing between her legs, ready to fuck her until she couldn't see straight. She hoped one day she'd get to find out.

Chapter Four

Thrace stood inside the doorway, his jaw slack, as he stared at Avelyn's bedroom door. He'd come home early, thinking he might surprise her since he knew she was alone and possibly bored, but he was the one getting the surprise of a lifetime. As she cried out his name, his hands clenched and unclenched at his sides. He wanted nothing more than to burst through her door, strip his clothes off, and really give her a reason to cry out his name. He'd fantasized about pinning her to the bed and fucking her long and deep ever since the first time they'd met.

He knew he should make his presence known, let her know she wasn't alone any longer, but something held him in place. Maybe he wondered if she'd do it again, or perhaps it was more that he was afraid if he moved, he'd go to her. Would she throw him out if he were to go into her room right now and offer to make her fantasy a reality? He knew having sex with her would be a bad idea, if he wanted to keep her as his nanny, but truthfully, he'd much rather have her as his mate.

Thrace found himself crossing the room and pausing with his hand on her doorknob. One little twist and he'd be inside. Was she naked? Was she sprawled across her bed, just waiting for him to take her? His cock throbbed in his pants, begging to be set free. He ached with how much he wanted her, and yet he held himself back. It was obvious that she desired him, but why hadn't she made that known to him? Was she worried he would reject her? Did she fear for her job if she made a pass at him?

He removed his hand and stood staring at the door for several long minutes. Heaving a deep sigh, he took a step back.

"Avelyn, I'm home."

He heard a squeak and the sound of someone getting out of bed.

"I'll… I'll be out in a minute."

He waited and heard the sound of running water and imagined she was washing her hands. Pity. He'd love to know her scent intimately. He already knew she smelled like sunshine, but arousal? That was a scent he'd love to experience, if only she'd give him a chance.

"Avelyn, I think we need to talk."

She opened the door, her hair mussed and cheeks flushed. "About what?"

He looked from her down to his hard cock, which he couldn't have hidden if he'd wanted to, then looked her in the eye again. He watched as she took in his aroused state, watched her cheeks flush an even brighter pink and her eyes sparkle with undisguised lust.

"You heard me?" she asked softly. "I thought I was alone."

"I gathered that. How long have you wanted me?"

She paused.

"Be truthful, Avelyn. How long have you wanted me?"

"Since the day we met. I noticed how attractive you were when I took Lily from you, and after spending time with you on the flight here, I got to know more about you and realized what a terrific guy you are. It just made me want you even more."

"I've wanted you since the moment I saw you. I've never reacted to a female that way before."

"What are we going to do? We can't sleep together. It would jeopardize our working relationship, and I love Lily too much to walk away. I want this job, Thrace. I need it, and not just for the money."

"The chemistry between us isn't going to go away, Avelyn. If anything, it's going to reach a point where we either sleep together or you have to walk away, and I really don't want you to walk away. How many nights do you think you can pleasure yourself before you realize that maybe part of fate's plan was for us to be together intimately? Maybe you weren't sent into my life to be my nanny. Maybe you were sent here to be my bride."

He watched as his words sank in. There was a brief moment when a light entered her eyes and he thought he'd won her over to his way of thinking, but all too soon that light dimmed and hopelessness entered the blue depths instead. She shook her head and took a step back, folding her arms around her.

"I can't be your bride, Thrace. You know that as well as I do."

"Why not?" he demanded. "Do you love Lily?"

"You know I do."

"And you desire me?"

"Yes, but… "

He raised a hand to silence her. "But nothing. What more do you want, Avelyn? You care for my daughter as if she was your own, and I heard myself how much you want me. Is that not enough to start a relationship together?"

"I can't have children! Did you forget that part? Your council would never approve a match between us. The entire reason you're here is to find a mate and have children, and I can't give you that." Silent tears trickled down her cheeks. "Don't you think I want to give you that? I want it so badly I ache, to hold a child in my arms that came from my own body, to share that experience with you, but it's never going to happen."

"You said getting pregnant would be difficult, not impossible. And while your doctors may have said it wouldn't be advisable, they don't have our technology. There's no reason for you to assume you wouldn't carry to term while under a Terran doctor's care."

"Are you really going to take a chance, Thrace? Throw away your opportunity to have a family? Because I see how you are with Lily. You're wonderful with her, and you would make a fantastic father to many more children. But you won't have those children with me."

He frowned. "We could adopt. There are many kids placed with the intergalactic adoption agency, infants and older children needing a home. There's no reason we can't adopt more babies, as long as you don't care what race they are."

She wiped at the tears on her cheeks. "You know their race doesn't matter to me, but your government is never going to approve a match between us."

"You don't know that. Not for certain."

"If I apply and they deny me, will you let the matter go? Will you finally realize that we can't be together like that?"

He thought about it a moment. He couldn't say with any honesty that he would give up, even if the council decided they couldn't be mated. Did he want children of his own? Of course! But even if Avelyn couldn't carry a baby to term, he would still want her.

The joy she would bring into his life far outweighed the loss of not having children of his own.

"Come to the station tomorrow and meet with Xonos. Let him do an exam, something he'd have to do anyway if you applied to be a bride. If the results come back that you can't, or shouldn't, have children, then we'll talk some more. But if he says there is no reason you can't bear children, will you stop arguing with me and let me put in the paperwork to make you my bride?"

"You truly want me?"

Thrace stepped closer, placing his hands on her hips. "I truly want you, Avelyn, and not just because you're so wonderful with Lily. She would be lucky to have you as a mother, and I honestly think she already believes you *are* her mother. But most importantly, I would be lucky to have a woman like you in my life, someone to share my days and nights, someone... someone I could come to love."

She placed her palms against his chest; her fingers were cool against his heated skin. He felt a tremor rake her and wondered if it was from longing or something else. If she denied she wanted him, he'd call her a liar. His arms enfolded her, bringing her closer. How many times had he wondered what it would be like to hold her just like this? The warmth of her body pressed against him; her skin was like silk to the touch. As he breathed in deeply, her scent wrapped around him, drawing him further under her spell.

"Promise me you'll see Xonos tomorrow," he said. "Promise that you'll give us a chance. I know it may not work out, that he may say you'll never have children, but at least give us a fighting chance to see where this thing between us could lead."

"All right," she said softly. "I'll see Xonos tomorrow. If I come to the station during lunch, could you watch Lily while I meet with him?"

"I'll sign Lily up for daycare tomorrow. I want you at the station by eight o'clock. That's when Xonos opens his clinic and you should be the first one in the door."

Avelyn frowned. "You said that Lily didn't like daycare, that they told you to never bring her back there again."

"It's an emergency. I'll make them understand."

"Very well. I can see this is important to you, so I'll go see Xonos in the morning, but I've already told you what he'll find. If he says the same thing my regular doctor told me, will you let it go? Will you give up on the idea of my becoming your bride?"

He smiled. "No. But I look forward to having many discussions with you about it."

She gave him a disgruntled look and it just made him want to kiss her even more.

"Now," he said. "Why don't you go put on something dressy and I'll take you out for a nice meal?"

Her gaze dropped to his chest. "I don't have anything nice to wear. I was wearing the nicest thing I own when we met, and I haven't had a chance to wash it yet. I was going to send our clothes down to be washed tomorrow."

"Then we'll have to rectify that. What size do you wear?"

"A ten."

He pulled away, but only long enough to place a call to the boutique downstairs, asking them to send up a size ten in a dress that would be appropriate for the restaurant he had in mind. Then, after getting her shoe size too, he asked that they send up a pair of shoes to match. Avelyn tried to snatch the phone away from him several times, telling him it was an unnecessary expense, but in his mind, it was a very necessary expense. He wanted to show his potential bride that he could take care of her, that he *would* take care of her.

"It's going to cost a fortune," she said.

"Do you doubt that I can afford a dress and shoes for you?"

"You didn't just order a dress and shoes. You ordered them from a boutique store in a hotel. Do you know how much that's going to cost? Hundreds, if not thousands. This place has to be insanely expensive."

He sighed and pulled the communicator from his pocket. A few taps and he turned it to show her his current balance. On one line was his Terran funds and the other was the amount he'd had transferred into American dollars. He watched as her jaw dropped and her wide eyes rose to meet his.

"I didn't realize being a guard paid so well."

"I believe your people would call it hazard pay. I'm part of my planet's military and being stationed here comes with certain perks. I'm paid handsomely at home, but here I make almost twice as much. Not only do I face potential danger every day, but they are compensating me for having to make my home off-world."

She looked at the screen again then back at him. "I won't complain about the dress anymore, but you can't buy costly things like that all the time or you'll run out of money."

He frowned at the screen. "Do I have enough to purchase a home?"

She made an odd sound like she was being strangled, then coughed. "You can purchase a palace with that amount of money. Maybe two of them. What are those odd numbers above it?"

"That's how much I still have in my account on my world. I only transferred part of my money here. On the off chance I went back home, I wanted to still have enough funds to get by on Terran. I already have a home there, although it's been sitting vacant for nearly a year. If I'm here much longer, I may sell my home there. Two of my friends have made their permanent home here on Earth, and I don't see why I can't do the same, unless the council denies my request. Would that make me a better potential mate? If I were to make my permanent home here?"

"Oh, Thrace." She sighed and placed her hand on his cheek. "You're a wonderful potential mate, regardless of where you call home. Any woman would be lucky to have you, whether she lived with you here on Earth or back on Terran."

He nodded and studied her a moment. "Then your only problem with a mating between us is the fact you believe you can't have children. And when I prove that's an incorrect assumption?"

"Then we can discuss the mating again. But not until then."

Thrace smiled. "Then we'll be discussing it tomorrow. I have faith that everything will work out."

"You know, you can't always have what you want just because you want it. Life doesn't work that way."

"Maybe not, but you have to believe that your dreams can come true, or they never will."

Her gaze softened. "It's your dream to be mated to me?"

"Ever since the day we met."

She stepped closer to him again, wrapped her arms around his waist, and hugged him tight. He'd been hugged by females before, but never one he wanted to claim as his mate. His body responded to her soft curves being pressed against him and he wondered if he'd be out of line to steal a kiss or three. He'd dreamed of her lips and wondered what they would taste like.

Tomorrow. She said they would discuss it tomorrow and that would be soon enough for him to find out. He wanted their first kiss to be perfect, something they would remember for a lifetime. Thrace didn't have much experience with kissing, having only been with the whores at the floating brothel near Terran, and they typically didn't include kissing with their services. He hoped he wouldn't disappoint her.

Chapter Five

Avelyn felt her heart break as Lily cried, reaching out for her. The daycare woman looked irritated that the baby was crying, but there wasn't anything Avelyn could do about it. She'd promised Thrace she would go to the clinic for tests and she couldn't very well do that with Lily in tow.

"How long will you be?" the woman asked with a Russian accent.

"I'm not sure. I'm meeting the doctor at the clinic for some tests, but I don't know what all he needs to do. It could be an hour or it could be a few hours."

"I told Thrace last time he brought this child here she was not welcome back. I do not have time to cater to a wailing baby when there are others needing attention."

Avelyn felt her anger spark as she narrowed her eyes at the rude woman. "That wailing baby, as you call her, is the sweetest child I've ever met. Maybe she cries the entire time she's here because of *you*. Perhaps if you weren't so cold and abrasive, she would react differently to you. She knows you don't like her, so she doesn't like you either."

The woman's lips twisted in a sneer and she thrust Lily back into Avelyn's arms. "I will not watch her."

Before Avelyn could respond, the door was slammed shut in her face. She looked down at sweet Lily, who was hiccupping but no longer screaming. Avelyn comforted the baby and walked away from the daycare center. She had a choice to make. She could either go to Xonos' office and ask if the baby could stay, or she'd have to make other arrangements for Lily and come back. Since she was already at the Terran station, she figured she might as well start with Xonos and see what he had to say.

As she approached the clinic, she saw Thrace leaning against the wall, one booted foot propped and his arms folded over his massive chest. He frowned when he saw Lily in her arms and shoved away from the wall, walking toward her. Lily babbled and cooed at him and he smiled at the sweet girl.

"I thought she was staying at daycare?" he asked.

"There was a slight problem. That wretched woman might have said some disparaging things about Lily, which *may* have led to me losing my temper and going off on her." Avelyn shrugged. "Neither of us is welcome at daycare now. Which was driven home by the door being slammed in our faces."

"That woman needs to be replaced," he grumbled. "You can't very well go through with your appointment if Lily is clinging to you, and I can't take her because I have work to do."

"Then I'll have to make other arrangements and either come back later today or maybe tomorrow. I can always see if Victoria would watch her for a little while, if she isn't too busy."

Thrace curled an arm around her waist and pulled her tightly against him, Lily cradled between the two of them. "I don't like the idea of having to wait. I want to set your mind at ease on the issue so we can move forward with our lives."

"I know, and I want that too, even though I'm not as confident about the outcome as you are, but I have to think of Lily first."

"And that is why I love you." He stiffened and his eyes went wide, his face paling a shade.

Avelyn had no doubt that the words had just slipped out, and there was a good chance he didn't mean them. She went up on tiptoe and kissed his cheek before pulling away. That brief contact of her lips against his warm skin was enough to make her want a proper kiss, the kind of kiss that curled her toes and made her forget everything around her.

"I should go home and call Victoria."

"Let's step inside and speak to Xonos first, that way he'll know to expect you either later today or in the morning."

Avelyn followed him inside the clinic and smiled at the very pregnant redhead in the waiting room. The woman looked up, saw Thrace, and smiled. Jealousy bit into Avelyn, but she forced it back. Obviously, the woman was already with someone, considering her current state.

"Thrace!" The woman managed to stand and waddled over to them. "It's so good to see you."

"Good morning, Brielle."

Avelyn watched as the petite woman hugged Thrace and fought the urge to bare her teeth at the woman.

"Brielle," Thrace said, "this is Avelyn. We're hoping to become mated, as soon as Xonos can examine her and we complete the paperwork."

The redhead's smile widened. "How wonderful! Were you hoping to see him this morning?"

"That was the plan," Avelyn said. "Until the daycare refused to watch Lily."

Brielle frowned. "They won't watch her? But… isn't that their job?"

"They said she requires too much of their attention because she cries the entire time she's there. I may have had a few choice words to say to them as well."

Brielle nodded. "As you should have. Well, I think my appointment is going to go by quickly. I don't have any plans today and I could stay and watch her if you'd like? I could take her to the employee lounge."

Avelyn looked at Thrace. "There's a lounge?"

"Yes. I didn't get to finish our tour yesterday." He smiled. "But I think Brielle has an excellent idea, if she's sure she doesn't mind watching Lily."

"Not at all," Brielle assured them. "I know she can be fussy, but it will be good practice for me."

Thrace frowned and pressed a finger to his ear. "Tell them I'll be right there."

"What is it?" Avelyn asked.

"Work. I'll come check on you as soon as I'm free." He pressed a kiss to her forehead and took off at a run.

"I don't see how you do it," Brielle said. "I'd worry about my husband every time he walked out the door if he worked security around here. With so many alien races in one building, and not all of them friendly toward one another, and also the humans who kick up a fuss things can get scary. There was a bomb threat just last month."

"He said he was with the military on his world, so I'm assuming he's been trained for this kind of work." Although, she had to admit the idea of a bomb was terrifying. Thrace might be good at his job, but he wasn't invincible.

Brielle nodded. "I'm sure he is."

Xonos entered the waiting area and smiled at them. "Morning, ladies. Brielle, I know you had an appointment, but to what do I owe the pleasure, Avelyn?"

"Thrace and I had a discussion about mates and he would like for you to run some tests on me. I told him your council would never approve me as a mate because I can't have children anymore. I had a miscarriage and there was some internal damage."

"And Thrace wants me to verify or disprove what your doctor told you?" Xonos asked.

"Yes. That is, if you have time this morning. If not, I can make arrangements to come back at another time. Brielle offered to watch Lily once her appointment is over."

"I can work you in this morning. My schedule is pretty light until closer to lunch. Well, barring any emergencies. They don't happen often, but they do crop up here and there. It's bound to happen when you thrust together so many different people from different backgrounds. Not everyone gets along, even if they are all here for the same reason. I think the competition just makes it worse."

"I'll wait out here while you see Brielle, then I'll hand Lily to her while you do whatever it is that needs to be done to me."

Xonos laughed. "Very well. Brielle's appointment shouldn't take long."

Avelyn sat as Brielle went into the back. With Lily in her lap, she pointed at the large screen on the wall and tried to interest the baby in the movie that played. Lily, however, was more fascinated with Avelyn's hair, and wound it around her chubby little hands and yanked.

They didn't wait for very long. Brielle hurried out and scooped Lily up into her arms. The baby looked momentarily startled and looked from Brielle to

Avelyn, as if deciding whether or not she should cry. Avelyn stood, kissed Lily's cheek, and handed the diaper bag to Brielle.

"Sweet girl, Momma will come get you shortly. Okay?"

It was the first time she'd referred to herself as Lily's mother, but it felt right.

"Ma, Ma, Ma, Ma." Lily reached for her.

Avelyn felt a rush of pleasure that her sweet girl's first word was momma. Sort of. She didn't think Thrace would be too thrilled with the news though. He'd spent months with Lily, and by all rights, it should have been Da-Da that she said first. Maybe that was something they could work on and surprise him, hopefully before Lily called her momma in front of him.

Avelyn waved bye as Brielle walked out with Lily. The baby didn't look too certain about being taken away, but at least she wasn't screaming. Yet. Xonos motioned for Avelyn to follow him. The room they entered was stark white with a counter, several cabinets, and a bunch of gadgets she couldn't identify.

"Why don't you tell me a little more about your situation?" Xonos asked. "I know you said there was a miscarriage, but that doesn't usually result in damage that is irreversible."

"I was married to an abusive man. We argued one day and he shoved me down a flight of stairs. I was about four months pregnant at the time and I miscarried from the fall. I had some bruised ribs, a fractured wrist, and some other slight injuries from the fall. The doctor who patched me up told me that either I would never have children again, or if I did become pregnant, there was a chance I wouldn't carry to term."

"I see." Xonos frowned. "I'm going to pull out a gown and step out of the room while you change."

He pulled a garment from a cabinet and set it on the table next to her, then stepped out of the room just as he'd promised. Avelyn quickly changed clothes and got back up on the table. When Xonos entered the room again, she felt a nervous flutter in her stomach. Whatever he discovered today, would mean the difference in her having a happily-ever-after, or possibly having to find a new job. She didn't think she could continue to work for Thrace if it meant getting more and more attached to Lily and him, only to lose them to another woman when he selected a mate. Someone as handsome and kind as Thrace wouldn't be alone forever. It was too depressing to even think about.

"Why don't we start with a bio scan?" he suggested. "Lie back on the table."

While she did as he requested, he went across the room and pulled a blanket from the cabinet. He draped it over the lower half of her body before raising her gown to just under her breasts. She watched as he pulled a small metal cylinder from his pocket and then scanned her stomach with it.

He frowned as he studied the gadget and then rolled a bigger machine over toward her. He levered the arm over her and she watched as a bright green light scanned her abdomen after which the machine gave him a readout. Xonos studied it a moment and then looked at her, as if contemplating what to say.

"I'm not sure how to tell you this. You're certain the doctor said you wouldn't have children because of the accident?"

"Yes. He said they had to operate."

"Was this doctor a friend of your mate's by any chance? Someone who might do you harm if your mate had requested it?"

She opened and shut her mouth several times before answering. "I don't know. I guess it's possible. The fall knocked me out and I woke up in the hospital after my injuries had been taken care of. I only know what the hospital did because the doctor told me about it when I woke up."

"I'm going to step out again and let you get dressed; then we need to have a rather serious talk."

Dread filled her, but she nodded and sat up. After Xonos left, she got dressed quickly and then opened the door so he would know she was finished. He was leaning against the wall in the hall and stepped inside when he saw her.

"Maybe we should have this talk in my office. And I think Thrace should be present, if he's able to attend."

The feeling of unease tripled as she followed Xonos to his office in the back of the building. She settled into a chair and waited while he called Thrace. The doctor's expression was grim while they waited. When Thrace burst into the room, she fought to hold back tears, certain they were about to hear something unsettling. He lifted her out of her chair, sat down, and pulled her into his lap. With his arms wrapped around her, she supposed she was as ready as she'd ever be to hear the news.

"Thrace, I asked Avelyn some questions about her past and the miscarriage she had because it didn't make sense to me that there would be severe damage. I don't know much about human medicine, but I figured they would have come far enough along that something like a miscarriage shouldn't prevent her from having more children."

"Is the damage extensive?" Thrace asked.

"That's just it. There's no damage." Xonos looked uncomfortable. "I don't know how to say this, but… they performed a hysterectomy on her. I'm not sure how they did it without her noticing. There should have been hormone pills she needed to take."

Avelyn was in a state of shock. "Hysterectomy?"

"Either your mate ordered it done because he thought you would return to him, and he didn't wish to have children with you, or he knew you would try to leave and wanted to ruin your life. Either way, it's irreversible."

Thrace's arms tightened around her. "Is there any way you can write up something for me to present to the council showing that this was done to her and she is in no way at fault for her inability to have children?"

"Thrace, they'll never approve of me," she said, tears sliding down her cheeks. "It's over. We just need to move on and figure out what happens now. Obviously, you'll find a mate one day and I'll be in the way. Maybe I can stay with you long enough to earn some money to sustain me while I search for another job. I'd like to see Lily occasionally, if that's okay."

He growled. "You're not going to see Lily occasionally, you're going to see her every day. I don't care that you can't have children. I told you before that there is always adoption. Having you in my life is much more important to me than being able to have children of my own blood."

"I'll get something written up and ready for you by the end of the day," Xonos said. "And if you need me to speak to them, I'll be happy to do so. I'm sorry I didn't have better news for you."

"How could he have done this to me?" She sobbed against Thrace's chest.

"I don't know, but we won't let him get away with it. As soon as we're mated, I'll make sure he's prosecuted for what he did to you. As the mate of a Terran, you will be deemed far more important than him, despite his money."

"They'll never let us be together." She blinked up at him tearfully.

"You need to call Kelvyk," Xonos said. "You can ask him to speak to his uncle on your behalf. If Chief Councillor Borgoz approves the mating, it will go through without issue."

"I'll place the call as soon as I escort Avelyn and Lily to a limo. I only wish I could take the day off to be with them."

"I'll be fine," Avelyn assured him. "It's upsetting news, but it isn't something we can change. And if your council comes back and says we can't be mated, then you'll have to accept it, Thrace. I don't want you to anger them by pushing the issue."

"I will fight back with everything I have, Avelyn, because you are worth having, at any cost. The worst they can do is ban me, in which case I will appeal to Earth's government to become part of their society. And if they won't have me, then I will find us another world to live on, but what I won't do is give up."

Avelyn's eyes teared up again at his words. In that moment, she knew that love wasn't going to come someday. She loved him already. Who wouldn't fall in love with such an incredible male? He was the stuff dreams were made of. So what if his skin was a lilac color? Or if his eyes were purple? Truthfully, she found him to be breathtaking and loved those things about him. She was saddened by the fact they couldn't have children together because they would have been beautiful babies.

"If you're willing to fight, then I will fight by your side," she said softly. "If you're willing to give up everything to be with me, I will do the same for you. All I want is for us to be a family -- Lily, you, and me. That's all that matters."

He smiled. "Come. I'll take you to Brielle and Lily, and then walk you to the limo. You should go home and rest until I get off work. Maybe we'll go out somewhere nice for dinner. Stop in one of the shops at the hotel and ask them to charge your purchase to my room, and don't argue about it. I'll have to make sure you have access to my funds so you can buy more clothes. I'm sure Lily needs things too."

By now, she knew better than to argue with him. He could be so stubborn! But she knew he was doing it because he cared. Everything Thrace did was for Lily's benefit, or hers. He seldom did anything that was just for him. She'd have to make arrangements for him to have some male bonding time with his friends. She knew he liked Xonos and hoped Victoria would know of other friends she could contact, or perhaps their mates. The women could arrange something for all of their men. Did alien men like movie nights, watching sports, or playing video games? Thrace almost always put something on that either Lily or she wanted to watch so she didn't know what he did or didn't like. She'd have to rectify that.

When they entered the lounge, Brielle smiled and carried Lily over to them. The little girl was fussing a little, but it wasn't an all-out scream fest just yet.

Avelyn held out her arms and Lily practically threw herself at her.

"Ma. Ma. Ma. Ma," Lily babbled.

Thrace's eyes widened. "She called you momma."

"It was an accident. I swear I haven't been training her to say that." Avelyn worried he would be angry, but a huge smile diffused her worries.

"Can you teach her to say Da-Da too?"

"You're not upset she called me momma?"

Thrace wrapped an arm around her waist. "Of course not. You *are* her momma. I think that's been apparent from the moment she went to you at the station in Las Vegas. She chose you, Avelyn, just as I have. We're yours, and you're ours."

Avelyn knew she needed to get out of there before he made her cry again.

"We'll see you at home. You don't have to walk us out." She brushed a kiss against his cheek. "I promise to stop in the shops before heading up to our suite. I'll buy something appropriate for dinner out, and I'll make sure Miss Lily is dressed appropriately too."

Brielle bit her lip and lifted her hand. "I don't mean to interrupt, but I can tell you received bad news. What if Syl and I took Lily for the night? I could bring her back in the morning and have breakfast with you, Avelyn. That way we can get to know each other better. My husband is Thrace's friend so I'm sure we'll see more of each other."

"Oh, but you look so close to your due date, and she can be so fussy when she isn't at home." Avelyn frowned. "I don't want to impose on you like that. I'm sure you need your rest."

Brielle smiled. "I can always make Syl get up with her. It will be good practice for him."

"Are you sure?" Thrace asked.

"Positive. I can ride with Avelyn back to the hotel and pick up a bag for Lily, then head home so she can shop without having to tote a baby around. Besides, I think the two of you could use some alone time tonight. Am I right?"

Thrace smiled faintly. "You would be right. It wasn't good news today, but I'm not going to let that stop me from claiming Avelyn as my mate."

"I'll walk with her to the limo and you can get back to work. Don't want to anger anyone with you taking an extended break or anything, although I'm sure they would understand if they knew the situation." Brielle smiled. "Go. They're in good hands."

"Very well." Thrace cupped Avelyn's face between his hands and stared into her eyes. "I will be home just as soon as I'm allowed to leave. Relax in the tub with those bubble things I've heard you Earth women like. Watch your favorite movie. Whatever it is you do to relax, and try not to think about what Xonos had to say today, and know that I will stop at nothing to make you mine. This is merely a… what's that Earth phrase?"

"A speed bump?" Brielle answered.

"Yes." Thrace smiled. "This is merely a speed bump. We'll get through this, and in the end, we'll be together as a family, just the way we were meant to be. And once Lily is a little older, and you're ready for another baby, we'll contact the intergalactic adoption agency and we'll see what infants they have available. With you as a stay-at-home mom, and since I have such a secure position, they are guaranteed to place a baby with us. Look how well it's turned out with Lily! They would be stupid to refuse."

Avelyn nodded. "I'll do as you say and wait for you to come home."

He hugged her gently, careful not to squash Lily, then gave her one last smile before returning to work. Brielle lifted the diaper bag and motioned for Avelyn to follow her. For someone carrying so much extra weight, the redhead moved surprisingly fast. When they reached the limos, Avelyn selected the one she'd arrived in, buckled Lily into her car seat, and then settled across from her so the baby could see her at all times. She'd found that worked best when Thrace wasn't with them.

Brielle chatted on the way to the hotel, telling Avelyn how she'd met her husband, Syl, and how they'd come to be on Earth. It made Avelyn worry that Thrace really would have to break ties with his council in order for them to be together, but Syl seemed to be managing just fine and was working for the council again, so maybe it wouldn't come to that. Perhaps they had learned their lesson? She nearly snorted. Since when did government officials ever learn anything?

When they reached the hotel, Avelyn carried Lily up to their suite with Brielle by her side. She entered the suite and set Lily in the playpen before she went to get a bag together for her; two changes of clothes, pajamas, enough formula to keep her full, several clean bottles, a few of her favorite toys, and a fresh stack of diapers. When everything was packed, she handed the bag to Brielle.

"I think I covered everything. If she gets too fussy, or really wants to come home, don't hesitate to call us. We'll come get her at any time."

Brielle smiled. "I'm sure we'll be fine, but I promise to call if I think she's getting too distressed."

Avelyn picked up Lily, hugged her tightly, kissed her soft cheek and then handed her to Brielle. The baby looked confused for a moment, but shoved her fist into her mouth and sucked on it. Avelyn waved bye as they stepped out into the hall, and as she closed the door, she heard, "Ma. Ma. Ma. Ma."

Avelyn leaned her forehead against the door and blew out a breath. Saying goodbye to Lily was never easy. She wondered if it ever would be, or would it just get harder the closer Avelyn and Lily got toward one another? How did parents ever send their kids off to school? She already knew she'd be bawling on the day Lily started school. It was guaranteed.

Pulling herself together, she made sure she had her room key in her pocket and decided to go do some retail therapy to find the perfect dress and shoes for dinner tonight. If Thrace and she were going to have some alone time, she wasn't going to squander it. She wanted his jaw to drop when he saw her. She contemplated buying make-up, but realized neither of the mates she'd met had worn any. Maybe Terrans didn't like make-up on their women? She'd have to ask Thrace.

Chapter Six

He pounded his fist on the table as he stared at the Vid-Comm. "Dammit, Borgoz. You owe me! I've given a year of my life to service on Earth and haven't asked for a single thing from you. You can read Xonos' findings yourself. It isn't Avelyn's fault she can't have children, and who's to say that I'm able to father them anyway? You're always so concerned with whether or not the females can give birth, you never stop to question whether or not the males mating them have the ability to plant a seed."

Borgoz snorted. "You know it's a rare occurrence for our males not to be in top performance. We excel at everything we do."

It was just the type of sexist remark he expected to hear from the Chief Councillor.

"Well, let me ask you this. How am I supposed to attract a bride you'll approve of with a Drelthene baby in tow? Avelyn loves Lily as if she were her own daughter. You know as well as I do that the adoption agency is overflowing. I want to give those babies a home, and so does Avelyn. We can provide a service that other couples don't or won't want to do."

"Those unwanted brats can find homes on other worlds. You'll do as you're told, warrior."

"Not this time. I love Avelyn, and if I can't claim her as my mate, then I won't take one. You can't force me to marry someone, not even the council has that much power, not when it comes to my personal life. I'm not your nephew. You can't arrange a match for me."

The Councillor's face flushed.

"Yes, I know all about the woman you're trying to force on Kelvyk. We talked about it in some detail before I made this call. And since forced matches are frowned upon in our society, you're going to do exactly as I want or I take your little misdeed before the entire council. How would you like to lose your position?"

"Don't you dare threaten me!"

"Then approve my mating request. In the grand scheme of things, does it really matter if I'm mated to a woman who can't have children? What's the difference in a Terran taking a non-Terran mate and possibly having non-Terran children, compared to my mating with Avelyn and adopting non-Terran children? Either way, our society is going to change in the upcoming years. You know we only breed true with humans, but there are only so many human brides to go around."

Borgoz looked disgruntled, but he didn't deny Thrace's claim.

"Very well. I'll consider the matter, but that's all I can give you for now. I'll take it before the council next week and we'll vote. Until then, maybe you should enjoy your time with her, in case this doesn't end the way you want."

Seemed reasonable enough. He signed off and made his way outside to a waiting limo. He was more than ready to go home, shower and change, and take Avelyn out to a nice dinner. He thought about Borgoz's words. If his time was limited with Avelyn, he definitely wanted to make every second count. He couldn't afford to be hesitant around her any longer. He would take what he wanted, what he knew she wanted, and he wouldn't have a moment of regret.

And if the council was unwise enough to take Avelyn from him, then he'd move forward with the next step of his plan -- forgoing his place in Terran society and going out on his own. Granted, when Syl had left, he was one of a very few scientists and his skills were greatly needed. If Thrace left, he'd be one of thousands of warriors. It wasn't likely his home world would ask him to come back. If he took those steps, it would very likely be the last time he was welcome in Terran society.

At the hotel, Thrace made his way up to his suite, trying to dispel his feelings of unease over the situation. He rolled his head on his shoulders, easing the tension built up there. Pushing open the door, he froze before he could take a single step across the threshold. Avelyn stood with her back to him, looking out the window. Sunlight streamed through the glass, forming a halo around her body. Her hair had been partially pinned up, with long curls hanging down her back.

A back that was completely bare. The sight of all that creamy skin made his cock harden. He'd asked her to purchase a dress, but she seemed to have forgotten part of it. Did she expect to go out like that? Where men could gawk at what belonged to him? She must have heard him and turned, a smile adorned her face. His gaze skimmed down her body. The black material of her dress cupped her breasts lovingly, draped over her hips, and fell to her calves, the slinky material leaving little to the imagination.

"Do you like it?" she asked.

"Where's the rest of it?"

Her eyes twinkled in merriment. "I assure you, this is a complete dress. Look! Matching shoes." She stuck a leg out and pointed her foot. A long, curvy leg and a small, delicate foot with some sort of strappy thing attached to it. He had to admit, the shoe gave him naughty ideas... of stripping her bare except for those shoes.

"You actually go out in public in that?" he asked, not sure he liked the thought.

The smile dimmed from her face. "You don't like it."

Not like it? He liked it so much, he wanted to remove it from her body -- with his teeth -- but he wasn't sure he should tell her that. She'd obviously gone to a lot of trouble to dress up for him and here he was making her feel bad.

"I'll take it off and return it," she said, a dejected look on her face as she turned from him.

Thrace reached out and placed a hand on her arm, turning her to face him. He stepped closer, curled his fingers under her chin and lifted her face. There was uncertainty in her eyes and he wanted to erase it, but he was a little nervous. He wanted to kiss her, more than anything, but what if he wasn't any good at it? He didn't exactly have a lot of practice.

"I like the dress, Avelyn. A little too much. What I don't like is the idea of other men seeing you dressed in it."

Thrace lowered his head and pressed his lips to hers. Just a gentle brush. He did it again and felt her melt against him. As her lips parted, he deepened the kiss, curving an arm around her waist and pulling her tightly against his aching body. His cock throbbed in his pants as the softness of her back brushed against his skin. It was so easy to imagine her naked, spread out before him like a buffet. And feast on her he would! All damn night if she'd let him.

He felt her hands fist his leather vest as her curves pressed against him. He wanted her touch so badly he ached for it. Thrace pulled away, knowing if he didn't stop now, nothing would keep him from stripping her and taking her right there on the living room floor. He didn't think they'd even make it to the couch; he wanted her that badly. He'd been tormented with dreams of her nightly since their first meeting and now he was so close to making it a reality -- if he didn't screw up.

"I should shower and change." Was that his voice? He cleared his throat. "You spent a lot of time getting dressed up. I'd hate for us not to make it out of the suite tonight."

"I wouldn't exactly call it a loss if we didn't," she said, a soft smile curving her lips. "But yes, it was a lot of work to look this way and I'd like to enjoy it a little bit longer."

"I'll hurry."

He walked away while he still could and closed his bedroom door behind him. He pulled his light gray leather pants out of the closet, tossed them over the foot of the bed and then flipped through the silk tunics he owned, which were few. He selected a soft teal and placed it on the bed with the pants before stripping out of his clothes. His shower was the fastest in the history of showers, and he made sure every knot and tangle was out of his hair after drying it and then braided it.

He typically didn't wear artificial scents, but someone had gifted him with a nice bottle of cologne. He spritzed a bit on his neck and wrists, hoping Avelyn liked it. The female who had given it to him as a thank-you had winked and said it smelled divine, had even tried to get him to put some on right then. Of course, he wasn't entirely certain she hadn't wanted him to wear her too.

In the bedroom, he quickly dressed, but paused over his boots. He couldn't wear work boots with his nice clothes, but he hated the dressier ones required at banquets and such. They tended to pinch his toes. Then again, what was a little pain if he got to spend a nice evening out with Avelyn? He'd called to make a reservation at what he had been assured was a top-notch seafood restaurant. He hoped she liked shellfish and wasn't allergic, he hadn't thought to ask.

He paused with his hand on the doorknob. His heart was racing in his chest. It wasn't so much due to nerves as it was anticipation. This was the night he was going to make her his in every way possible. The council may not have given their approval yet, but he had no doubt they would. He'd given them sound information. Borgoz was the only one he'd worried about, but he felt sure his little bit of blackmail would sway the man in his favor. He was tempted to leak the information anyway, just to save Kelvyk from an unpleasant future, but honor forbid him from doing it. It was one thing to put a little pressure on the Chief Councillor but another to make trouble for Kelvyk.

Thrace opened the door and smiled when he saw her standing at the window, watching the moon rise. She was so beautiful; she took his breath away. He'd read that saying in an Earth book and it had stuck with him, though he had not really understood it until this moment. He was experiencing a lot of firsts with Avelyn.

He'd never felt desire before. He'd had a need, but it hadn't been because of any particular woman. The females at the floating brothel were all right, but nothing special. Convenient, that's what they were. He'd gotten hard seeing their naked bodies, but he'd never ached from wanting someone so much. Never before had the mere thought of a woman touching him, even innocently, been enough to set him on fire. His cock stayed hard all the damn time around Avelyn. A smile. A glance. The way she brushed her hair away from her face. Every move she made was seductive.

He cleared his throat to get her attention. "Are you ready? Our reservation is for seven and it's nearly that time now. I don't want to be late or we'll lose our table."

"I'm ready."

He crooked his arm, like he'd seen men do in the movies, and waited until her delicate hand settled on his forearm. Thrace escorted her out of the room, down the elevator, and out to the waiting limo. He'd made sure his regular driver was available tonight and would be able to wait for them at the restaurant. On the drive there, he watched her, but covertly. She fascinated him, especially this side of her. He'd never seen her look quite so elegant. He was nearly afraid to touch her, for fear of messing up her hair or the touch of make-up she wore. He hadn't seen any in her bathroom the other day and assumed she'd just purchased it. Usually he detested make-up on a woman, but the little bit she wore just accented her beauty.

The limo drew to a stop in front of the restaurant; Thrace slid out and then held out a hand for Avelyn. After helping her from the vehicle, he placed her hand in the crook of his arm again and escorted her inside. A doorman opened the elaborate doors for them and they swept inside, drawing the attention of everyone nearby. For once, he doubted it was his unusual coloring. Avelyn was stunning tonight, and he knew he was the envy of every man there.

The hostess showed them to a table near the window; a small candle flickered in the center. Menus were placed at their settings and Thrace held Avelyn's chair for her. He'd seen men do that before and hoped it was the right thing to do. He wanted this night to be special -- perfect -- and hoped he didn't mess up. He'd studied for this moment and ordered a bottle of red wine. Did Avelyn like wine? If not, lesson learned. He'd never tried it himself, but humans seemed to like it well enough. It seemed every couple in the restaurant had a glass of the stuff.

"Are we celebrating something?" she asked as she took a sip.

"In a manner of speaking. I called the Chief Councillor this afternoon, once I had the paperwork from Xonos. He's going to present our case to the rest of the council, but it may be a week before we hear anything."

"So, we're celebrating that our case is being presented?"

"That and… I did some thinking. If the council won't approve our mating, then I will break from the council. Either way, we're going to be mated. If you'll have me."

She stared at him, blinking several times.

He set his glass down. "Did I say something wrong?"

"No, it's just… you'd leave everything you know just to be with me?"

"Of course." He frowned, not understanding what she found so confusing about it. He wanted her. She wanted him. They would be together. It was that simple. At least, in his mind it was. He'd heard Earth females could complicate a situation if given the opportunity.

"But, Thrace… you can't leave your people, your job. Where would we live? Where would you work? I… I can't be the reason you lose everything."

He reached across the table and took her hand, noticing her distress. "Avelyn, I would do anything to be with you. Don't you realize that I don't care about my job or anything else if you aren't by my side? You're perfect for me in every way. I want you in my life, and as more than my nanny. I dream of going to sleep at night with you in my arms. Of waking to your smiling face."

A trace of a smile graced her lips. "You might rethink that last one. I don't wake up smiling. I don't smile until I've had my coffee. I'm actually very grumpy in the morning, but you're usually gone by the time I get up with Lily. I know it's only been a few days since you brought me here, but sometimes I forget that. It feels like I've been watching over Lily longer than that."

"Then I'll have a cup waiting for you when I wake you in the morning." He smiled. "I'll even serve you breakfast in bed."

"Oh, now you're just taking things too far." She laughed. "But I may hold you to the cup of coffee. I'm a bear without it."

He smoothed his thumb along her hand. "Avelyn, will you have me as your mate? I don't care that you can't have children; there are plenty out there who need homes, like Lily. I promise to do everything in my power to give you a good life. I may not be as rich as your previous husband, but I promise that you'll never want for anything. I'll buy a house. Clothes. Give you anything your heart desires, if you'll only agree to be mine."

"Thrace." Tears shimmered in her eyes. "You don't have to promise to buy me things to win my affection. Do you know why I would say yes? It isn't because you have billions of dollars, which by the way is more money than my husband ever had. It isn't because you want to buy me whatever my heart desires. I would say yes because of the respect you show me, the gentle way you touch me, and the wonderful father you are to Lily. I know that if we are blessed enough to adopt more children, you would treat them the same way you treat Lily and me, and they would be very lucky to call you dad."

"Does that mean you're saying yes?" he asked, his heart pounding in his chest.

"It means I'm saying yes. But… I really hope your council comes through. I would hate for you to turn your back on everything you know just to be with me. I'm not sure I'm worth that."

He lifted her hand and kissed the back of it. "Avelyn, you're worth that and so much more. I don't understand the emotions I feel when I'm around you. There's always this anxious feeling in the pit of my stomach; my heart races out of control, and I'm always afraid of saying the wrong thing. But most of all, not a moment goes by that I don't think about kissing you… " He kissed her hand again. "And making you mine in all ways."

He felt the tremor race through her.

"I think about those things too."

A waiter came over and took their orders. Neither had looked at the menu, and at that particular moment, Thrace couldn't have cared less what he ate. Even Avelyn seemed to open the menu and order the first thing she saw. Did she want this meal to end as quickly as he did? Suddenly, the most important thing in the world was getting her back to the hotel and out of that sexy damn dress. Not the shoes though… he wanted those on.

"I wonder how Lily is," Avelyn mused. "Brielle assured me she would call if there was a problem."

Thrace hoped like hell there wouldn't be a problem, not tonight. He had plans for Avelyn, plans that involved no clothes and lots of naked skin -- and no babies! If things went the way he hoped, he'd make love to her all night and into the morning. He wanted to watch the sunrise with her, feed her breakfast, and then take her back to bed. Just the thought of having her completely at his mercy was enough to make his cock thicken. He may only have experience with prostitutes, and there might be a small part of him that worried he wouldn't be able to please her, but he knew that being with Avelyn would be earth shattering. Another Earth phrase he couldn't wait to experience.

Their food arrived and he noticed that she ate as quickly as he did, with little conversation between them. He nearly jumped and choked on a shrimp when he felt something slide up his leg. Judging by the naughty look in Avelyn's eyes, it was her foot. As discreetly as he could, he reached under the tablecloth and snagged her foot. A smile blossomed across her face and quickly changed to one of pure longing as he stroked the delicate arch with his thumb.

Avelyn jerked her foot away and he smirked, knowing he'd gotten to her. She got to him every damn day, but it was fun playing with her like this, seeing just how far he could wind her up before getting her back to the hotel. The limo ride home would prove interesting.

With her eyes fastened on his, she licked her lips, and then used the tip of her tongue to lick the butter sauce off her shrimp. His cock jerked and his grip on his fork tightened. She teased the morsel along her lips before gently sucking it into her mouth and chewing, her lips glistening from the butter. It made him wonder if she'd look the same way with his cum on her lips. Ever since he'd seen the video of the woman taking the man's cock in her mouth, he'd wanted to try it. And he couldn't think of anyone he'd rather share it with than Avelyn, assuming she didn't find it distasteful. He'd never force her to do anything.

As she pushed her plate away, he waved to the waiter and asked for their check. The bill was around one hundred dollars and he had no idea how much to tip, so he just stuck two one hundreds on top before rising to his feet. Anxious to get Avelyn home, he hoped the money was adequate. She smiled as she slid her hand into his and he wrapped an arm around her waist as he guided her out to the waiting limo.

Thrace had no sooner closed the door and settled on the seat than he found his arms full of soft, willing woman. She plastered her lips to his, her hands roaming his shoulders and chest. Thrace kissed her with a hunger he'd never before experienced, devouring her lips as his hands slid up and down her bare back before settling on her rounded hips.

Avelyn squirmed in his lap and then threw one leg over him. As she straddled his legs, his cock pulsed in time with his heartbeat. Her palms slid up his chest then down before returning to his shoulders. Her eyes glittered in the dim lighting and he stared at her plump lips, wanting another taste. But there was something he wanted even more.

His hands fell to the hem of her dress and slowly eased it up, exposing her creamy thighs and baring more of her than he'd ever seen before. He tugged it up further until he saw the scrap of black satin between her legs and his breath left him in a *whoosh*. His mouth suddenly ran dry and his pulse pounded in his ears.

Thrace fastened his gaze on hers as he reached between them, his thumb sliding over the slippery material, feeling her heat through the thin scrap. She wiggled her hips and he felt the heat radiating between her legs. He slid his hand down until he cupped her mound, the dampness taking him by surprise. It seemed his Avelyn wanted him very much. He'd read enough about Earth women to know they became wet when aroused.

"What do you want, Avelyn? I'll give you anything you want, just name it."

"I want you to touch me."

He smiled. "I am."

"I want... I want you to make me come."

He stroked her with a finger, feeling the seam of her pussy through the material. "And how do you want me to make you come?"

"I... I want you to touch me, to stroke me, until I come. I want to feel your fingers inside of me."

If his cock got any harder, he'd never be able to walk through the hotel lobby. Her words were enough to make him come in his pants like a young boy. But he wanted to do as she asked, wanted to do that and so much more.

"How attached are you to these panties?" he asked.

She shook her head, either telling him she wasn't attached, or that she didn't understand. Either way, he didn't give her a chance to do much else. The sound of fabric tearing filled the air as he ripped her panties from her, leaving her bare to his hungry gaze. The sight of her shaved pussy made him growl softly and he licked his lips, wondering if her nectar tasted as good as she smelled.

He teased her slit, sliding his fingers along the slippery flesh before parting the lips and finding the little bundle of nerves he knew would give her the most pleasure. He stroked her softly, just a brush of his fingers against her swollen flesh, and she gasped, her nails biting into his shoulders. He watched as she parted her legs further, giving him better access.

Circle, flick, stroke. Circle, flick, stroke. He set up a rhythm that had her pulse pounding into her throat and her heart beating so loudly he would have sworn he heard it. Sweat gathered along the back of his neck as his control was tested. Her hips jerked against his hand and he remembered her words. She wanted to feel his fingers inside her.

As this thumb teased and tormented her little clit, he eased a finger inside her tight passage. Heaven! She felt like silk wrapped around his finger, her wet heat enough to make him buck his hips in anticipation. She groaned and pressed down tighter against his hand. Thrace stroked her, in and out several times, before adding a second finger. While he stretched her inner walls, he watched in fascination as she lifted her hips, and then lowered them, fucking herself on his fingers.

It was the most incredible thing he'd ever seen. Faster. Harder. Her breath came out in pants as she rode his hand to a climax, her walls fluttering around his fingers, trying to suck him in further. Her teeth dented her lip where she held back her cries of passion and he wished she didn't have to. Thrace wanted to hear every moan, every scream, and every cry of passion that left her lips.

Her body twitched as he slowly stroked her, wondering if he could bring her back to that frenzy before they reached the hotel. She moaned again as he pressed a little harder against her clit. Her movements became frantic as she clawed at the top of her dress, dragging it down her arms. Exposed, her breasts swayed with the motion of the vehicle.

"Taste me," she whispered. "I want your lips on my nipples."

With a groan, Thrace couldn't hold back. The feel of her on his fingers, the scent of her in the air, and her naughty words were enough to make him come in his pants. Leaning forward, he took one rosy tip in his mouth. The point pebbled against his tongue as he lapped at her. She tasted sweet and felt incredible as she ground herself against his hand.

Thrace knew the hotel wasn't much further so he stroked her faster as he switched to the other breast, the nipple every bit as responsive as the other one. With a gentle nip, he sent her over the edge, her soft cries filling his ears as she was unable to hold back this time. As she trembled in his arms, he stroked his fingers in and out of her, slowing and then withdrawing his fingers.

With his gaze fastened on hers, he stuck his fingers in his mouth and licked them clean, sucking her juices from the digits.

"You taste even better than I'd imagined."

"You didn't get to come. I shouldn't have been so selfish."

He chuckled. "A male should never admit this, but you were so hot and so damn sexy that I came in my pants just feeling you climax. I'll be sticky when I get out of these pants."

A blush tinged her cheeks. "I made you lose control?"

He nodded.

"I like the sound of that." Her hand stroked his chest, down toward his abdomen, and was heading for dangerous territory when he stopped her. For the moment, his cock wasn't hard and he'd be able to walk through the hotel lobby without garnering too many stares.

He helped her put her dress to rights just as the limo came to a stop. Thrace exited the limo first and then helped Avelyn out. With an arm curved around her waist, he led her into the hotel, up the elevator, and to their suite. He shut the door with a *click*, tossed his keycard aside, and prowled toward her.

Her eyes were still bright from her orgasm, her expression soft. He felt proud that he'd been the one to put that look on her face. It had never mattered to him before if a female came when they were together. But with Avelyn, it mattered.

She pulled her dress down her shoulders, did a little shimmy, and he watched as the material pooled at her feet. Completely bare except for those damn shoes, she crooked her finger at him. Thrace stalked toward her, wondering what the little vixen had in mind. She helped him out of his shirt, and as she reached for the button on his pants, he toed off his boots.

Getting his pants off took a bit of effort, but they managed and he kicked them aside. Now every bit as nude as her, his cock once more awake and ready for action, he wasn't sure how to proceed. In the limo, instinct and her need had driven him to do the things he'd done. Here, under the bright lights, he wasn't as sure of himself.

Avelyn placed her hands on his hips and he watched as she slid to her knees at his feet. His cock jumped at the implication and he hoped like hell she was going to do what he thought she was going to do.

Avelyn licked her lips and looked up at him, wrapping a hand around the base of his cock. His breath froze in his lungs as she opened her mouth and took the head inside, stroking the underside with her tongue.

Thrace thought his head was going to explode it felt so damn good! She hummed a little then took more of him in her mouth, her tongue stroking his shaft. His fingers threaded through her hair, but he was careful not to hurt her. She pulled back, sucking long and hard and he damn near came from the pleasure. When Avelyn swallowed him down again, he held her there for a moment, hoping he wasn't hurting her but not wanting the sensations to stop. She pulled away and he allowed it.

The pull of her lips and the stroke of her tongue were enough to make him lose his mind. After a few more strokes, he found himself holding her head steady and fucking her mouth with long, slow strokes. She allowed it, even seemed to enjoy it, if the noises she made were any indication. He felt his balls draw up against his body and knew he was about to lose control, but he just couldn't stop himself. He wanted her to taste him, the way he'd tasted her, wanted to see his cum on her lips.

He quickened his pace and groaned as the first spurt hit the back of her throat. Before he emptied himself, he pulled back enough to bathe her lips in the pearly liquid. She looked up at him and licked it off, damn near making him hard again.

Thrace didn't give her a chance to stand. He scooped her into his arms and carried her over to the sofa, where he tossed her onto the soft cushions. She landed on her ass, legs sprawled, and a beautiful smile on her face. Thrace knelt on the floor, her legs on either side of him, and leaned down to trail kisses between her breasts and down her soft belly.

She spread her legs further, the closer he got to her pussy. Already she was wet and ready for him, apparently not having gotten enough in the limo. Using his thumbs, he parted her pussy and just looked at her. She was all pink and soft -- beautiful. Leaning down, he lapped at her, gathering her cream on his tongue. Avelyn wiggled her hips and he dipped his tongue inside of her. Gently, he pressed his finger against her clit, lightly stroking the little nub.

"Yes, just like that," she panted. "More, Thrace. I want more."

He growled. "What do you want, sweet Avelyn?"

"I want you to fuck me with your mouth, to feel your tongue inside of me. I want to come on your tongue and feel you lick and suck every bit of my cum from me when I'm finished."

His cock pulsed between his legs as he stroked her with his tongue, delving inside on every other stroke. As she whined and thrashed, he fucked her with his tongue, mimicking what he wanted to do with his cock. A little more pressure on her clit and she came, screaming his name. He drank down everything she had to give him and then rose over her.

"Are you ready for me, Avelyn? Can you take me now or do you need more?"

"I just need you, Thrace."

"We're taking this somewhere else. I can't get to you very well from this angle."

She cast a glance around the room and pointed to the chair. "Can you bend me over the back of that? Am I tall enough that you could fuck me that way?"

Without answering, he pulled her from the sofa and led her to the back of the chair. Thrace placed his hand in the middle of her back and eased her down until her ass stuck out in a most inviting way. Her pussy teased him, parting to let him see what he so desperately wanted.

He braced a hand on her hip and wrapped the other one around his cock, leading the hungry beast to her sweet pussy. He slipped between her lips and eased into her tight channel, her body gripping him like a glove. With both hands on her hips, he pushed forward until he was buried inside her. His heart hammered in his chest and he wasn't sure how gentle or slow he could be.

"Stop teasing me," she said, pushing back against him.

"I don't have much control right now, Avelyn. I'm worried I'll hurt you, or that it won't be good for you."

She looked at him over her shoulder. "Thrace. I want you. Now. If you need to take me fast and hard, then do it."

Her words eased his tension and he thrust inside of her, slowly at first, then faster. It seemed the harder he pounded into her, the more vocal she became, begging for more. Sweat slicked his skin as he watched his cock disappear into her sweet body again and again, her cream coating the shaft, until he felt his orgasm fast approaching.

He didn't have time to warn her before he was shooting deep inside of her, groaning as he emptied himself. The flutters around his cock told him she'd found her release, and for that, he was grateful. He'd have felt like such a failure if he'd left her behind.

Thrace knew she had to be uncomfortable, but he was loath to pull out just yet. When she wiggled against him, he disengaged their bodies and helped her stand up straight, wincing as her back cracked.

"Maybe we shouldn't do that again."

She smiled. "I'd be disappointed if we didn't. But I'm definitely not as young as I once was."

"Let's rinse off in the shower, then you can pick a movie and we'll cuddle for a while, get our second wind."

"You want me again tonight?" Her eyebrows rose and the surprise on her face almost comical.

"Of course I'm going to want you again tonight. Did you think once would be enough? I've been aching for you for days."

"It's just… " Her hands fidgeted at her waist. "My ex, he never… I mean, it was always just once, maybe once every other week, and it usually didn't last more than ten minutes. We've been fooling around since the limo and… "

He placed a finger over her lips. "Hush. I'm not him. You're desirable and sexy, and if you let me, I would make love to you all night and all morning. I'd keep you awake until you passed out from exhaustion."

She looked pleased with his words and took his hand, leading him through his room and into the bathroom beyond. Turning her back to him, she started the shower, then propped a foot on the toilet and unfastened her shoe. Unable to resist, he reached for the other one, his fingers fumbling with the tiny buckle before freeing her foot. He studied the shoe a minute then smiled at her.

"I like these."

"Then I'll be sure to wear them again."

"And only the shoes?"

She gave him a bashful look. "If that's what you'd like."

Oh yeah, he'd very much like! He assisted her into the shower then followed, pulling the curtain shut behind them. Thrace had never showered with a woman before, but his instincts hadn't led him astray so far. He helped her lather her hair and then washed her body, his hands caressing her soft curves. When he was finished, she turned the tables on him and washed him from head to toe.

After they had dried off, they donned the *His and Hers* robes hanging on the back of the door, robes he'd never had a reason to use before now. Hand in hand, they returned to the living room and cuddled on the couch while they watched a movie. Thrace couldn't remember the last time he'd felt this content. Avelyn completed him and he looked forward to many more nights like this one, even if he had to con his friends into babysitting more often.

Chapter Seven

Avelyn stretched, smiling at the aches and twinges she felt from her head to her toes. There wasn't an inch of her body that Thrace hadn't explored and loved well into the morning light. She looked at the bedside clock and bolted upright. 2:00! She glanced at the other side of the bed and found it empty. Tossing the covers aside, she cracked the bedroom door and peered into the living room. She didn't see Thrace and nothing looked out of place.

Dashing across the living space, she sprinted into her room where she quickly scrambled into some clothes. Avelyn went back into the living room and looked everywhere to see if Thrace had left her a note. Anything to tell her where he'd disappeared to. Had he been called into work?

A sound outside the door drew her attention and a moment later it swung open.

"Ma. Ma. Ma. Ma." Lily clapped her hands and smiled at Avelyn.

Thrace smiled when he saw her, a warm light entering his eyes. "Yes, I see. Your momma is awake."

"I didn't know where you'd gone," Avelyn said, reaching for Lily.

"Brielle called a little while ago and said Lily had been crying and asking for you all morning. She held off as long as she could before calling me. I didn't see the point in waking you just to go pick her up, so I left you to rest."

She smiled. "I appreciate it. Someone I know kept me up all night."

He laughed.

"Ma. Ma. Ma." Lily tugged on her hair.

Avelyn pressed a kiss to the baby's chubby cheek. "Momma is here. Did you have fun with Brielle?"

The baby babbled at her some more.

"I know you're probably tired, but I thought maybe we'd do something with Lily today," Thrace said. "Now that you've agreed to be mine, regardless of what the council says, I don't see why we shouldn't act like a family."

"Is there a ceremony or something we need to go through?"

"For a Terran warrior, if the council says we're mates, then it's so. I've seen the ceremonies you have here on Earth. Do you want to have something like that? I'm not opposed to it."

"You would go through a wedding ceremony for me?"

He nodded. "I'm not sure if it would be considered legal since I'm not a resident on Earth, but if it would make you happy, then yes, I will do it."

"I don't need a wedding, Thrace. I just need to be yours. I don't want there to be any question that Lily and you belong to me, and that I belong to you. As long as no one is going to try to separate us, then I'm happy."

He growled. "I would never let anyone take you from me, Avelyn. Not even my council."

His words warmed her and she smiled brightly. "You said you wanted to do something with Lily. What did you have in mind?"

"Well… I bought her what I could when I adopted her, but as you know, I'm still struggling with being a father. I'm sure there are things she needs or wants that I have missed. Would you be opposed to taking her shopping at one of those huge baby stores?"

"I bet Lily would love that! We can buy her some more clothes. The ones she has now are getting a little tight on her. I think she's ready for the next size up. Same for diapers. Wouldn't hurt to buy a package or two of a larger size, just to have them."

He looked around the suite. "And toys?"

"I'm sure she'll talk you into something." Avelyn smiled. "You don't expect to take a child shopping and come home without toys, do you? She may be small still, but you'd be surprised how many things she'll try to grab. If you get her close enough to the shelves, I'm sure she would put a dent in your wallet."

"No." He laughed. "I suppose not. When I went shopping with her before, she didn't do much but scream. I think they were quite happy when we left. I made sure to tip them."

"Well, let me get my purse and we can head out. Miss Lily looks ready to shop to me."

"You don't need your purse." Thrace held out a hand. "You have me."

Sliding her palm along his, she felt his fingers close over her hand and tingles shot up her arm and settled in her heart. No words of love had been spoken the night before, but she could tell that he really cared about her, that he desired her, and above all, he wanted her -- forever. For now, that would be enough. She knew she had the love of Lily, and she could be content with that. If Thrace didn't love her yet, she was confident that it would grow over time.

As for her? She was definitely in love with the big alien.

Throughout the day, they went from one baby store to another, filling the limo with way more than Lily would ever need, but Thrace was a force to be reckoned with. They bought clothes in several sizes, trying to anticipate her growth spurts, developmental toys to help make her smarter -- not that she wasn't already exceptionally bright -- and Avelyn had found the cutest patchwork doll that was brightly colored. Lily had grabbed onto it and had yet to let go. The cashier had tried to take the doll to scan it and Lily had screamed until the doll had been given back.

"Tired of shopping?" Thrace asked.

"A little. My feet are starting to hurt."

He looked down at her feet and frowned. "You need better shoes."

Avelyn glanced at the shoes in question. They were plain sneakers, but she'd gotten them used and the padding inside was pretty much shot. She had to admit, he was right; she did need new shoes, and something told her that the long strides he was using to eat up the sidewalk were taking them to a shoe store.

As she stared up at the sign above the shop, she arched a brow at him. "There are cheaper shoe stores. Can't we just go to Payless or something? I don't need an eighty dollar pair of shoes."

Thrace folded his arms over his chest and frowned at her. With a sigh, she relented and went into the shop. As she browsed the shoes, she winced over the prices, even though she knew Thrace could more than afford them. It was the principle of the thing. Yes, there was a time in her life she hadn't batted an eye at spending hundreds, if not thousands, of dollars on a pair of shoes. But after having all of that taken away, she had a better appreciation for money. It wouldn't last forever.

Thrace held up a pair of purple and teal ones. "What about these?"

They were cute, and a good brand. She hunted for a pair in her size and tried them on, but they pinched her toes. Another half hour of looking and she was the proud owner of a new pair, and she found Thrace shopping for other shoes... in the women's department.

"What are you doing?" she asked. "I thought we were paying for these and taking Lily home for a nap."

"I've studied Earth women. You need more shoes. They all seem to have hundreds of pairs."

"Not all."

He held up a pair of ballet flats. "These look like they would be comfortable."

She couldn't help but smile. "Very well. I'll look at a few more pair."

"Two. I'm not walking out of this store until you pick out at least two more pairs of shoes."

With a shake of her head, she picked out two more pairs, then followed Thrace and Lily to the counter to pay. She tried to hide her wince when she saw the total, even though she knew it was pocket change for the big alien. They loaded her bags into the trunk and then she climbed into the back of the limo and helped fasten Lily into her car seat. The little angel was asleep before they even reached the hotel, having had a very busy day.

"We should probably order room service for dinner," Thrace said. "I'm not sure Lily can handle another trip out. And you've been rubbing your foot for the last ten minutes."

She looked at her hand wrapped around her foot and released it. "It's a little sore."

Thrace sat on the couch and held out his hand. "Give me your feet."

She balked for a moment, then stretched out across the couch and put her feet in his lap. As his thumbs dug into her arch, she couldn't hold back the gasp of pleasure. Avelyn groaned as he worked out the knots in her feet. By the time he moved to the second foot, she thought she might melt into the couch it felt so damn good. It also made her wonder if anyone had ever given him a massage. Was it a common practice on Terran?

"You do that really well," she said.

"I'm worried I'll squeeze too hard and hurt you. I've never done this before."

"Have you ever had someone massage you?"

He looked hesitant to answer.

"It's all right if you have. I won't be mad. People pay good money here on Earth for a good massage."

"I haven't had one, but there was a woman who tried to massage my shoulders once. I didn't like the feel of her hands on me and tried to brush her off."

"What happened?"

He looked away before swinging his gaze her way again. "She tried to disrobe in the middle of the Terran station and told me she could offer me more than just that. I didn't like her."

Avelyn bit her lip. She could just see some woman trying to come on to Thrace and him backing away in horror. He was such a sweet guy and probably didn't have a clue how to react to an aggressive Earth woman. And something told her the woman didn't want anything more from Thrace than his wallet. Although, word was out that the Terrans were well hung, so it was possible she'd just been after him for sex.

The smile slipped from her face. She didn't like the idea of women throwing themselves at him for sex.

What if someone better came along? What if there came a time that some beautiful female caught his attention, one who could give him children, and he decided he'd made a mistake taking Avelyn for his mate?

"You look worried. I didn't want that woman."

"I believe you, but it did make me wonder what would happen if someone came along that you did like in return. What if you take me for your mate and then one day decide you've made a mistake?"

He gave her a patient look. "That isn't going to happen, Avelyn. You're the only woman I've wanted. Ever. I never felt desire until I met you. I never felt all these intense emotions until you came here to live with me."

"I came here to be your nanny," she pointed out.

His jaw tensed. "I see. Are you regretting what happened between us last night? Have you changed your mind about being my mate? Would you prefer that I pay you for the services you do around here and keep my hands to myself?"

"No! God, no. Thrace, that isn't it at all. I just… look at you and look at me. You can do so much better."

He tugged on her feet until he'd dragged her down the couch, then he scooped her up and placed her across his lap. "Listen to me and listen well. There is no woman out there for me except you. I've never felt these things before, and I know I never will again. Lily and you mean everything to me, Avelyn. You're the perfect mother for her, and the perfect mate for me. And together, we'll rescue more orphans and make one big happy family."

"There's something you should know." She nibbled on her lower lip, questioning whether or not she should tell him. Was it the right time? "There's a reason I'm nervous around you, that I feel so insecure."

"You have no reason to be insecure, Avelyn."

"It's because I love you," she blurted. "I love you and I'm scared that you can never love me in return. I'm broken, Thrace, and that's never going to change. Yes, it was done to me without my knowledge, but it doesn't change the fact that I'm not a whole woman. I'm defective."

"Don't make me turn you over my lap and blister your ass." He grinned. "I learned that from television."

Tears gathered in her eyes.

"Avelyn, you exasperate me at times with the way you view things, but it doesn't change how I feel about you. You mean the world to me. Do you think I would fall to my knees and worship at the feet of just any woman? I've never tried to pleasure a woman before last night and I was terrified I would do it wrong, but I was determined to follow through. I wanted you to feel the things you make me feel. My blood heats when you're around and all I can think about is stripping you bare and getting you under me as fast as possible, because my cock aches to feel you wrapped around it. And it isn't just lust. I've felt lust before. This is so much more than that, Avelyn. Do you know why?"

She slowly shook her head.

"Because I love you." He smoothed her hair back from her face. "I love you so damn much. It's why I won't let you go, even if the council says we can't be together."

She toyed with the buttons on his silk shirt. "You know. Lily is sleeping soundly. Maybe if we're really quiet, you could take me to the bedroom and show me just how much you love me?"

"I could do that." He smiled and kissed her softly. As his hands delved into her hair, there was an incessant beeping in the room. "Damn."

"What is it?" she asked.

He pulled the little tablet looking thing from his pocket. "The council wishes to speak to me. They asked that I bring you with me, which means I have to find someone to stay here with Lily. That could take time."

"Will they be that patient?"

"I can only hope." He sighed. "I'm going to call Victoria and Xonos to see if one of them can watch Lily for a little while. I'm not sure how long a conversation this will be. The fact they want to see both of us worries me somewhat. If they had good news, wouldn't they only need to see me?"

Her stomach knotted. "You think they're going to deny our mating?"

"It's possible."

"Make the call and let's hurry to the station. I don't want to keep them waiting. What if they become angry? They surely won't approve our mating if we make them wait for us."

"I'm calling now. Put on some of your new shoes so your feet won't bother you, and then, despite what the council has to say, we'll come home, and hopefully, Lily will still be asleep so I can show you just how I feel about you."

Avelyn brushed a kiss against his lips again, before going to get a pair of her new shoes while Thrace made his call.

Chapter Eight

Thrace stood before the Vid-Comm, Avelyn's hand clutched in his. He would never tell her, but his heart was pounding in his chest and his stomach didn't feel so hot. Yes, he would defy the council, break from them and find his own way if they said he couldn't be with Avelyn, but it would be so much better if they would say yes. He didn't want to give up everything he knew, but he would gladly do it for her. There wasn't anything he wouldn't do for Avelyn.

"Thrace, it's good to see you," Larimar said. "As you can see, the council has convened over the matter of your mating. Everyone is present except for Borgoz."

A feeling of unease slid through him. Why would the Chief Councillor not be there unless they knew Thrace had blackmailed him?

"Borgoz is dealing with some family issues today, but he's given his opinion and we took that into consideration as we deliberated over the matter. As you know, the bride program was set up so we could further our existence once our females stopped being born. It was only going to be a matter of time before we died out, and it's been proven that Terrans breed true when it comes to human women. Granted, there are a few males who have found matches in other female races and those children, while half-Terran, look nothing like us."

Thrace wasn't sure where this was going and his nerves hadn't eased. He tightened his grip on Avelyn's hand.

"We will approve your mating with one stipulation. During our studies of humans, it has come to our attention that sometimes, when a female is unable to have children, they bring in what is called a surrogate mother. Would you be willing to provide a sperm donation for a surrogate mother? Everything would be handled clinically, and once the child was born, you would have the option of raising it yourself."

He was so stunned he wasn't sure he could draw breath. Looking down at Avelyn, he tried to judge her reaction to the situation. She didn't look quite as surprised as him, which meant she was at least familiar with the practice, but how would she feel raising another woman's child knowing he was the father? At least if they adopted, the child had unknown parents on both sides.

"He wouldn't have to have sex with her?" Avelyn asked. "Just give a donation like at a sperm bank? And the woman would have no rights to the child?"

"She would be paid for her services, but she would be required to sign a paper stating she gave up all rights to the baby," Larimar said. "We've thought about this a great deal and it's the only way we'll approve your mating. I know it's a lot to ask of you, Avelyn. The baby would be Thrace's by blood and not yours, and I know that has to be painful, but furthering our existence is very important. If he can't have children with you, then he needs to contribute in some other way. Do you understand?"

"I do," Avelyn said, giving Thrace's hand a squeeze.

"If this is going to hurt Avelyn, I won't do it," Thrace said. "I could never cause her pain."

Avelyn tugged on his hand. "Perhaps they'll let us interview the women and select one together? Maybe there's a young woman out there trying to save for college who isn't ready for kids, but would be willing to do this for us so we could have a baby that was yours in every way. As long as she won't get emotionally involved, I don't have a problem with it."

"But, Avelyn... "

She placed a finger over his lips. "Just agree with the council, Thrace. It's the only way for us to be together without turning your life upside down. It's a good deal. And you can't deny you want a child of your own."

"I want a child that is part you and part me," he clarified. "I don't want a child with some stranger."

"As you know," Larimar said, "the Helios from Helon-9 have been working with DNA. If you'd like, we can wait on the donation. Perhaps, in a few years, there will be a way to add Avelyn's DNA to the mix and the baby would be a part of both of you, even if she is unable to carry it. Just because you agree to this, doesn't mean you have to go through with it right away. As you know, Terran sperm is viable until we're in our eighties. There may be many changes between now and when you follow through that will allow you to share this experience with your mate. It is not our intention for her to feel left out or inadequate."

"And if I agree, we will be mated?" Thrace asked.

"If you agree, we'll sign the mating papers today and have them processed by tomorrow. You'll be an official couple by breakfast." Larimar smiled. "We would never do anything to bring harm to your mate, Thrace. This is a good deal. You should take it."

He looked down at Avelyn, saw the hope shining in her eyes and knew what his answer would be. He didn't like the idea of having a child with another woman, but as the council said, there was time for changes to be made, for them to find a way for the child to have a part of Avelyn as well.

"Very well," Thrace said. "I'll agree."

"Then congratulations," Larimar said. "You are now a mated couple. We should discuss where you intend to live. Several of our human-Terran pairings have decided to remain on Earth so their mates will not become stressed. Is this something you wish to do as well?"

Avelyn tugged on his hand again. "I don't care where we live, as long as we're together."

"If the council doesn't mind, I would prefer to spend most of my time on Earth. They are very accepting of different races and Avelyn and I wish to adopt more children. If we were to do so on Terran, the children would not always feel welcome."

"Then you may remain on Earth. I will note your preference. However, in times of war, we may ask for your assistance here on Terran, but as a mated male with a family on another world, we would not ask you to be an active soldier. Your input would mostly be about strategy, and could possibly be done from Earth. But that's a matter to discuss another day." Larimar reached for the Vid-Comm. "Enjoy your newly mated status. Congratulations to you both."

The screen went black.

"So… we're married?" Avelyn asked. "That's all there is to it?"

"That's all there is to it. There's a ceremony we can go through if we wish, but not everyone uses it. The council would have to perform it, but I guess we could do it over the Vid-Comm, if you want to do that. Some males don't feel mated without it, but I've felt like you were mine from the first day."

"I don't need a ceremony to tell me you're mine." She smiled and cupped his cheek. "There is one human custom I would like for us to use though, if you don't mind."

"What's that?" he asked, willing to give her anything.

"A husband and wife wear wedding rings, showing other people around them that they belong to someone. Could we do that?"

"We'll stop at a jewelry store on the way home to get these rings you speak of. I've seen the large shiny stones women wear. Is that what you mean?"

"I'd be happy with a pain gold band. I don't need a flashy diamond to make me happy."

He frowned. "But these rings, they are a symbol of power? The larger the stone the more the male loves his mate?"

Avelyn laughed. "Some people see it that way. It takes some human males years to save for one. Others can go out and spend ten thousand or more on a ring without doing more than writing a check. I don't have to have a flashy ring, Thrace. Just having something on my finger to show I belong to you is plenty for me."

He grunted. "Let's go look at these rings and I will decide which you should have. I want everyone to know you are mine and that I am able to take care of you properly."

He led her from the building and into the waiting limo, instructing the driver to stop by the best jewelry store in town. He knew she would be upset about spending more of his money, but what was the point in having it if he couldn't spend it on her? Thrace wanted to give her everything she'd ever dreamed of, and if that meant spending a large chunk of his money on a ring, then that's what he would do. He wanted other males to see her and know, that not only was she off limits, but he could care for her better than they could.

When they reached the shop, it took a bit of convincing to get Avelyn to try on the flashy rings, and he watched her face to see which she seemed to like the best. There was a large purple stone she said reminded her of his eyes, but she dismissed it as costing too much. As Avelyn looked at smaller rings, he motioned to the sales lady and asked her to pull the purple one out of the case. He studied it, deemed it worthy, and then snagged Avelyn's hand. He'd seen the women wearing them on their left hands and assumed she would wish to do the same.

Thrace slid the ring onto her finger -- a perfect fit! -- and decided that's where it would remain. Avelyn protested strongly, but he silenced her with a kiss. As she stared up at him with a dumbstruck look, he smiled at the sales lady and paid for the ring. The numbers meant nothing to him, but Avelyn assured him he was spending way too much on it. He hushed her protests and took her back to the hotel. He couldn't have cared less how much the shiny bauble cost, as long as he could get her home and naked.

"Thrace, the ring is gorgeous; it really is, but I don't feel comfortable with you dropping over fifty thousand on a ring."

"It's… what was that phrase you used? Pocket change? Yes, it's pocket change. If the ring makes you happy, that's all that matters."

"But you only picked out a plain ring."

"It's platinum, like your band. The sales woman assured me it was a nice ring and would be adequate to show we're married. Was that wrong?"

"Well, no… "

"Then this discussion is over. I'm not returning either ring, so enjoy your newly mated status and the shiny thing on your finger telling all males you belong to me."

She narrowed her eyes at him, but he flashed her a smile which seemed to make her melt a little. As they reached their hotel room, all seemed quiet and Thrace hoped that meant their daughter was still sleeping soundly. He pushed open the door and found Xonos with his feet kicked up on the table, watching some show on television with men in white coats like the doctor wore every day.

"Any problems?" Thrace asked.

Xonos stood and shook his head. "She never made a sound; I checked on her about ten minutes ago and she was still sleeping."

"Good." Thrace smiled. "This is where I throw you out." He held up Avelyn's hand showing off her wedding ring. "We're newly mated and I wish to celebrate with my woman."

Xonos laughed and walked toward the door. "Say no more. Congratulations to you both! If you decide you wish to have a honeymoon, call; Victoria and I will be happy to watch Lily for a few days."

Thrace frowned. "Honeymoon?"

"It's where you take your mate somewhere romantic and stay overnight for a day or two. You don't go to work and don't answer the phone unless it's an emergency."

Thrace looked down at Avelyn. "Would you like one of these honeymoons he speaks of?"

"Maybe we can talk about it tomorrow."

He nodded. "Thank you, Xonos. If she decides she wants a honeymoon, I will call."

As the doctor left, chuckling, Thrace scooped Avelyn into his arms and carried her into his bedroom. He pushed the door shut, but left it cracked so they would hear the baby monitor, which he'd left in the living room. He didn't want distractions and knew every time Lily made a sound his mate would be ready to jump up and go fetch their wee daughter.

"Strip." He folded his arms over his chest. "I wish to see you naked."

Avelyn gave him a bemused smile and did as he commanded. As each creamy strip of skin came into view, he felt himself grow harder. She stood before him completely bare, but there was no uncertainty in her eyes this time. She now knew the power she held over him, and looked very ready to wield it.

Thrace slowly removed his clothes, wanting to savor the moment. As he dropped his pants, he pulled Avelyn into his arms. His lips sought hers, his tongue sliding into her mouth, as he tried to tell her without words what she meant to him, how much she turned him on, and how very much he would want her every day for the rest of their lives.

"Have you ever had a woman ride you?" she asked, nipping at his jaw.

"You mean the way you did in the limo?"

A blush stained her cheeks. "Yes, except I'd be riding your cock and not your fingers. Are you willing to try that? Or is it a Terran thing to always be in charge?"

Thrace turned them, falling back onto the bed and taking her with him. "You may do whatever you wish with me. I'm yours, and you're mine."

She smiled and shimmied down his body. At first, he thought she was going to take him in her mouth again and his cock twitched in anticipation, but she pushed herself up, her thighs on either side of his. Her hands caressed his abdomen and chest and she licked her lips, as if she wanted to taste every inch of him.

"Your body is beautiful," she said. "I'll never grow tired of looking at it."

His hands cupped her hips. "I feel the same about you."

"I want to ride you, but I don't think my body is ready yet. Would you touch me?"

His lips tipped up on one side as he remembered something he'd seen in one of Earth's porn videos. "I have a better idea. Move up here. Put your knees on either side of my head."

Her mouth dropped open.

"I wish to taste you."

He felt her tremble as she followed his orders, placing a knee on either side of his head, her beautiful pussy hovering above him. With his hands on her hips, he lowered her enough that he could reach her with his lips and tongue. As her taste filled his mouth, he hummed in appreciation. He traced the seam of her pussy with his tongue before pushing it inside her.

Avelyn groaned and pushed down against him. His fingers dug into the cheeks of her ass, massaging the globes as he pleasured her. Her little clit stood hard and begging for attention. He teased it, skirting the little nub before flicking his tongue over it several times. It didn't take long before Avelyn was riding his face, taking as much pleasure as he could give her and demanding more. As she screamed out her release, he felt her cream coat his lips and chin and he lapped up as much of it as he could.

His sweet mate nearly collapsed and he eased her down his body, wiped his chin, and gave her a big grin. "You seemed to like that. We'll definitely try it again soon."

"I think you broke me."

"Does this mean you won't be riding me?"

"I don't think I can. My legs won't work."

Thrace laughed and rolled them so that she lay under him. Hooking her legs around his waist, he entered her slowly, giving her body time to adjust to his size. As her nails bit into him, he realized he wasn't going to be able to hold back or go slowly. Not this time. Maybe not ever. Every time he entered her, she felt so damn incredible that he felt like he would explode at any second.

His slow, easy strokes became frantic as he pushed both of them toward orgasm. He felt her tightening around his cock, felt her grow slicker, and knew she was about to find her release. Wanting to feel her shatter under him, he reached up and tweaked her nipples, pinching and lightly twisting them until she bucked under him and cried out. He felt her juices gush around his cock and he let himself go.

Thrace collapsed on his side next to her and pulled her into his arms. Kissing her sweaty brow, he murmured the words he knew she needed to hear. "I love you, Avelyn."

"I love you, too."

"Promise me that it will always be like this between us."

She cupped his cheek. "I could never grow tired of you. I'll desire you every day for the rest of our lives, and the sex will always be explosive because of how much we want each other."

Lily began to wail in the other room and she smiled at him.

"Good thing she didn't do that about five minutes ago. I don't think I could have stopped if I'd wanted to." Thrace kissed her again. "You go shower. I'll fetch our daughter and see what she needs."

"Thrace... I think we should have that honeymoon. I love Lily, but I want a few days alone with you, where clothes aren't required."

He smiled. "I'll make the call while you shower." His gaze skimmed her body. "We are definitely celebrating more later. I've seen so many videos and there is a lot we haven't tried yet. Expect very little sleep for at least a month."

Avelyn laughed and swatted him on the ass. "Go, before I decide to tackle you to the bed and let Lily fend for herself for another half hour."

Thrace snorted. "Woman, there is no way a half hour would be long enough. Not for what I have in mind. Rest while you can, my sexy mate, because you're going to get very little of it in the days to come."

Thrace gave her a wink, pulled on some sweatpants and went in search of his daughter. If this was what being mated was like, he wasn't surprised the males he knew were so anxious to try it. Avelyn was smart, sexy, and so damn beautiful he ached looking at her. Maybe after he settled Lily he'd find some more of those videos... *Never hurts to be prepared.*

Jessica Coulter Smith

Award-winning author Jessica Coulter Smith has been in love with the written word since she was a child writing her first stories in crayon. Today she's a multi-published author of over seventy-five novellas and novels. Romance is an integral part of her world and spills over from her professional life into her personal one. When she went on that first date with her husband, she never expected to hear the words "Marry me" pop out of his mouth -- and judging by the shocked look on his face, he hadn't meant to say them either. But, being the hopeless romantic that she is, Jessica said yes and they've been married since 2000.

Jessica firmly believes that love will find you at the right time, even if Mr. Right is literally out of this world. She's often gazed at the stars and wondered what, or who, else might be out there. Who's to say that hunky model on the hottest romance bestseller isn't really from some far off galaxy? Maybe that blue Martian you saw at Halloween wasn't really in costume. After all, there's an awful lot of space out there for us to be the only ones living in it. Jessica loves to hear from her readers! You can follow her on Facebook facebook.com/jessicacoultersmithauthor/ and Twitter twitter.com/kitcatjms.

Visit her website: jessicacoultersmith.com. Want to be notified of new releases or special discounts? Sign up for her newsletter eepurl.com/bwPvbT. Find more books by Jessica Coulter Smith at changelingpress.com/author.php?uid=144.

Changeling Press E-Books

More Sci-Fi, Fantasy, Paranormal, and BDSM adventures available in E-Book format for immediate download at ChangelingPress.com -- Werewolves, Vampires, Dragons, Shapeshifters and more -- Erotic Tales from the edge of your imagination.

What are E-Books?

E-Books, or Electronic Books, are books designed to be read in digital format -- on your desktop or laptop computer, notebook, tablet, Smart Phone, or any electronic ebook reader.

Where can I get Changeling Press e-Books?

Changeling Press ebooks are available at ChangelingPress.com, Amazon, Barnes and Nobel, Kobo, and iTunes.

ChangelingPress.com

Made in the USA
Columbia, SC
04 September 2023